Anonymous

Short stories by California authors

Anonymous

Short stories by California authors

ISBN/EAN: 9783744749169

Printed in Europe, USA, Canada, Australia, Japan

Cover: Foto ©Andreas Hilbeck / pixelio.de

More available books at **www.hansebooks.com**

SHORT STORIES

BY

CALIFORNIA AUTHORS.

SAN FRANCISCO:

GOLDEN ERA, 29 KEARNY STREET,

1885.

PORTRAIT OF A CALIFORNIA GIRL.

A jagged horizon of frowning cliffs against the blue sky ! Mountains to the east and west ! Mountains to the north and south, a mammoth herd of mountains all crowned fantastically ! Through the midst of this native wilderness ran a narrow cañon, the only outlet to the great world beyond, and here in this wild spot had been chosen a place for a habitation.

From the stage window, Judge Harville glanced out at the bevy of children that gathered round, and could not help but wonder at the refined mother of the group, and ask himself what fortuitous fortune had-cast so beautiful and delicate a woman so far above the level of civilization. And then his eye had been caught by a strange young creature by his side, who resembled her as the fawn does the deer-mother. It looked like a child that was masquerading as a woman, dressed in matronly style, with trained skirts and ample crinoline, but showing in her childish face and undeveloped form the marks of extreme youth, and yet in the self-reliant pose of the head and utter unconsciousness of the gazing eyes bent upon her, was very different from the preconceived idea of the child who stands where brook and river meet.

She was dressed for traveling, and as she kissed them all farewell, her trunk was being strapped on behind the stage with tremendous energy.

"Is she coming in here ?" asked one of the passengers with enthusiasm.

"No, she's booked outside with Dennis, the driver," was the reply. "She's one of the belles of Esmeralda. You wouldn't think it, would you. She's only fourteen, but she's had several proposals already. Women are mighty scarce in this part of the country, you know, and we don't let 'em waste much time."

"Good bye, Lorena, good bye !" cried the chorus of brothers and sisters as she mounted up the wheel and into the high seat by the driver, and they were off, the six horses prancing gaily down the canon.

Judge Harville had listened amused to this little colloquy and at the Half-way House where they stopped for dinner he took a closer look at the girl.

She wore a string of pearl beads around her hair, a sailor collar turned down in the neck with a picturesque knot at the throat, very full gathered skirts over a large crinoline, and a saucy little brown felt hat like a boy's. Certainly she was all out in her clothes.

In the city, he knew the ladies affected very high chokers, and their skirts were rather slimpsey, crinoline having been dethroned for some time.

Still there was a certain sweetness and dignity in the fresh young face that was very attractive. He saw her eyes glisten as he took up his magnificent fur-lined coat, and knew she had never seen anything like it before.

He handed her into the coach, for it was now growing cold, and found her the easiest place, and watched her fall into a baby-like slumber. The night was bitter in its frostiness, and the shawl around her seemed scarcely heavy enough. Very lightly he drew off his otter-lined garment, and put it around her, then wrapping himself in a blanket, he too had gone to sleep, maintaining meanwhile, however, a strong grip on the straps—those kindly-provided contrivances to keep passengers from mounting roofward at odd moments. In the grey light of the morning he saw her looking at him with an amused yet grateful pair of eyes, and patting the soft lining with evident enjoyment.

After breakfast they fell into a little chat, and he remarked the change in the landscape around them, for it was much more level and open on the road to Carson.

"It is very different," she replied; "yesterday it was like home all the way, nearly, for they were my own mountains, my very own, but I don't know my way here, at all. Which way are my mountains ?" and her eyes betokened the liveliest interest.

They were pointed out in the dim distance directly upon one side, for they had come in a sort of semi-circle. Air, light and shade commingling to invest them with a royal magnificence of color from the delicate pearl tints to rose and purple, and behind them the clouds lay piled like another succession of heavenly peaks till the eye could scarcely tell where earth left off and the portals of the sky began.

"Are those my mountains?" she said in surprise "Why, they are more beautifully purple than any of them and I have always been envying the far away mountains for being so lovely and hazy, and there all the time my own mountains were just as purple as any of them. Doesn't that seem funny?"

He was much amused by her naive remarks, for she was not afraid to talk upon any theme from politics to poetry, having an unusual fund of information upon these subjects, and showing that she had grown up among people much older than herself. And yet the childish idea would make its appearance every now and then, giving a most unique turn to the conversation.

The stage jolted violently over the rough road, and they fell into silence again. She rosy cheeks of the girl seemed to whiten out as a faintly perceptible odor began to steal on the air. It was an ill-defined, suspicious odor, that seemed to creep upon the senses insiduously, and yet not give the slightest clue to its origin. Being a man, perhaps it made less impression upon Judge Harville, but he saw the girl evince signs of the greatest discomfort.

When they reached the place for changing horses, and the men got out and stretched their limbs, he saw the girl bend forward eagerly, and with her teeth, bite the string that fastened a great demijohn of whisky to the side of the stage, put it under her shawl, and, at an unobserved moment, pitch it out the window.

He smiled to himself, at her resolution, and wondered how she would make it straight with the owner, getting back into the stage with renewed interest in the "child-woman," as he mentally dubbed her.

She sat smiling, wickedly happy, now; the color had come back to her round cheek, and she had a sparkle in her eye that told of her triumph. Presently the owner of the odorous treasure began to look for his demijohn. In a few moments he had accused the man next to him, which was resented on the instant. Words followed and a row seemed imminent, when, all at once, the girl laughed. They looked at her with indignation.

"I took it," she said, a little shame-facedly.

"You?" said the man, astonished, yet doubtful.

"Yes, the horrid thing was making me sick with its awful breath, and so *I pitched it out*;" her whole manner breathed of defiance. Then realizing faintly the difficulty she had gotten into, she said, apologetically, "Besides it was good of me to keep you from drinking it. 'Tisn't good for you, you know it isn't. Whisky makes people ugly, and if you hadn't been drinking it all the morning, you would laugh and call it a joke. Now, wouldn't he?" She appealed to the other passengers.

"Of course he would!" they laughed back.

"Better give in gracefully, old fel," said one, "you're beat this time."

"Got to stand the drinks next place," said another.

"Oh, bah!" said Lorena, her eyes flashing, "we don't want any more drinking. That's what I pitched that old thing out for. Can't you brighten up and be nice for the rest of the trip? Tell me, haven't you some nice little children?" she asked interestedly of the owner of the lost treasure.

"Yes," said the man, rather sullenly.

"How many?" her voice was eager.

"Three," was the reply, less sullen.

"Oh! have you? Boys or girls?"

"Two boys and a girl," replied the man, looking at her curiously.

"We have three of each at our house, and I have just the sweetest baby sister in the world," said the girl, joyously.

Judge Harville looked upon her with a new interest; she was certainly an odd little child-woman, with so much maternal affection in her nature. In a few moments she had found out the names of all the children belonging to the fathers there, and made a remark on each; then turning to him, she asked, artlessly, "What are your children's names?"

Judge Harville was taken by surprise. He was not over thirty years of age, was brown haired and brown bearded, and felt himself a very young man for the honors he had received. That he should impress any one as the father of a family struck him incongruously.

"I'm almost afraid to tell you"—he hesitated, yet in spite of himself, he smiled.

"Why?" she asked, emphatically.

"Because I haven't any." Everybody laughed, even Lorena herself, and good nature was immediately restored.

The rest of the stage ride was pleasant enough, and Judge Harville found himself more than once on the point of asking the bright little Lorena where she was going to stop in San Francisco, which she had inadvertently referred to as her destination. But there was a certain dignity underneath all that childish presumption and chattiness that made him hesitate. And when they arrived at Carson, he arrayed himself in his luxurious coat, and gathered together all his belongings and bade her good-bye, saying simply, "Farewell, Miss Lorena. I hope we shall meet again."

And she looked him in the eyes like a child, and said cheerfully, "I hope so, too."

"You won't forget me, will you?" said he with a little touch of vanity. She seemed too unimpressed by the notice he had taken of her.

"I'm sure I'll never forget your beautiful fur-lined coat," she said, mischievously, and he went off amid a shout of laughter from the other passengers.

Four weeks passed by. He had almost forgotten the little girl in the stage, when one day, near Christmas time, with the rain pouring in torrents, he suddenly met her face to face on Kearny street in San Francisco. He stopped and looked at her with a very pleased expression.

She was clad in city fashion, short trim skirts, ermine-bordered velvet jacket, and Tyrolean hat to match, with a scarlet wing setting it off jauntily, really a very charming picture of youth and freshness. He held out his hand. She hesitated.

"Why Miss Lorena, you haven't forgotten me surely?"

"No," she said, rather unwillingly, "but you see I've never been introduced to you."

"Well, I'll be blanked," said he to himself.

"Well? what difference does that make. We're acquainted all the same."

"I know," said the girl, "but at home—up in the mountains—we don't think it nice to continue an acquaintance without an intro-

duction. If I'm worth being acquainted with, I'm worth being introduced to. Besides, I don't know who in the world you are, you
know." And she laughed.

Finished man of the world as he was, Judge Harville was speechless. He looked down in wonder on this curious little woman with
the artlessness of a child, this child with the worldly wisdom of a
woman·

"With whom are you staying ?" he asked in a low voice.

"With my uncle, W. B. Lawrence of the firm of Lawrence and
Chester," she replied with dignity. "Good morning," and she was
on her way.

The spirit displayed by this comical little mountain belle, aroused
his deepest respect. "If she is worth being acquainted with, she
is worth getting an introduction to," he repeated. "The little girl
is right, and I'll take the trouble to get a first-class introduction that
will be without a flaw."

And then he fell to laughing at the absurdity of the situation, he
a man of high position and eagerly sought after by the finest circles
to grace their receptions, going to the trouble of getting an introduction to a comical little girl from the mountains in order that he
might set himself straight, and prove that he was not a gambler or
other suspicious character. "I don't know who in the world you
are, you know." It would make a funny story to tell some time,
he thought.

Nevertheless his pique was aroused and he sought the house of a
mutual friend, who during the call, casually, mentioned that the Lawrence family were to dine with them on Christmas day. "But I
suppose it is of no use to invite you, Judge Harville, you are always
engaged months beforehand," said the lady with a sigh, thinking of
her own marriageable daughter.

"Well," said he, stroking his handsome mustache, "I will tell you
what I will do. I will come late."

He resolved to dumbfound the nonchalant little Lorena, and teach
her a lesson. He would rather enjoy a harmless little revenge on
such a spirited young creature. In spite of his pride and high position, underneath all there was to be found a petty vanity in the
breast of the otherwise admirable Judge Harville.

The dinner was over, and the several little families were gathered

in congenial little knots, some singing at the piano, some looking at
the new gifts; but in the bay window, solitary and alone, sat little
Lorena. She had discovered already, in her short experience of city
life, that she was no longer a young lady, but only a little girl, and
was trying to adapt herself to the new position of being seen but not
heard.

The door suddenly opened and the hostess came in smiling, leading
Judge Harville as if he were a prize ox that had received the first
premium at a county fair. She introduced him to the few who did
not already know him, personally, while Mr. and Mrs. Lawrence
beamed upon him, renewing the slight acquaintance that already ex-
isted between them, and the others gathered around to show him
deference and respect·

All listened to his words of bright address, and responded with
animation—all but little Lorena, who shrank back behind the curtains and wondered at this remarkable coincidence.

Judge Harville saw her sitting there all solitary and alone, and
after he thought he had punished her sufficiently, he said, "By the
way, Lawrence, I believe I came down in the same stage with your
niece—a very bright little girl—is she here? I should like to be
introduced."

And Mr. Lawrence had gone to the window and had said,
"Lorena, Judge Harville wishes to be introduced to you."

"Does he?" she said, quietly.

"Yes. It seems he came down in the same stage with you from
the mountains," and he waited for her to come out from behind the
curtains.

"Well, why doesn't he come and be introduced then?" and she
turned to look out the window again.

Uncle Lawrence was somewhat startled, and then he smiled to
himself, remembering the trains to her dresses only a few weeks
before, which had to be cut off in order to make her presentable.
"She wasn't so much of a child as they had imagined."

In a moment the curtain was separated more widely than usual,
and Judge Harville stood there, with a quizzical smile in his handsome eyes, repeating gravely, "Miss Lawrence," after the ceremony
of introduction.

But the little girl, in her pretty short suit, with, however, the pearl bead fillet still around her head, did not seem dumbfounded in the least. She inclined her head with diguity, and then there came a bright sparkle of merriment into her eyes.

"You are lately from the mountains, I believe, Miss Lawtence."

"Yes," returned she, "like yourself."

"Did you have a pleasant trip down?"

"Delightful," returned Lorena, "especially when I pitched out that old demijohn! Didn't you?"

"Are there any more formalities to be got through with?" he asked, "if so, please mention them, and I'll try to secure them all."

"I can't help it," said Lorena, answering implied sarcasm of his words. "I have been taught that it is the only proper way."

"Do you know who I am yet?" His eyes looked mischievous.

"No," said she frankly, "I do not."

"Yet you talk to me."

"Ah!" said the girl, "but my uncle has assumed the responsibility, and I trust *him*."

Judge Harville stroked his moustache a moment reflectively. There wasn't much satisfaction for his vanity yet. "This is a great contrast to the country we left behind us four weeks ago, isn't it," pointing as he spoke, to the garden in front, which revealed great, white calla lilies, bright-red geraniums, and graceful, drooping fucbsia blossoms of purple and red. "I suppose you would be very willing to make the change."

"I?" said Lorena, with a flash of her eyes, "no, indeed! The city stifles me; I love my own wild mountains best."

He looked down at this small young person with a half smile on his face—"Ah, but if those brothers and sisters of yours lived here, it would be different, and you would soon forget all about the dreary desolation up there."

"No, I shouldn't," she persisted; "my dear old Mount Chalcedony is worth a dozen of these hills here. And besides, I have all the wild flowers to myself, and name them whatever I please. And then, too, we meet some of the most talented men in the country, up there. Why, I know Governor Nye, and J. Ross Browne, the traveler— when he was writing up Bodie and Mono Lake, for Harper's he vis-

ted our house—and there's Mr. Gough, the nephew of the celebrated
lecturer, who is almost as eloquent as his uncle; and there's Mr.
Clagget, and Mr. Kendall and several other Congressmen, and O,
judges! why, I know ever so many judges! There's Judge Boring,
who often lectures for us; and Judge Sewell. who is considered
really very fine; and Judge Chase—a real brilliant judge, who used
to be a student of Longfellow's, himself, and I guess that's more than
you can say, isn't it?"

Judge Harville's vanity was wounded in more ways than one.
He had no desire to be considered in competition with "those old
fogies," as he mentally dubbed them.

"You must think me a regular old grandfather," he said, passing over this extensive list of notables, his pride hurt more than he
would have confessed at her childish refusal to consider him of any
particular value, and also at the implied sarcasm which intimated
that he evidently felt he was condescending to talk with her.

"Oh! it's nice to be old," said she, reassuringly, "that's what
makes *you* so pleasant and agreeable," and then with a sigh of self-
importance, "I don't like *young* men."

Judge Harville took a long breath. He had thought to subdue
little Lorena, but, instead. be was himself subdued.

When he had recovered his breath, he looked at her curiously,
"I'd like to come across you about five years from now. I'd like to
see what sort of a woman you would make."

He was about to ask some questions about her mother, when
voices from behind appealed to him to settle some vexed question of
trivial importance, and he was drawn away, the little girl with her
pearl bead fillet looking out upon them from behind the curtains with
an ill-concealed smile of amusement at the way the young ladies hung
upon his words, and looked up into his eyes. It made him feel ridic-
ulous rather than triumphant, his vanity had received a blow.

The rain was falling in torrents when the gathering broke up,
and he could only say a conventional good bye to to the well-equi-
poised, little Lorena, who gave him a bright little nod in reply.

The next day he sent her an exquisite bouquet and a magnificent box of confectionery, mingling the gifts suitable to a child and a
young lady, but when he called a week or so later, little Lorena had
flown back to her beloved mountains, and so passed out of his life

and thoughts, leaving only a dim little memory of a strange child who played at being a young lady.

A number of experiences fell to Judge Harville's share in the years which followed, but fortune and fame continued to smile upon him, and the young ladies and their mammas. Still his heart remained his own, that touch of vanity made him well satisfied to remain as he was—the honored and welcome guest of a large circle of refined acquaintances.

*   *   *   *   *

Eight years had passed. He was still handsome with only a few silver hairs clustering in his brown locks. An intricate question of law had taken him up through the wild Sonora route into Mono county.

On setting out in the morning, some one had said, "Jedge, I'm 'fraid there's goin' to be be a snow storm. Ye'd better stay over till tomorrer."

He only laughed at the would-be weather-prophet, and thought no more about it, urging his horse along at a pleasant canter till he came into the rough mountain road, and gave himself up to the reflections that naturally come to a solitary horseman who knows he is likely to travel for twenty or thirty miles without meeting a human being.

The road wound around the hills, and then took a line through the only natural egress or ingress—a long, dark canyon, two gloomy walls of solid rock, that once fitted evenly together in a solid mass, but in some great convulsion of nature, had separated, leaving this narrow space between—barely room enough for two teams to pass with a little stream of water running alongside.

Stories of waterspouts, very frequent in this locality, came to his mind, and he wondered if one should strike this canon, whether the unfortunate caught between these walls could possibly escape drowning.

After a while, the walls lowered gradually, and he saw a wild horizon of jagged fantastic angles encircling him round. On the instant a picture came back to his mind of a house situated in the foreground of a wild mountain, and a group of children, and then a succession of pictures with a bright little girl figuring arching in the center.

"It must be the peculiar horizon that brings back such a faint little memory as that of Lorena," said he, musingly. "It was no wonder she didn't grow up like other children, with such a horizon as that around her. What's that? Snowflakes falling? The old man was a prophet, after all. I wonder if I can't make the quartz mill before it gets too heavy." And spurring up his horse, he hastened along. The weather had changed, the bracing air had given way to that strange, heavy atmosphere that precedes the snowstorm, so imperceptibly that he had not noticed it.

On leaving this uncanny place, the road verged about several small slopes, but the snow increased so suddenly and so violently, with a sudden gust of wind blowing down the canyon, that he became confused. Once he thought he had struck the trail because of the fresh horses' tracks before him in the snow, but he soon found that, in his confusion, he had been merely following in a circle upon his own trail.

To add to his distress, his horse stepped into a sudden gully and fell beneath him with a broken leg. Darkness now seemed to encompass the earth, and Judge Harville stood gazing into space utterly bewildered.

The violent efforts of his horse in attempting to rise called him back to himself, and after a moment's hesitancy, he drew out his revolver and put the beast out of his misery, performing this action of cruel kindness promptly and effectively.

He felt sure that the quartz-mill was not far away, and that he could make it within an hour. He lighted a match, and looked at his watch. It was six. He felt the need of food and shelter, and resolved to press forward.

The night was coming on fast, and it was bitter cold. He could not think of staying in this desolate spot when a place of refuge was so near.

But he soon found himself at the mercy of the pitiless elements. The snow still fell madly, the wind was beginning to throw up little drifts. Still he struggled on. Once he plunged into the creek through the shallow ice, and although wet through, and his clothes immediately stiffened, he exclaimed, "Thank God!" for it showed that the road was not far away. Bit by bit, step by step, he makes

his way. In three hours he has made a mile directly forward,
though five or six has been lost in retracement.

He is no longer the elegant and dignified Judge Harville. He is
only a man fighting for life—a pitable object of humanity. His
clothes are torn by contact with the rocks, or stiffened with frozen
water, his hands are bleeding, his feet badly frozen. Shall he give
up and lie down to sweet, coaxing sleep—sleep that knows no wak-
ing, or shall he struggle on?

A sound breaking on the freezing air attracts his wandering senses.
" Help ! " he cries.

The sound comes again, repeated thrice. If he was desperate before, now he was like one transfixed.

It was the bark of a coyote—a sharp, insolent bark. What an
answer to a freezing man's call for help !

" What ! lie down to die, and be devoured by those cowardly
brutes ? " And in answer he plunged along again with renewed
efforts, nerved with strength born of desperation. The barks increased around him; there was a pair of them; he could see their
dark shadows on the snow, waiting at a respectful distance. His
hands were so cold and numb that he could not get his revolver out,
and even then the water had frozen it stiff. " Great Heaven ! " he
cried, " was I born for this ? "

His ears now told him the voices were three, he wasted no time
looking for the shadowy forms on the snow. " I will keep them out
of their feast as long as I can," he thought, his natural stubborness
coming to his aid. And he did, but his powers were nearly exhausted, his endurance overtried. Gradually the stiffness was creeping
on him, he felt no more arms or legs, he was only a human clump
struggling onward. Still the snow fell. " Heh! heh ! heh !"
barked the cowardly chorus. Each moment seemed a year as they
gained upon him. One crept close to him; in an agony of despair he
made one great effort and struck at it, the cowardly thing slunk back.
It feared even the semblance of a man as long as there was a spark
of life in it.

Suddenly upon his ear almost dulled in its sense of hearing, came
another sound, he roused himself to listen. Could he be losing his
mind already,or was it a mocking human voice imitating the coyotes?

"Heb, heb, heb !" called the chorus around him. "Heh, heh, heh," called out a clear mocking voice from a distance.

"God !" said the man, and with soul swelling within him, forgetting his poor cumbersome, solid body he strove once more, with hope inspiring him. That mocking human voice was the sweetest sound he had ever heard. But his feet failed him, they would no longer do their master's bidding. Accepting this new distress, he fell upon hands and knees and crept painfully along in the direction of the voice, which seemed to take delight in mocking the voices of the night. " If it should cease !" thought the man in despair.

One more little turn of a bend, and there he saw, very near, a light; with one loud cry born of agony and despair, he cried, "Help, help !" and at that moment felt the breath of the coyotes upon his cheek.

He struggled to show there was still life in him, and in the breathing spell thus obtained, the door flung wide open and the figure of a woman rushed out, a lamp in her hand.

" Where! where are you ?" she cried. "Heh, heh," cried the chorus. "Here, here," cried the man with his last strength. "Merciful Heavens !" with this ejaculation, not pausing a moment she ran directly towards them, the coyotes shrinking back out of sight at the appearance of so much life and vitality. She found a clump of frozen humanity in the snow, speechless but with grateful eyes that looked up in her face and told of life.

Hurrying to the house, she brought out a flask of liquor, and by the light of her lamp made him drink. "There is no time to waste," she said in a quick way, "I shall have to depend on you to help me. My husband is at the mill, I can't wait to go for him." Putting a rope around his waist, she gave him instructions what to do. " Now when I pull, lift a little of your weight." Foot by foot they struggled along the fire obtained from the whisky as well as the light so near him, and the encouraging voice, gave him new energy. Who can tell where the strength comes from that enables a woman to grapple with burdens beyond her powers ? No one could ever tell how she got the helpless man into the cosy domicile where warmth and comfort awaited him. There was not much to remind one of the elegant scrupulously attired Judge Harville, in the poor piece of humanity before her eyes. Cold water was used to take the first agony out of the frozen limbs, and then warm drinks to comfort the inner man.

Then with a sigh of relief she said, "I guess you will do till morning, and then we'll have the doctor."

Judge Harville's eyes had been resting upon her questioningly through all this tedious process.

"It seems to me that I've seen you somewhere before;" he said slowly. "Very likely," was the response; "I've traveled all over California and Nevada since I was a child." "No, but it seems as if I had known you "

"If you will tell me your name," she said hesitatingly. A faint smile crept over his face with recognition. "You are the little Lorena who wouldn't speak to me without an introduction. Will the old one do, or must I get a new one?"

"Judge Harville!" she exclaimed, "can it be possible? I never expected to see you again, much less under these circumstances."

"How is it you are here, all alone?" he asked.

"Oh, my husband, Aleck Westbrook, is night engineer at the Silver King mill, a quarter of a mile away. I've lived here over a year. I never think o such a thing as being afraid.

"I often mock the coyotes just to amuse myself, they are a sort of company; but your cry, tonight, quite horrified me. They must have been starved to be as bold as they were tonight, but we wont talk of that anymore. You had better get some sleep before the doctor comes."

"What time is it?" "It is two o'clock, Aleck always gets a light lunch about twelve, and that accounts for my being up at such an hour and very fortunate it was." Judge Harville accepted all these statements as the most natural in the world, dining at twelve o'clock at night, and mocking coyotes to amuse one's self, why, of course, he wondered why he had never done these things himself, and in the sleep which crept drowsily on, dreamed he had turned into a coyote, and was tracking something to death.

Aleck Westbrook proved to be a tall, manly fellow, a little reserved, though cordial in congratulation to the stranger he found housed upon his return, and very prompt in bringing the doctor who pronounced the quick and efficient care the night before as likely to bring him through without an amputation, but his recovery from the shock and all would be slow.

Seeing that it was to be a long siege, Judge Harville sent for choice groceries to the city, as his contribution toward the household expenses, for provisions in the town where supplies were bought were incredibly high. He also sent for music and books.

Lorena Westbrook, as a woman, was the same arch, bright creature, with a strange dignity and fearlessness all her own, that Lorena Lawrence had been, and with the self-reliance that comes from frontier life.

Judge Harville from his place upon the bed-lounge watched her curiously in all her little duties, as she sewed, or tidied up the room, or in caring for the year-old child which clung to her skirts. He was lost in admiration of her. To his weary, sated eyes, in her freshness and vivacity—she was a revelation. Day after day crept by, and his admiration grew till it passed the limits of admiration. He allowed himself to break the tenth commandment. He coveted.

"Do you never wish that fate had placed you in a beautiful home in the midst of civilization?" he asked Lorena, one day.

"O, I don't know. I'm very happy here. I have my piano, and baby and husband. I don't know of anything else I want very much. I love this wild place better than the trammels of society."

"But you would find congenial society, and an opportunity for those accomplishments which make a woman so charming and delightful," said Judge Harville, insidiously. Lorena gave a little sigh. "It *is* nice to be accomplished," she said.

Many were the visitors that came in of an evening. Mrs. Westbrook's simple little parlor seemed an earthly paradise to those rough diamonds who had left civilization far behind them with all its comforts to battle with the wilderness. Some of them were fluent talkers, some were geniuses, some were bores, yet each was respectful and kind in his admiration of the engineer's wife. Occasionally a lady from the town, four miles distant, favored her with a call, or a family who lived a mile away, but these were exceptions, and men almost exclusively formed the society that gathered around her.

This curious state of affairs was not altogether new to Judge Harville, but it had never affected him as unpleasantly as now. "A bright, intelligent creature like Lorena to be wasted on the desert air," he thought to himself, impatiently—and even a species of jealousy took possession of him, to see how freely and frankly she met them, and how sweetly she talked to them all.

"Say, Westbrook," said he, one day, after they had been discussing one of the habitual bores, "aren't you afraid you'll have to straighten out some of these fellows some day. First thing you know some of them will be in love with your wife."

"Oh, no," laughed back Westbrook, "Lorena straightens them out as she goes along. I'll never have any duels to fight for her."

The fierceness of the winter was over, and spring began to assert her sway, sending down great freshets ladened with boulders from the mountains, and touching into life the sparse vegetation. "Here is the harbinger of spring," said Lorena, one day, bringing in a branch of willow, which had commenced to sprout in tiny buds of wool. "And in California the roses are blooming, the lilies shining white, and the whole earth covered with green," said Harville.

She turned upon him fiercely, "Why are you always trying to fill me with discontent? I never thought of such a thing till you came."

Harville smiled to himself. "Because I cannot bear to see you satisfied with such a life." Lorena looked at him in bewilderment. But he said no more, and she had nothing to say being puzzled to catch his meaning.

The roads were now in good condition, and Judge Harville's crutch almost unnecessary, everything pointed to there being no further excuse for his remaining in such a wild, desolate spot. But Aleck told him to be in no haste, he was glad to have such good company for his wife, and had enjoyed the time spent together. They did live delightfully in that strange place, with music (Harville was an accomplished musician), with reading (he was a fine reader), with communions with Nature and the charming little suppers at twelve every night, and sleeping in the morning, turning day into night, and night into day, with no bustle of the outside world, no weary seekings after pleasure, no mingling with great crowds of people, utterly indifferent to each other, but each new human being a study and a revelation.

One day, together, they went to the Indian Camp, quite near, and watched the dark-faced creatures prepare their meals, and try the steps of the Indian dance, preparatory to the grand pow-wow on Walker's river.

"I wish we both were savages like these," said Harville, in a low tone.

"Why?" she responded, "what idea have you in that?"

"So that we should not be bound by these laws civilization puts upon us."

"I am glad that your wish cannot come true, for I love law and order" she laughed back in reply. But something in his tone alarmed her.

The next day, with her baby, she went out seeking new flowers that she knew where to find, and stayed beyond her time. Meanwhile Aleck, who had waked before his usual hour in the day, was out of temper for no particular cause, as a man can easily be sometimes, and stepping into the kitchen, saw the bread, forgotten in its capabilities for expansion, a great frothy roll over the sides of the pan, and even dripping on the floor.

At this moment Lorena and the baby came in the back door, both trimmed with wild flowers, a pretty bloom on their faces, and a smiling look in their eyes.

"You had a d—n sight better stay home and tend to this bread," said Aleck, crossly, yet touched by the pretty picture of his wife and child, and regretting his temper on the instant.

Without a word, but the bloom blanched in a moment, Lorena walked past him into her room.

Judge Harville observed this little scene and wondered what she would do, but in a moment she came out and got supper quietly, after Aleck's departure taking up her sewing.

Harville sat and watched her. Since he had allowed himself to covet that which was his neighbor's, he had, with many dallyings with conscience, proved to himself that his ultimate object was a good one, a real kindness, cruel perhaps—like the shooting of his horse to put him out of his misery—but a kindness, a good deed, after all; such tricks does pure, unadulterated reason, untouched with conscience, play with a man's judgment! He was no worse, no better, than many men we know and believe to be honorable.

He would not sully by a word Lorena's purity of soul; he loved her too deeply for that; he wanted her for his wife. He was a law-

yer, and a crafty one, and knew well the meshes of the law and how
he could disentangle her from her present position and make her his
own.   And he had convinced himself that it would be a kindness to
her in the end.

"To think of such a rare creature condemned to these dismal
things of life, such a barren, miserable outlook ! I'll place her in a
sphere more fitted to her charms and graces, for where will not Judge
Harville's wife be welcome?"

And so he sat there, thinking all these things, how lovely she
would look in a beautiful home, and what a joy to free her from all
this toil and hard work, this lovely creature who had saved his life—
what would he not surround her with to soften life for her?"

"Lorena," he said, softly. .

"Well," she responded, as if nothing strange were suggested by
his familiar method of address.

"Do you never tire of this dreary life ?"

She looked at him a second, as if measuring him.   "Oh, no," she
responded, carelessly.

"Lorena," he said again, and his voice was thrilling?y low, "listen
to me."

"I'm listening," she repeated, carelessly again.

"Lorena, don't you see the love shining out of my eyes ?   Don't
you see that I adore you?"

"That's nothing new," she laughed back; "I've always been
adored.   I can't remember when I wasn't adored."

"But I want you for my own," he whispered, yet not coming any
closer—he knew he dared not.

"That's nothing new, either," she laughed, again, "there's always
been somebody who wanted me for their own; in fact, if that's intended for a pleasant remark, I'm dreadfully tired of it."

"But seriously, Mrs. Westbrook," said he, in a different tone,
"how can you be happy in such a place as this, and with a man who
swears at you ?"

The pretty chin quivered, still she kept up her play of speech,
and said, most innocently, "One would suppose that you had never
heard anybody swear before," and then, rising, "I must see to
Aleck's supper; poor fellow, he'll be very hungry when he returns."

And soon she was busied with the fire, and preparing an oyster stew for him.

His step was soon heard, and after a bright little talk around the table, he went back again to his work. Lorena, hurrying away the dishes, and clearing up, retired to her own room and locked the door.

Judge Harville soon sought his own couch, but not to sleep. He was restless, irritated, but more determined than ever.

In her room, Lorena acted very strangely; she seemed suffocating; she kissed the sleeping babe, then, drawing a shawl over her head, cautiously opened the window and crept out, and dropping to the ground noiselessly, she walked up the narrow road in the waning light of the old moon.

' Oh, I could kill him, I could kill him !" she cried to herself, passionately, "but I shall have to deny myself that pleasure." For an hour she walked up familiar pathways over the rocks, looking down upon rocky gorges and black, abysmal shadows between the mountains, and sat down to rest a moment.

She heard a faint rustle, a chasing movement, and in its terror, a white rabbit that had not yet changed its winter coat for grey, crouched close to her foot, and from behind the rock below came a shadow—a coyote. Quickly she threw a handful of stones, which made the ugly beast skulk away. Lorena stooped to stroke the trembling, terrified little creature at her feet, but in an instant it had leaped away and was gone.

"O God !" exclaimed the lonely little human creature on the rock, as a similar picture to the scene just enacted before her, came to her vision. "Can I come close to your foot for protection, as this rabbit has done to me? You are so far away, God ! If you had left me mother she would have helped me. I am so lonely, and the Bad is so near."

This solitary, little human-being on the bleak and craggy Sierra, without knowing it, expressed, in her deep despair and anguish, the true Persian theory of belief—that Good and Evil (Ormuzd and Ahriman) are contending for the mastery, and the human being is free to choose one or the other; and no worshiper, at the old-time altar of incense, could have prayed more earnestly nor passionately to be delivered, than this untaught mountain child of the wilderness, trusting to her intuitions alone.

The wise and cynical may smile or sneer, but to the end of time, the despair of prophets and philosophers can never carry them beyond the Persian theory of belief, nor the despair of hunted souls find greater consolation than that strange instinct which bids them creep close to His foot.

Suddenly her tears ceased, she laughed hysterically, "If I haven't mother, I have my baby," and her tears flowed again, but they were sobs of joy. Those tears washed out all blur or spot that, like mould or rust, was beginning to faintly touch that pure, young soul.

She arose, and with impatient step made her way down from the frowning mountain, with its abysmal shadows and deep gorges, and running down the road to the little cabin home in the canyon, hastened in, and with the key which she had taken with her, unlocked the door and seized her treasure. Wrapping it warm in shawls with motherly instinct, she carried it out into the night, and kissed it again and again. What an experience for a babe! But it was used to its mother's eccentricities, and was always ready to accompany her to the deepest gorge, the highest peak. It was sent to be her comforter, and its trust in her was infinite. The darkest night it looked up in her face and smiled, not knowing whither it was going, and caring not whither so that it was with her.

Harville could not sleep, and the sound of her coming in and going out attracted his attention. Looking from the small-paned window, he saw her hurrying away. In an instant he had flung on his clothes and was following. What rash thing was she about to do—three o'clock in the morning straying through that bleak wilderness? He would follow and protect her from a distance.

What a picture of strangeness and unreality! The waning moon shone with a sickly glare, and looking down saw amid the rocks and fantastically-heaped mountains, a little open gulch, through which passed a small woman with a large baby in her arms, hurrying along, small but brave, and at a distance a man following, anxious and full of dread. But the moon faintly smiled as she saw the red light beaming from the mill, and the mother and child seek entrance.

But the man frowned, and hastening, saw, unobserved, a picture of domestic bliss—Aleck with his arms enfolding the two, Lorena, whose head was pillowed on his shoulder, and the babe which crowed its joy in the strange accents of the baby language, that tongue which doubtless contains cognate sounds with the first and original language of the human race.

The protective feeling first aroused in his breast gave way to jealous hatred and ugliness of feeling, and he swore an oath to himself—an ugly oath—that he would destroy this happiness, or—"

Human nature is so strange ! From love comes hate, from protection, destruction, in only a moment. From the kindly, loving friend of five minutes before, wishing to avert danger from Lorena's path, he became transformed into a subtle enemy determined to destroy her happiness. Love is an awful thing. It ccoes like a dove, it coils like a serpent.

Not daring to trust himself at the window farther, he returned to the house, his iron will bent relentlessly on subjugation.

"Lorena," said Aleck, "you don't know how badly I felt today—and you took it so quietly, and did the work so cheerfully. You have a hard time, little woman," he said with feeling. "And I've been thinking it all over. I'm going to make a dead set to get out of this business, and let you see something of the world. And we'll go to San Francisco, and go to all the operas and concerts—how we'll enjoy the music—and baby there shall grow up a civilized child instead of a savage. How did you know I was wanting you so ?"

"O, Aleck," cried Lorena, full of happiness, "I wanted you." What truer answer could be born of love ?

They sat there in the flickering light of the lamps, the ponderous fly-wheel whirling around, the shining steel machinery sliding backward and forward with its subtle intricacies of mechanism, and pleasant noise, so strangely out of proportion with the clamp, clamp of the stamps and the hissing of the pans in the body of the mill. The engine-room was retirement in comparison.

Aleck made a little nest in the corner with his coat and a blanket, and the baby was allowed to finish its nap, going to sleep as obediently as it had wakened.

"I never realized until to-night, Lorena, how you would shine in society, you have such good taste and are so bright and clever. And I thought if I didn't tell you of it, somebody else might get in

ahead of me, sometime. And the first thing I'd know, my little
Lorena might be running away with some other fellow;" and Aleck
laughed.

"Oh, Aleck," said Lorena, reproachfully.

"Well, we'll fix that all right, I'm going to run away with you
myself; I'm going to be that other fellow."

Then they both laughed. Was it a childish happiness that made
the rafters of that mill re-echo with merry laughter!

"Say, Aleck," said Lorena, "how much happier we are alone. I
wish Judge Harville would go. If he speaks of it again, don't urge
him to stay, will you?"

"Why, no!" said Aleck, looking surprised, "but I thought he
made it pleasant for you. Why? has he commenced to talk silly?
If he has forgotten himself"—what a threat of vengeance was conveyed in that tone!

"Oh, no," laughed Lorena, "only he bores me, a little of his
style goes a great way, you know. It is six o'clock, isn't it? How fast
the time flies in this dear old engine-room. Come, baby, it is time
to go." And together the three wended their way home in the grey
and chilly dawn. Certainly her husband's love was a charm that
encompassed Lorena round, yet if he had not been so kindly, she
would possibly have fought her good fight against Ahriman, though
not so well armed for the fray. She had resolved to meet him in
open fight, disarm and overcome him if she could. There must be
no scene, no trouble, no scandal, it must be subtly, silently done.

Judge Harville was courtesy itself all day. Aleck almost forgot
Lorena's instructions on the matter, and certainly his faintest suspicion.

But when evening came and Aleck was gone, he turned to her
with supplication in his eyes that was almost irresistible. He commenced to tell the story of his life, garnished with brilliant bits of
philosophy, it had even an element of pathos in it. Lorena's fancy
was kindled unconsciously. Her work lay neglected in her lap, the
baby, after sleeping all day, refused to sleep any more and amused
itself tumbling blocks around upon the floor.

He went on, the deep love he felt for her coloring everything he
touched upon, the impression she had made upon him as a little girl,
till finally he reached the snow and her strange appearance with the

light. "Oh, Lorena, Fate has ordained this from the beginning of the world, that we should meet and mingle our lives. You cannot escape from fate."

"Well," said she laughing, though it sounded strangely hollow, "I shall spoil fate for once—I'm just stubborn enough to defy it where my will is concerned."

"It seems wrong to you now," said the voice of the tempter, "but a year from now in a high and noble position, Mrs. Judge Harville shall find that she has escaped from a galling slavery and bondage. In her beautiful and lovely home with congenial friends and time for culture and improvement, she will wonder at the tame and profitless existence she led in the years forever past, and rejoice that she had had the ambition, the wisdom to grasp the opportunity which had lifted her from that condition which presented happiness as the happiness of a sheep, dull, quiet, aimless; enough to eat, but nothing else." Harville was nothing if not subtle.

"Is this what I saved you from the coyotes for?" asked Lorena quietly, yet a little dazzled by the picture he so brilliantly painted her.

"I know I stand in a bad light at present," he said rapidly, "but you are too lovely and dainty a blossom to blush unseen, and should see something of the world."

"That's what Aleck said, to-day," said she artlessly.

"I am the instrument of fate sent to interfere in your behalf, and in the years to come you will thank me for the interference. You have saved my life. It belongs to you rightfully; take it then and do what you will with it."

Lorena looked into his eyes hopelessly. Where were her subterfuges, her little arts to cover her feelings, where were the subtleties with which she was going to disarm him? All seemed in a daze around her.

"All conventionalities shall be observed. There shall be no scandal. I know enough of the technicalities of the law to set you free from this bondage without a mar to sully your fair name; and after that—for I shall be patient—the justice or the minister, which ever you like, shall give me the right to care for you." He spoke in a low, thrilling tone.

"Judge Harville, it has always been the great desire of my life to

exert a good influence on those around me. Are you deliberately
going to make me feel that I am responsible for all this terrible, terrible thing that you are talking about?'' It was a direct appeal,
and should have awakened his better self. But that vanity of his
was underneath all, strong and exacting. He was irritated by her
resistance, and threw off the mask which he had so carefully worn.

"I don't know anything about your good influence, I only know
that you waken the very devil in me when you come near me. And
I cannot endure to see you tied to a stupid dolt of a man who cares
nothing for you. It simply maddens me.'' His voice was hoarse
and his eyes were full of evil light.

Lorena's eyes were riveted on him, a strange little red flame
seemed to burn in their depths. Was she going to succumb?

"If I should be in great distress,'' she said in slow, measured tones,
her pupils dilated beyond their usual size, "if some one was hound-
ing me, and driving me to death, could I claim your protection?''

"Claim my protection?'' he repeated in surprise, and rising to his
full height, he spoke, "Lorena, I'd protect you with more than my
life if there were anything more to offer.''

"Then, Judge Harville,'' said Lorena, slowly, rising also, "*I
claim your protection*''—her voice faltered, her eyes fell, sobs choked
her while her heart surged up in mighty throbs—"*I claim your protection from yourself.*''

Turning to the table, she fell upon her chair, burying her face upon her arm, and cried like a broken-hearted child, the babe at her
feet clinging to her dress, and sobbing in unison with its stricken
mother.

Judge Harville drew a long breath. He walked up and down the
room a moment. The evil light died out of his eyes. He felt himself a black-hearted fiend—a Mephistopheles—all the false reasoning
in his premises stood out like lightning in the black night—his vision
became clearer—his selfishness more apparent. He walked to her
side, laid his hand gently upon her soft hair.

"Don't grieve,'' he said, "*you have my protection.*''

And that was all.

Daily lives must go on, and daily tasks must be done, though the
heavens fall, or earthquakes rend the world. Very quietly Judge
Harville took his departure, but he never forgot for a moment, a

certain purpose which took possession of him, and after much wire pulling and utilizing of secret influence, he had the pleasure of hearing that Aleck Westbrook had received an appointment from the Governor of the State, which placed him in a position of trust and well on the road to fortune.

Years have passed since that act of selt-abnegation, and last winter Judge Harville was called to Washington to attend to an intricate matter of law.

At one of the receptions, where he went merely as a spectator, he stood gazing at the gay throng with weary, careless eyes, when suddenly a profile among the throng carried him back eight years in his life.

He saw the gloomy canon covered with snow, a light shining from a window, he felt again the breath of the coyotes upon his cheek.

The face turned. It was indeed Lorena, bright, arch, as ever he pictured her, clad in a shimmering satin robe of white, leaning upon her husband's arm, and leading by the hand a beautiful little girl in daintiest lace, erratic a mother as ever, taking the child as naturally with her to a reception, as out into the blackness of the night in the wild Sierras.

A gladness came into Judge Harville's heart, and overflowed at his eyes. He felt a strange sensation of nearness to that beautiful, womanly figure. It was Lorena, and she was resting under his protection still. ELLA STERLING CUMMINS,
Author of "The Mountain Princess."

QUARTZ.

(FROM A MINER'S MEMORY.)

CHAPTER ONE.

STRIKE.

The men who strike for silver mines in the arid country of the State of Silverado are called "prospectors." They are a curious compound of the laborer, the speculator and the scientist. Your "prospector" is not, usually, when you meet him, what he has been. You accost him, or he you, and it becomes at once evident that the man before you belongs to no class or province, and you cannot guess at his position in life with any certainty. He has upon his person the commonest of "store clothes," generally well worn, coarse woolen shirts, open at the sun-tanned neck; no coat, slouch hat, pants in rough boots. But his dress and address do not go together in harmony; his conversation is just whatever your own may invite, until you strike the subject of mines or silver ores; then he leads into a world of travel, speculation, rise, progress failure, until you find this sun-burnt man has handled coin in his day, and means to do it again.

He may have been a minister of the gospel, a lawyer, a physician, politician, merchant, etc; but not often do you find him to have been a day-laborer, save on compulsion. Wiry, tough, irrepressible, and far-traveled, patient yet excitable, his experience is large and various, and his love of adventure with hope of great gain is as boundless and often as barren as the region of mountains he loves Poverty and privation he bears like a philosopher; while affluence is to him only "for the fun of it," and he makes short work of spending thousands of dollars on old and new sensations.

He talks about a home which he has, or wishes to have; but, generally, he has no home, and never will have any, outside of the clothes he happens to be wearing. And where he goes when he must lie down and die I have never discovered. That he does die I take for certain; but, except in a fight or by accident, I have never known of a dead "prospector."

He is the creator of new states and the driving power of the Stock Boards; yet people endeavor to treat him, unless he is flush of money, as a person of little importance. The merchant, the lawyer, the ranchman, physician—everybody — lives in Silverado, on the results of the prospector's exertions; yet even the camp-followers think themselves more respectable and higher-toned than he, the Moses who leads them about in the wilderness.

Almost always he has a faithful partner in his joys, journeyings and sorrows, and that partner is a man. This fellowship is imposed by the fact that it takes two to sink a deep hole in the ground or a drill in the rock; and it requires two to accomplish such an experience as shall now be presented.

It snows heavily as out of the sage-covered wilderness two men, riding, urge a laden mule into a beaten road and turn toward a mining center, shifting in their saddles to give the wet and driving snow a cold shoulder.

Pushing steadily onward, a farm-house near the roadside rises out upon the horizon. Boy in front of the house rushes in to say: "Mother, two men a-comin'!"

Woman (outside of house)—"What, in a buggy?"

Boy.—No; on horses an' drivin' a mule."

Woman. "Pshaw! only prospectors."

By this time the two rough, ragged fellows, with beards awry, hair uncut and unkempt beneath the slouched hats, ride to the door.

Prospector (to boy.)—"Well, but ain't this winter?"

Boy.—"You bet, it is!"

Prospector (at the open door.)—"Cold, bad day, madam."

Woman (inattentively.)—"I reckon it is."

Prospector.—"Madam, could you let us have about two loaves of bread? And, tell you the truth, we haven't a cent in our clothes, but we're likely to be along this way again soon, and we haven't a bite."

Woman.—"I haven't got none baked, and something's the matter with my yeast. I won't have no bread till most night."

Prospector (turning away.)—"It would accommodate us very much, but you know best, madam, about your own affairs. Good day."

Prospector (remounting.)—"Couldn't make it, old boy! We'll have to ride for it."

Old Boy—"H—l! Couldn't you git nuthin'?"

Prospector.—"Not a snoot-full. I spoke a lively piece to the old gal, but she wouldn't come out. Go ahead, we may be happy yet."

Woman (inside.)—"Johnny! Johnny, do you hear?"

Boy (outside.)—"yes'm. What yer want?"

Woman—"What'd them fellers say?"

Boy.—"One of 'em called yer an old gal."

Woman.—"That's cause I wouldn't turn to and bake for 'em; 'zif I hadn't nuthin to do but bake for people who are flat broke! Them prospectors is allus flat broke. Why don't they stay at home and work, like I do? Fetch in your wood, Johnny; it's going to be a cold night when it stops a-snowin'."

Boy.—"Yes'm. Them men's got to make Simmins' ranch afore they git a bite, an' that pack mule's mighty nigh petered out, if you hear me."

Woman.—"That's none o' yore business; you git yore wood an' come in the house an' dry yore feet."

Time passes at the ranch, time passes on the road; time passes in the nearest mining town; time passes in the lonely mountains where the rich earth lies about the open shaft; time passes in the great commercial city, where trade and science sigh for silver; and amidst the the great city, past the ranch, along the road, through the mining town and to the open cut in the lonely mountains, there moves the love of gain—that subtlest of spirits. So, on a day of bright, white winter sunshine, the boy outside the ranche, gazing up the road beneath his own shading palm, shouts, "Pap! buggy comin'; high steppers, you bet!"

Pap (drowsy, frowzy, red-faced and smoke-scented, appearing at the door), "Which way, from town? (Looking townward) I say, Symanthy, I'll bet that's them fellers what's found them new mines out yander. They'll want dinner in a hurry."

Woman—(looking over old Frowzy's shoulder as both stand in the door), "Them's liberty stable stock, and coyote-robes; high-flyers, you bet! Yer sir! Johnny, make a fire in the stove this minit!"

All in one moment there happens here a multitude of incidents, chief among which "old Frowzy" finds his hat, puts it on, comes to the door again in time to say to the newly arrived party, as the "high-stepping" team drives up, "Fine day, gents."

Man in carriage—"Yes, tip-top day. How about something to eat for man and beast?"

Old Frowzy—"Lots of hay and barley; and I reckon the old woman kin give you enough to eat—sech as we've got.

The man who holds the reins smiles, and without making the least motion to alight or drop them, remarks: "Yes, but boss, we're flat broke—havn't a red."

Old Frowzy, with eyes on the fine turnout, "Oh, that makes no odds in a new country! we all get that way at odd times."

Here the man above hands the reins to old Frowzy, and the whole party alight. On moving near the door they are met by madam of the rancho with, "Walk in gentlemen, and take a seat. Did you say you would have dinner?"

He of the reins—"Yes madam, if you have bread enough baked, we'll all take a bite."

Woman—"Bread enough? Why certainly, I allus have that."

Reins—"Well, excuse me, madam, I didn't know. Sometimes people in these out-of-the-way places, get short of convenient grub."

Woman—"I don't never fail to—oh! I see! You're mebbe the man as come by here about six weeks ago. Well, now, you see, I can't allus tell whose a joshin me and who isn't. Why I thought you was a-a jokin' that day; you prospectors are all the time on the josh!"

Reins—"That's all right, ma'm; I expect I did look sort o' gay and festive that day, and we had a jolly time after we passed here."

By this time madam is away in the adjacent room of the cabin, deep in the mysteries of bacon, canned salmon, black coffee, etc., but Reins goes on with the story thuswise:

"We rode (Sam and me) from here to Simmins'; that's the first ranch this side of town, on horses that we had already pushed hard to reach this place, and we hadn't a bite of anything to eat that day, and d—d little to eat for three days, because we were holding out to the last minute to develop the prospect, and working on short rations. But we left here at late dinner-time, rode all night, and it a-snowing for keeps, and the horses stilted up on snow-balls, till next day about noon we struck Simmins. Lord God! I was never so happy in my life as when old Dan Simmins looked me square in the face and says he: "Well if h—l ain't a-goin' to pop then I'm no Christian!" (you know how old Dan talks.) "Where in h—l have you been?" says he. "Why, you look like a sick woman's baby! Take a horn, you'll find it in that there jug in the corner." I don't ever expect to be so happy again as we all were that afternoon! We ate and drank and sung, and told yarns, and had a bully time inside the house, while the snow was attending to its job outside and a-coming down as steady as clock-work. Sam sort o'went out of his mind with the sudden change—mebbe the whisky had a hand in it—and he thought he was back home in the States, telling his mother all about his ramblings for fifteen years; and he thought old Dan was his daddy—so, as he was telling his mother, and crying and laughing and talking it was better than any theayter. And when old Dan would put in to help him out, Sam would say: "Never you mind, daddy; you let me tell it." Then old Dan would laugh till the tears ran down his face, and say, "Go on, my son, go on! Your ma and me will listen to you." We knew the poor fellow was wandering but it was funny for all that—particularly when one comes to consider what a maguif' old dad could be panned out of Dan Simmins."

"Gents, dinner is ready—walk out! We haven't got no great variety, but its the best we have. Yer pap (to old Frowzy) cut up and pour out for 'em, and if yer want anything more, holler. I've got to go in the kitchen."

After Frowzy helps the party to such as there is, he proceeds to ask a few leading questions of a nature just such as his kind are most loth to answer—questions looking to a share of some sort in the county of the new mines.

"Hev you enny ranche-land or good hay-land out near them new prospects?"

"Yes. There are several spots where a man might find a lay-out for ranching."

"How is it for wood?"

"Plenty of wood."

"Well, do you reckon to go ahead out there ennyways soon?"

"We can't just say about that. The Professor here will be able to tell, mebbe, as we come back."

"When do you 'low to be back again?"

"Well, if the Professor can see as much in the same place, and in the same time, as we can, we may be back here in three days."

"What are you goin' to do about hoss feed and grub while yer there?"

"Oh, Sam's out there. Didn't he stop here as he went by with a team—four horses, high load, doors and windows at the side and hay bales on top—about two weeks ago?"

"No; he didn't stop yere. I seed him goin' past, but he never stopped."

Here Reins smiled over his cup of black coffee, and said: "Sam's a little curious about some things."

Dinner over, bill paid, the "high-stepping" stock is buckled to, the party are seated. Frowzy passes up the reins, and says: "Well, I hope you've got a good thing out there; I'm half a mind to come out and see you."

"All right, old man; I'll introduce you to Sam." Then turning toward the door where Madam Frowzy stands, with hands on hips and arms akimbo: "Bye, bye, madam; keep a sharp lookout for prospectors. Why, hello, sonny; what are you looking up at me so for? I'm not a pinto circus horse."

Boy (near the wheel)—"You're the fellow 'at went past yer about a month ago, and called ma'am an old gal—that's what you are!"

"Well, but I'll take it all back, and I wouldn't have said it if I had known you were around."

Away rolls the light wagon, as back into the house goes Frowzy, to smoke and stew over the fire, while he considers the chance of making something for himself out of the new discovery.

"I say, Symanthy, I'm a good mind to go over to that new place."

"Well," snaps Symanthy, "if yer goin', you'd better go airly.

Fer if them fellers really hez struck ennything big over ther', ther'll
be plenty a-goin' in on the chances mighty soon. I wouldn't wonder
ef you'd see some of the sharps a-follerin' them fellows up afore
mornin'"

"Well, I reckon I'd best strike out in the mornin'. I fergot to ax
'em how far it was, but I kin foller in their tracks."

In the morning, early, Frowzy is off with saddle-horse and pack-
mules, for, although Frowzy is the very picture of uncombed and
smoke-dried indolence, and as a general thing, goes about on foot
with the dragging sprawl of a work-ox, yet when it comes to exertion in the saddle, or endurance in the hope of sudden gain, he is as
tough as a lariat.

The day is bright and warm as only some odd days in Silverado
can be, the very essence of beautiful weather and pure air, for the
climate in the State is like the human fortune in the State—either
lovely and serene, with an "elevated goose," or else detestably bad
and flat broke.

The day is splendid, and though the season is winter, the dust
whirls in spiral, electric columns along the highway and rises in a
cloud about Bub and his dog as they romp in the road in front of
Frowzy's ranche house.

"Mam!" shouts Bub, "that 'ere buggy's a-comin' again! and
there's 'nuther dust acrost the valley, and I'll bet that's Pap."

"Well, it's a-most night, and yore wood ain't in yet! Ef enny-
body's a-comin', they'll cum 'thout your starin'."

Nevertheless, as to the staring, madam comes out into the road to
stand with Bub and the dog for a prolonged stare into the valley.

The light wagon halts this time only long enough to refresh man
and horse, and then away toward the town; for the eye of science
has seen what the man of science is in haste to lay before the men of
money and speculation. Time, time is now the prime object, and
horse-flesh is a second consideration; so, drive, driver—send 'em!
the love of gain grows into a fever.

Away goes the vehicle from view, and the dust cloud of its rolling
settles down as Frowzy dismounts at his own door, where his sage-
brush cherub and his dog vie with each other in jumping around for
purposes of undefinable joy.

Madam begins to feel some thrill of anxiety about the new state of affairs, and so, without waiting, she appears at the door to ask, "Well, how is it over ther?"

Frowzy, big with the throes of a new hope, and the consciousness of new knowledge, answers not, but continues to unpack and strip his animals in silence, save when he says to the dog, "There, that'll do now. Git down!"

But once the animals are out to graze, and one saddle flung on one side of the door and the other on the other side—things begin, thereby, to be made neat and comfortable—he says, "Well!" some Western people always say "well" to start with, "well, that's a mighty big thing over ther. Things'll be a bilin' yer in a mighty short time, ef ye hear my gentle voice. I'm hungry."

"I'll giv ye yore supper in a minet—it's all ready. Did you see every show fur a ranche?"

"You bet I did! I located the purtiest place fur a ranche and station you ever seed—not more'n three miles from where the town's got to be. That Purfesser feller says there ain't no better silver mines in the world."

"Was they all located?"

"No. That feller as was a talkin here as they went down, he showed me wher' I could take chances on an extension."

"Didn't ye take it?" asked madam, eagerly.

"Well, he said before he'd show it to me that I must locate, and record it as the Old Gal, or he wouldn't show it to me."

"Durn his imperdent picter!"

"So, I located it, and it's the 'Old Gal;' and that Purfesser says it's as good as enny of 'em, when it's opened once."

"Don't it crop out nowheres along?"

"No; but it's right on the line o'them best leads—that's wher' the 'Old Gal' is. I can't make out what that feller wanted me to call it the 'Old Gal' for."

"I know!" exclaimed Johnny, dumping on armload of fire-wood into a corner of the cabin, "it's 'cause mam wouldn't bake bread fur him when he was flat broke!"

"You, Johnny! you jist keep yore mouth shet an' speak when yore spoke to, will ye! You don't know what yo're talkin' about."

"Enny how," says Mr. Frowzy, "the feller seemed mighty tickled about some durned thing or other! But you can't make him

out very easy. He's smart—he is. He knows more in a minit
about them mines nor what that Purfesser knows in a day; but he
pertends to leave it all to the Purfesser. I see him a-winkin' at that
Sam, when Old Spectacles and Big Words was a settin' it in steep
on the lingo. He knows what he's after!—that feller does."

With which piece of wisdom Frowzy finished his supper and commenced cutting "plug" to fill his pipe; after filling and lighting
which, he proceeded to puff awhile in that odorous smudge of silence which the European man has borrowed from his red brother.
But he soon broke forth again with "Symanthy!" That vigorous
female being in the kitchen said, "Well?"

"I've an idee I'd better take the tram an' go back ther' and put
up a cabin. And you'd better send over to Reese river for yore
brother and his wife to help you run the house while I'm gone."

"Oh, Bub an' me kin run the house! 'Taint worth while to be
bringin' people till ye need 'em. They'd only growl ef ye didn't divide the new lay-out with 'em. You go ahead; I'll run the house."

By this time it had grown dusk outside, as the shortening winter
day dropped behind the dark silhouette of mountains, and the family
conversation was broken by a strange voice:

"Hillo! Haeow is it about here?" To which Frowzy shouts
back, "Aye, aye! Comin' in a minit!" And he peers about by
the firelight for "that everlastin', durned, old hat" that he never
can lay his hands on, save when his head is in it, while Mrs. Frowzy ventures to whisper, "That's a Yank—you bet he's a-smellin'
after them mines."

Before Frowzy can find that much-maligned head-gear the new arrival, or one of them, has entered the door, with that terrible im-
patience and fussy attention to details peculiar to some of those citizens who say the word, "haeow."

"I waant to staybil teow hawsis with yeow."

"All right," returns Mr. Frowzy, by this time under "that hat."
"Symanthy, gimme the lantern."

While the horses are being cared for, Enoch rattles around as if
he were helping to do the work, though really he knows nothing
about it, having been brought up to oxen and a good stick in the
State he calls Neow Hawinsheer. But he keeps his tongue and wits
at work with numerous questions, such as: "Who were the party

we met back a piece?" "Prospectors—ah! Rich, I s'pose?"
"Clus about here? Ah—no. Never du strike anything near
hand, any one. Sing'lar, ain't it? Quite so."

Frowzy, busy with the team, answers as clearly as he deems best;
but, as he closes the stable door and starts, lantern in hand, for the
house, lazily asks, "Which way might you be travelin'—if it's a
fair question?"

"Wal, we've got a little bizniz acount Nowth. I fergit wich way
yaeou sed the neaw mines were."

"Like as not I didn't say. I'm not clear which way they are—
som'ers out south-east tho,' I think they said. Do you want supper?"

"Wal, no; we've got foud an' beddin', thank ye. There's my
friend strikin' a fire naeow. When we've eatin' a bite we'll cum
over an' chat a bit, ef its agreeab'l."

"All right," assents Mr. F., as he blows out his light and enters
his domicile; while Mr. Enoch Southchurch repairs to his wagon, his
friend and his supper—at which locality he says in a low voice to his
companion: "Aeour old naybor sez thet the neaw mines are saeouth-
easterly from here."

"No odds what he says," remarks the other in a graff voice. "I
cain follow that wagon track wherever it may go. If I cain't, I'll
go straight back and die in Texas."

"Jes so, Kernil, I depend on yeou for that." What further was
said out of doors at the fire, or in the house at the other fire is not
important to us, except that Frowzy hurriedly told Symanthy that
"them fellers is after the new diggins, hot-foot."

To which Samantha responded, "I know'd it."

"Yes," says F., "they've mighty smooth ephs; but they don't
pump me; not much."

Morning dawns once more upon the wide fields of Artemisia, cold,
calm and clear; the blue smoke of the camp-fire by the roadside
curls up among the early rays of the sun, and everything about the
hithertofore drowsy rancho is made awake. The prospector has made
his track in the wilderness, and the keen and silent noses of Mam-
mon's blood-hounds are down upon the trail.

Frowzy is away before the dawn; up to the mountain-slope of the
foothills, to secure his team—horses—ere they cease to bask in the

fringes of the morning sun, warming away the chill of night from their shaggy, winter coats.

The bacon in the fry-pan at the camp-fire of Enoch Southchurch sputters to the tune of "Haste thee, son of Plymouth Rock! God helps those who helps themselves."

The "high-stepping team of "liberty-stable stock" has rolled the glittering wheels all night through the glancing moonbeams along the road, toward the mining town, passing "old Dan Simmins" with a slight halt, long enough to shout "how-de-do!" and bring "old Dan" to the door, in unpresentable haste, for a brief chat—and then away again, with his last, "Be good to yourselves! Make my regrets to the Young Men's Christian Association, on account of my absence last Sunday, and tell Gage to send me two gallons of whisky. I'm about out. S' long, boys!"

Away, again—and away—till down the mountain road, heralded by the golden glow that tips the topmost peaks with new born morning's flush, into the busy mountain town, along whose plank side-walks the heavy boots of the earliest risers thump, thump, thump, the light wagon rolls and ceases to roll. The party leap out as the horses snort that grateful recognition of home wherewith the faithful servant expresses his satisfaction.

And now, as Frowzy says it, things begin "to bile." The assayer's fire glows a white-fever-heat as it leaps and licks the precious ore in presence of the anxious eyes that watch the boiling-pot. Deftly the assayer handles his tongs, coyly he toys with the blistering glow, and then carefully pours, pounds, batters, rolls and weighs the "button."

Eureka! millions of earth's treasures loom up before the eye of speculation. The news flies; men gather on street corners, in stores, in saloons, everywhere, to inspect samples of rock and hear the story of the new discovery; while the prosp ctor, his pocket lined with "eagles," slouches with a newly, well-dressed, easy grace along the polished board that bears the glasses in front of the pretty young man whose back hair shines in the big mirror in all the glory of tonsorial art, and slapping his "heavy sorrel"* on the counter, says, "Come up, boys, come up."

* Twenty dollar gold pieces.

CHAPTER TWO.

The discovery and location of new silver-mining centers in the wild semi-desert regions of North America will soon be a matter of the past; but it was once a very exciting business. First there was the desert valley and the wild, rocky, rugged mountains; then across the valley came the earliest "prospector," making his devious way among the "sage-brush;" guided by no previous track in the dry gravelly soil; steered solely by the contour of the surrounding mountains; riding on his mule or wiry, wild broncho and driving before him, or leading behind him, the grunting animal upon whose back are girted and corded the needed bedding, food and implements for preliminary mining purposes. It is a serious and a silent procession under the hot sun of a summer-day, or the cool star-light of night when the shadows of the pointed mountains fall dark and long across the arid waste, or in the wind-driven snows of altitudinous winter. If the search is successful and the winner crowned with reward, then the single track of the prospector becomes a beaten trail, like an ashen-colored thread stretching from civilization toward the unknown; the trail in time gives way to the wagon-road on which the slow-moving ox bends his unwilling, calloused neck to the inspiring needs of speculative industry; soon to be followed by the more aristocratic mule marching in silent, solemn, long-eared processions of dust-covered pageantry; and the mule at length to be followed by the swifter whirling stage-coach team with its cloud of dust and its crowded passengers.

People—mostly, if not entirely, bearded boisterous adventurers—take to the new road and flock into the new mining camp which is hidden away on the slope of a cañon, or at the water giving head of a ravine. Heavy loads of lumber for house-building underlying an imposed stratum of merchandise unload under the direction of the "gentleman from Judea;" while the manager and dispenser of alcoholic amusements erects his tent and, behind a rough board, begins the grave exercise of polishing a tumbler with a napkin; the boarding house, the lodging house, the needed mechanical houses and all other houses arise in so short a time that the aspect of the scene changes, as if by magic, from all that make the irksomeness of solitude to the moving, shifting, humming, habitable picture of energetic industry. Thus has been initiated, under varying aspects, that great aggregation of representative commonwealths commonly called the United States of North America. Later in the years comes the ready school-master to his appointed task; still later the church building, with its echoing bell in pointed spire with weather-vane a-top to show how blow the winds of Heaven and which way waft the clouds.

It might be a useful, certainly a curious, study to find out how much alcohol in its various drinkable forms—mostly whisky, however—has had to do with the advancement of civilization and the establishment of good government; for it seems to be a fact, that the drinker of the more fiery potations, however much they may have damaged themselves, have always been the staunchest creators and supporters of good government. The maxim about "the sober second thought" implies that the previous thought was not sober and, therefore, drunk.

Is the strong-drinker's liking for good and free government the remorseful expression over the ruin of his hearth-store felicity? Let that pass; it is an open question; but there is no question that in a new silver-mining camp the political and social center is the alcoholic saloon; neither is there any question that in the camp whereof this vivacious history treats one Alexander Crowder kept the "Head Quarters." It has often been remarked, by the uninitiated, that it looks singular to see so many of the largest and most able-bodied of our fellow citizens engaged in the light-handed avocation of filling fluids into bottles and glasses; but such persons should be informed that the saloon-keeper is liable to have heavier—vastly heavier—work upon his strong hands. He may not often need the heft of his heavy shoulders, but when he does need it he needs it very much. Yet there are retail alcoholic dispersers on the Pacific slope—life-long veterans at the bar—who have never laid a hand harshly on any mortal. These be the few men of high administrative ability—stranded statesmen wasted by the wayside; probably the lineal descendants of the "publicans and sinners" with whom Christ the

Saviour used to talk, or, at least so it reads, was accused of it by
the righteous Pharisees; and of such was Alexander Crowder, formerly
of various other localities, but now a resident of the new and thriving
camp yclept Mountain Brow.

At the Head Quarters was held the first meeting to raise a fund to
institute a school and prepare the way toward establishing that insti-
tution in a permanent school-house; because, by the school laws
passed by the keen legislators of the State of Silverado no public
money for school purposes could be obtained by any camp until the
"said camp shall institute and support a school, of not less than ten
pupils of the proper age (exclusion of Indians not twenty), for a
period of time not less than three months," etc. At the Head Quarters were taken the initial steps towards providing the camp—the
new town or city in mining parlance is always "the camp"—with a
supply of good water and for the creation of a volunteer fire company,
of which latter, by the way, Alexander Crowder was unanimously
elected foreman.

At the Head Quarters the Central Committee of both our great
political parties met—each committee on a different day in the week,
however—to plant the seeds of national dispute and presidential
fervor along the advancing highway of "our glorious institutions."
Here the night-flying orator was wont to point out the dangerous
rocks of national navigation in tones of unmistakable alarm supple-
mented by the soothing scintillations of patriotic promise and political
hope. Whoop la ! The stars and stripes shall wave over a country
that must be saved. The little springs of far-off mountain-bowed political power shall borrow the white-souled purity of the shining
snows, and in the glad dance of the sparkling fluid follow the music
of the mountain stream down and away to where the great river of
our political power bears upon its bosom the commerce of a world
and the hopes of all mankind. (Cheers, but no note taken of the
miner who mutters, "'cept the dam Chinaman.")

At the Head Quarters—which gradually come to be known as
"Crowders"—was preached the first sermon from any Protestant
preacher at Mountainbrow; though the Catholic Padre had been
around first—as he usually is in such places—to look after his
flock and get the Church's dutiful "divvy" on the young prosperity.
The reason the Protestant preferred to preach at Crowder's was

partly owing to the fact that the Head Quarters was the building in camp best adapted to congregational purposes; but mostly, it was surmised, because Crowder, out of the abundance o. his mountain experience, was too wise to permit the smaller games of gambling to be carried on under his roof. He rather contented himself with private poker and faro rooms at the back end, with billiards in all styles, in the bar-room and social cribbage in the corners. So, when Brother Magath dropped into the Head Quarters on a wintry Sunday forenoon, the house was full, the billiard balls clicked their way through the pool-pins, the game-keepers cried the score, the glasses clinked at the bar from time to time as the hearty "here's to us" preceded the usual imbibation; and the string band of three, with the cornet player, behind the piano and the heavy German pianist (male, of course) discoursed musical gems from the composers of all lands. The musicians were present out of regard (financial) to the day of the week. Sunday is a fine large day all over Silverado.

Upon this scene entered Brother Magath, and modestly waiting for an opportune moment to catch Mr. Crowder's ear approached the highly polished bar-board in front of that worthy fluidical dispenser who instinctively looked the preacher interrogatively in the eye and "set up" a glass tumbler.

"Ah, no-ah ! Not anything to drink; thank you."

Crowder put out the cigar-box.

"Thank you; but I'm not a smoker. Excuse me; but I merely wished to talk to you in private a moment."

"Want to strike me for a piece?" and Crowder opened his money drawer. "Broke, I 'spose ! How much ?"

"No, sir, I want no money."

"Well, what do ye want? Spit it out."

"I want permission to preach a sermon in this room this afternoon at 2 o'clock sharp. That's all I want."

"Want to preach h'yer?"

"Yes, sir !"

"Well. That'll depend on what the boys say. I've no objection, myself."

"Would you be good enough to announce it to them, and let us hear what they say about it ?"

"Well, I'm not much on the announce—but I'll try it a whack," —he walked to the outer end of his long bar and in a big voice said—"See yer, boys. I want ye to lissen."

The games and the noise consequent upon them gradually subsided. Pool-players dropped the butts of their cues to the floor and stood at rest—the music of the band lapsed into silence.

"This gent wants to preach and pays us the compliment by sayin' its the most respectable place in camps for his business; an' I've told him I'd leave it to you fellers."

"When d's he want to preach? Right away, now?" said a tall cue-holder.

"No; this afternoon at 2 o'clock. What d'ye all say? Preach or no preach?"

"Preach—of course. D'ye 'spose we're dam heathens?" said one.

"Preach! why cert'nly," said another.

"Of course," assented another.

Brother Magath whispered to Crowder.

"But he wants ye all to attend. Will ye do it?"

"You bet we will," said the tall man turning to take the shot he had omitted, and added, "give him a drink and charge it to me."

When Brother Magath appeared in the Head Quarters, promptly at 2 o'clock, P. M., he found the billiard tables draped in their white night-clothes, the bar and its bottle-holding shelves clothed in similar attire, the musicians dispersed and the audience silently, though a little uneasily, waiting for him. He took his stand behind the piano using that musical furniture as a sacred desk, and thereon, as a "sport" phrased it, "spread his tricks to buck against the devil"—which "tricks" consisted of a Bible, a hymn-book and a white linen pocket-handkerchief. Then first, as was his custom, he read a hymn, but before, the reading he remarked:

"Gentlemen, among my misfortunes, one of the greatest is that I have no ear for melody and no talent for singing; I shall therefore, be compelled to call upon any person who can sing to raise the tune for the lines I am about to read.

"Am I a soldier of the Cross,
A follower of the Lamb?

> And shall I fear to own his cause,
>   Or blush to speak his name?
>
> *   *   *   *   *   *
>
> Are there no foes for me to face;
>   Must I not stem the flood?
> Is this vile world a friend to grace
>   To help me on to God?
>
> *   *   *   *   *   *
>
> Sure I must fight if I would reign;
>   Increase my courage Lord;
> I'll bear the toil, endure the pain,
>   Supported by the word."

"Part of the seven-hundredth hymn; common metre; please sing."

There was a deep and depressing silence that followed the spirited reading of these martial lines broken at first by no sound save the low whisper in which one miner conveyed his idea into the ear of another, thus:

"I think the parson's dead game—there's a heap o' sand in the hymn."

"Cannot some one raise the tune? Surely there are several persons in this room whose early training and musical talent fits them to sing these sacred lines."

"What is the tune?"

"Unfortunately I cannot remember that either, but it is a very common one," and still he stood with his book in his hand open before him as if supplicating some one to come forward and take it away; but the tune did not arise.

"Where's them doggonned musicians gone to? They'd ort to be able to h'ist 'er up," said a new voice.

"What duz a durn Dutch musical cuss know about hymn-singin'?" exclaimed another.

Here the front door of the saloon was thrown open, wafting into the room a sharp breath of the winter air:

"Hello! There comes Wash White an' he's a reg'lar camp-meetin' psalmist. Yer Wash, come in an' h'ist the tune."

Wash took a hasty stare about the room as he closed the door behind him and asked:

"What the hell's up?"

"H-u-u-s-sh. This's meetin'."

"Miner's meeting?"

"No; prar meetin'. Church. Religion. Ye dam fool, don't ye know nuthin' pious!"

"I-o-h. Whew!" responded Wash as he eyed the preacher and took in the invitation,

"Yes, my friend," said Parson Magath still holding the open book in his hand, "we desire to sing a few lines preparatory to a continuance of Divine worship and we are waiting for some one to voice the music.

"What is the hymn!" asked Wash.

"Am I a soldier of the cross," began the preacher to read, but was interrupted by Wash continuing—

> "A follower of the Lamb ?
> And shall I fear to own his cause
> Or blush to speak his name ?

—o' course I can sing them lines like a licensed exhorter. I was brought up on that music. My ole dad used to fold his arms of a Sunday morning an' walk up and down singing them lines till hell howled an' Satan shook in his irons. But if I start the tune I want all hands to chip in an' jine the uproar—an' I don't want no squeakin' nor no half-mouthed mumblin'. Go ahead, parson; line 'er out."

Brother Magath once again read the initial stanza Wash, with a voice trained from infancy to "revival" airs, launched boldly out upon the melodious stream, and at first, was assisted in a wavering way; but at length the crowd, seeing and hearing that he was fully equal to the occasion, joined in with a will and boomed the lines, couplet at a time, as Brother Magath, smiling blandly, delivered them. For up and down the hills the echoes sped bearing with them the true spirit of the Soldiers of the Cross. It was an able-bodied noise not devoid of a rude spirit of harmony.

After the singing Brother Magath nodded his thanks to Mr. White and proceeded with the subsequent spirituality, the general tenor of which was that, whatever might be a man or woman's place in this life it was a duty, and ought to be a pride and a pleasure, for such person to do that duty boldly, cheerfully, respectfully and firmly for righteousness sake; "nor God, nor man, nor devil loves the coward or the quitter."

"Them's my sentiments," said Mr. Crowder, and Brother Magath wound up the exercises with a fervent short prayer.

"Three cheers for the parson, Hip, hip, Hurray!" and the cheers were given with a will, while Crowder disrobed the bar, the bottles and glasses.

"Come down," exclaimed a short active man. "Come down handsome in the contribution box," and he went about through the crowd extending his hat to everybody. "'Taint no real genoowine church 'thout a kerleckshun. Parsons kaint live on chin enny more'n other folks. Come down!" and while the hat grew heavy with silver, the imbibations went on all around, and in the midst Brother Magath was receiving hand-shaken congratulations, also refusing numerous invitations to participate.

"There she is, parson"—said the volunteer collector—"salt 'er down," and he placed his heavy hat on the nearest billiard table.

"Gentlemen, this is, indeed, very kind of you and I hope God will bless this gift in my hands to his own great uses; and I pray that you may gather again, tenfold, this bread thrown upon the waters," all the while as he talked, loading his light pockets with heavy coin. Then at last, he politely returned the hat to its owner, bid his unique congregation an effusive farewell and went out upon his way rejoicing.

Again the games went forward, the instrumental music resumed its sway and, sorry to say it, Wash White, proud of his opportune assistance was fast approaching the meandering edge of inebriation. And so ended the first lesson. Were these seeds of salvation, sown by the wayside, lost—all lost? Who shall say? Is the vim of good in the evil of Nazareth worked out? *Quien sabe?*

CHAPTER THREE.

I was sitting in the saloon to-day reading the papers when a man about fifty years old—a heavy man, stout, stooped and hard-handed, came in with a kind of weaving, slouchy gait, having his hat in one hand and an empty smoke-pipe in the other. He stopped in the middle of the floor, gave a sort of goggle-eyed gaze around the room, swung his body with the sweep of a weak old willow in the wind, slapped his hat on his head pretty well over his eyes, put the stem end of the empty, short pipe into his mouth and pushing his hands down into his breeches pockets, took a weaving step forward and said:

"H're ye, Crowder, old b-hoy!"

Crowder stood behind his bar with a napkin polishing that perpetual tumbler, but made no reply.

The man took another nearing step forward toward the bar, paused and said:

"I say, h're ye, Crowder? Can you s—peek—t—feller? Wh'a'r puttin' on dog wi' me for?"

"How are you, Daniel!" said Crowder. "you look sleepy, you'd better go and take a big sleep."

"A'r right. I'm go'n to whe'r ge'r ready, no—t b'fore."

"Better take a spin around the square, then," suggested Crowder, still polishing the tumbler.

"No z-sir," and proceeding to pull up a chair by my side, he added: "I'm goner talk sense to the old boss here."

"That's a man of family, Dan. If you want to talk some one to death, go hunt up a single man. What'll his wife say when she sees his corpse?"

Dan saw the old joke even through the fumes in his brain, and, looking at me, smiled one of those twisted smiles which are not to be described. Then he sat down on the chair, threw his hat on the floor at his feet, commenced in a fumbling way to fill his pipe, and said: "Crowder's g-ome! Knows been on a bust! A—as all right. Crowder's 'noll friend—use't wore 'gether in 'noll T'wolloinme."

While Daniel was fishing up from the depths of his vest pocket tobacco fine-cut, pinch by pinch, between his work-calloused thumb and finger, and boozily crowding it down into his pipe-bowl, nothing was said; but Crowder looked at me then at Daniel, as much as to inquire if I was being badly annoyed. Seeming to see that as yet I was not, he continued to gaze out in the sunny street, as he stood erect with that ever-active tumbler and napkin in hand.

Daniel, after finally filling his pipe, hunted throughout all his pockets twice over, and then said to me: "Boss, got'r match?" I gave him a lucifer match. "Boss, you're a gem-man! Don't put on dog." Then fixing the match perpendicularly between his thumb and finger, he raised his right thigh at an angle of forty-five degrees, and rapidly drew the match from the hip forward toward the knee over the woolen pantaloons, until it snapped and blazed into a light, as he brought it around with a single motion immediately over the tobacco in the pipe that was in his mouth. Silently puffing away until his dim senses were satisfied with the result, he proceeded to address me upon the subject that was uppermost in his mind. Why he should have desired to tell me what he did, seeing that I was a stranger to him, I know not. Who, indeed, can know the unconscious impulse that intoxication starts in the brain? Disrobed of its inebriate blur here is what he said to me:

"Yes, Crowder knows Old Dan! We used to work together and cabin together in California. The last place we were at was in Tuolumne. From there we came over in the Washoe excitement to Virginia City, in Nevada Territory, and that's where Crowder left me and went to selling whisky. Crowder can sell whisky, he can; but I can't. What do you suppose is the reason I can't sell whisky, eh, boss?"

"Well, really, I can hardly say."

"Did you ever read Shakespeare, boss?"

"Yes, in a scattering way."

"Look here," said he, in a mock dramatic style, pointing first at himself, then at Crowder, "upon this picture and this! That's the reason I can't sell whisky."

"I think I see it."

"All right, boss! I left Virginia City and went north to Montana; and kept going north until I could nearly see the top of the north pole. Then I roamed around again and got away down into Arizona and New Mexico; and from there went to New Granada in South America, where there is more trees and roots and vines and bushes and brambles and snakes and bats and spiders and bugs and things than you ever saw to the acre in any country—and rains; je-e-whillikens ! Why, it rains there down and up and cross-legged.

Then from there, I worked away further down into South America and back again, like a walking bag o' bones, into California. But California wasn't like home any more, so I weaved my way back to Washoe to hunt up my old pard. I was flat broke, and wanted to strike him for a stake. Crowder always opens out when I strike him for a piece. Eh, Crowder, ain't that so?"

"Yes, Daniel, such is the fact so long as I've got a cent."

"But my old pard was gone. I wasn't able to work a lick; so I rustled around among the ole-time boys, and they came out, and kept a-coming out to me, until I got onto my working pins again; got a job—saved up, paid 'em all back and put out again. And now I've worked round through Colorado, part of Arizona, and all of eastern Nevada, and here I am, flat broke."

"What was the point in all this traveling?"

"Gold, sir, gold. Placer diggings, with gold in 'em. Ah, God! give me once more the old days of placer diggings ! I don't care if I find it on the middle line of the equator, where the sun will cook eggs on the top of a fellow's hat—or I don't care where it is. That's all I ask—just once more."

"How does it come that you didn't get a better advantage of it when you had it?"

"Boss, that's what my lawyer called a leading question. Ain't it the scripture says 'every soul knoweth its own sorrow?'"

"I think it is in the scriptures, or ought to be," said I.

By this time, he began to speak much more plainly, and to the point. He put his pipe into his pocket, and throwing his legs over the arm of the chair that was next to mine, he asked me:

"Did you ever look into the face of twelve men for three days inside of a court-house, while a lot of lawyers were pulling and hauling over a case, and your own life was the interesting subject of discussion?"

"No; I can't say that I have."

"Did you ever marry a girl in the old States, and come to California, and work in the water, underground, and every way, like a wild working machine, to make money for her and one little gal baby; then be tried on a d—m false charge of murder, and get clear by spending half you'd made; and go home with the other half to her, only to find out that she had throwed off on you, and that the law back there wouldn't give you your own child?"

There was a fierceness in his expression that drove away entirely the drunken look, as he paused in his link of interrogation.

"No, my friend, I'm thankful to say that I have never passed through such a trial as that," I replied.

"Well, you may be thankful. I've gone through all of that. Ain't that so, Crowder?"

The saloon-keeper, as business was dull during the sunny summer afternoon, leaning on his white-shirted elbows over the counter, patiently watching Dan in his increasing earnestness, went back to his tumblers, simply saying, "Such are the facts, Daniel."

"Now, boss, there is nothing underhand about me. I'm up and up, on the square, all the time. I never cheated any man, or woman, or child, or Indian—not even a Chinaman. I never went forward to hunt a fight, nor backward to get out of one; and I don't think that I ever throwed off on a pard, or left a debt behind me in all my travels that I didn't pay. How's those statements, Crowder, are they true?"

"The man who says they are not true is no friend of mine, Daniel."

"There, now, boss! I'm drunk, you see, but he ain't; and he'll tell you if I strike the wrong lead, or go off on a spur. Now, what I want to know, and want you to tell me if you know, is, why it is, when a man wants to do the square thing, and does about do it, that he has such infernal luck?"

"Indeed it is hard to say. Perhaps you, being strong yourself, were severe upon others who were weak-spirited, and sternly demanded of them to stand up against all odds when they were not able, and sneered at them for weaklings, when they failed in courage and endurance, thereby raising up against you numerous weak but silent and busy enemies. Such things have been, and such may be your case."

" No; I think you must out there boss, that's too preachery. I never meddled with other people. I went about my own business."

"Very true, no doubt; and you, perhaps, left all other people, save a very few, to think they might go to hell for all you cared. Whereupon, these small people hunted for the weak place in the strong man's arms, and found it; because there always is a weak place."

He threw his legs off the arm of the chair and stretched them out to full length, with his boot heels resting on the floor, reached down for his hat, put the hat on his head over his eyes, put his hands deep into his breeches pockets, and plowing his heels along the floor slipped as far down into his chair as its form would permit, and in that posture remained silent for some moments, while Crowder, with one elbow on the end of the bar-board, partly pursued a newspaper, but mostly eyed his friend.

I was about to resume my reading, when he threw one of his legs over the other, with a heavy thump of his heel on the floor; then, thrusting his hand into his breast coat-pocket, he drew forth a letter, handed it to me without moving his hat off his eyes or further changing position, and said:

"Read that out loud to Crowder and me."

Baltimore, Md., July 10, 1864.

MY DEAR PAPA: Oh, my dear papa, mother is dead, and I am living with uncle John! Mother died about a year ago, as I wrote to you about, but never got any answer, and her husband has gone away in the war, and uncle John says he thinks he is dead, too, for he saw it in a newspaper that a man by the same name was killed in Luray Valley. I'm working along with Mrs. Ellicott and her daughter Mary, making soldier clothes at the factory. Uncle John was thrown out of work at Harper's Ferry when the arsenals were burnt down, and he has been working wherever he could get work, mostly in the car factory for the Baltimore and Ohio, but he is going now to Pittsburg to work on government wagons, because the railroad is all torn up by the war, and, oh, dear papa, Uncle John is poor now and I will have to go with him, or else stay here with strangers. Do let me come and live with you. I have got fifty dollars saved up to come to you and, oh! dear good papa, do let me come. It is so lonesome here except for Uncle John, and now he is going away; and we do not know what minute Baltimore may be burnt to ashes, and there are so many soldiers here coming and going all the time, and marching and drumming that it is not a bit like the nice, old place you took me to see when you came home here once before the trial, and when mother took me away.   Do let me come, papa.   I'm a big girl now, and can work and help you if you haven't got much money, and I do want to see my own, dear father, and be with him all the time.   I read in the papers all, every single word I can find, about California and Nevada Territory, and sometimes I am so afraid that you will get killed in the mines, and I will never see my dear papa any more.   Do let me come to you.   Oh, please do.   Uncle John says it is not a fit place for me out there, because it is so rough, but I do not care; I can stay wherever my papa can and I will, too, if you will let me.

I wrote to you a long, long letter all about mother's death, and about how the money you left for me in Alexandria is lost, because Mr. Smith has gone to Richmond with the Confederates.   Uncle John says may be it is not lost, because Mr. Smith is an honest man and your best friend; but I hear that everything at Richmond will be lost and I think it must be, because the Federal soldiers are just swarming into Virginia.

Uncle John says our nice home in Alexandria is a total ruin.   Mr. Smith was very good to me and sent me to school and told me to learn everything, because you liked your people to be educated, and I did try to learn as well as I could when I was at school, and Mrs. Ellicott says I am the best needle-woman and know more about a sewing machine than any girl in the factory.

Papa, if you will let me come and live with you, I will be the best girl I can, and never give you any trouble if I can help it, because my poor, dear papa has had trouble enough.

Now, papa, do answer this letter soon, and let your poor, only, lonesome daughter know how you are and if you are well, and if I may come and be with you.

God bless you, my dear papa!   No more at this time, from your affectionate daughter,   CALIFORNIA CALVERT.

Without saying a word, I handed the letter back to Dan, who was mopping his eyes under his hat, never having altered his position during the reading; while Crowder, with one foot on the lower round of Dan's chain, had stood listening with a sad face.

Dan took back the letter, replaced it in his breast coat pocket, and springing to his feet, dashed out of the saloon, exclaiming in a husky, choking voice:

"I'm the damnedest old fool in the world!"

He was gone, and Crowder said, partly to me and partly to himself: "That's what's the matter with him!"

"Singular character, your friend seems to be," I remarked.

"Well, no; he's not so singular—only a little odd just now. As a general thing he's one of the levelest-headed men in the mountains; but he's been on his gin for two or three days—an unusually long drunk for him—and I could see something bothering him ever since he came to this camp, now about three months."

"I should say his home affairs are working on him."

"Yes, sir," said Crowder, giving his bar-counter an extra flourish in the way of polishing it off. "That daughter—a good girl she is, too, I reckon—has been winding close round his tenderness, and bringing a heap of trouble on the old man's mind. That's just what he never could stand up under. Fight him—buck against him, and he's all iron and steel-pointed, come under, and cotton to him, and you've got him—got him, dead as a fish."

"Why is it that a letter written so long ago should just now affect him so keenly?"

"Why he never got the letter, I think, till he came here to me, about three months ago. That same letter, if I ain't mistaken, has been in my trunk since it was sent to my care, while he was away in South America working for Harry Meiggs, and the devil only knows who else."

"Did he not tell you of it after you had given it to him?"

"No, sir; that's not his gait. I gave him a whole lot of letters when he first come, and he went away, I reckon to read them. Then in about an hour he came back, looking as solemn as an owl, and says, 'Alec, have you any money?' I said I had. 'How much?' says he. 'Well,' says I, 'a few hundred.' 'Then,' says he, 'for Jesus Christ's sake, lend me two or three hundred dollars, if you can spare it!' I gave him the money in a minute, and he never said a word to me what the matter was with him. But I know now—that letter tells the tale."

"Queer idea in him to show it to me, was it not?"

"Well, now, do you know, I think he's been trying to get that out of himself, for my information, for two days; and after he sat down there alongside of you it just popped into his boozy old head that he could get the yarn off through you."

"What is his business—miner?"

"Miner! not much. He's the best general mechanic that ever gripped a hammer. There is nothing in machinery that he don't know or can't do. Did you ever notice his big, square head, and the heavy bumps right over his great wide eyebrows? If I knew as much as there is behind them bumps, I'd shut up this gin-mill so quick people would think there was a funeral on hand. He's a poor talker with his mouth—don't run much to jawbone; but he can make wood and metal say his say, like a poet and a philosopher. Humph! no wonder his girl can get away with all the points on a sewing machine."

"He seems to be a man of big feelings and a bitter sense of wrong."

"Yes, sir. Inside of him he's the biggest-feeling man you ever saw. It cuts him to the raw to have a man deceive him, and it cuts him deeper to have any one suspect him of trying to go back on anything; and when you cut him he don't heal up by licking his wounds with his tongue. He can't talk away his trouble, as some can."

"I have noticed the same trait in other mechanics, particularly those who have to do with steam-boilers. Steam is an exacting master, who will not be put off with a lick and a promise. Such work must be honestly done, in the smallest details, or the results are disasters which ought to be called crimes."

"Well, that's Dan! Anything that's not done to a hair—correct—worries him like a ghost; but when he puts his finish on a matter, and says 'that's all right,' then it's off his mind. What's worrying him now is that girl, after he'd fixed for her, being thrown out by the war."

"Ah! he has found out that when a government gets into trouble, even private affairs will not stay fixed."

"I suppose so," said Crowder, whose instincts as a publican prompted him to avoid drifting into matters political.

CHAPTER FOUR.

Daniel Calvert—honest old Dan—is dead. Crowder still dishes up the drinks for the convivial parties who come and go in front of him; but the effort he puts up to wear a smiling face only make us, who know of the shrouded sorrow that lies prostrate across the threshold of his heart, all the more sensitive to his bereavement.

We are a rude set of fellows—little schooled in the pretty combinations of crape, and rose-wood grief—and we don't know how to speak glibly the sadly-rounded sentences of symbolic sorrow for our departed brother whom "It has pleased an all-wise God to take from our midst;" but if you think we do not sympathize with Crowder,—for he was Crowder's pard,—you ought to have been present when Dan died, and when, without preacher or prayer-book, we buried him—we, a little squad of men only—on a lonely knoll among the sage-brush at noon-tide, when the sun was painting shadows of the trees upon the crags.

You see, the way of it was, something got the matter with the patent pump on the big mine of the Silver Cup Company, and they sent for Dan to come there and see if he couldn't find what ailed it and fix it. So Dan went out, and the next thing we heard was that he was fatally hurt. Crowder got one of the boys to look after the saloon, and taking Dr. Duugleson and myself with him, hurried to Dan's bedside.

On our arrival in the wild little camp up among the rocks and crags of a steep canyon, we found a few log and rough stone cabins clustering around the boarded-up frame of the hoisting-works and the company boarding-house; and in one of these little log cabins, with a mud roof and a dirt floor, lay old Dan, mashed up but still alive, upon a bunk made of peeled cedar-poles,

He had his senses; and when he saw Crowder before him, his eyes looked the welcome which his paralyzed hands could not extend, and the tears came big and fast down upon the coarse pillow.

Strange, strong men were there, going in and out, and the big nails in their heavy boots made queer pictures in the dust of the dirt-floor; but there was no noise, no useless fussy moving about—only quiet, patient attention. They had kept constant guard over him for two nights, with that aching suspense that waits, not knowing what better to do, and watches wounded life, and listens for the Doctor's wheels among the echoing aisles of mountain crags.

As the Doctor went forward and bent over Dan's prostrate body, the men formed unconsciously a new circle behind him—their heads only a few inches from the low roof—and looked and listened, each chest heaving with silent, suppressed breathing, until the Doctor said;

"There is not enough air in this place."

Then, instantly and quietly, each man left the little room to stand outside and whisper, or gaze reflectively down the bank upon the willows in the canyon, until the Doctor came out. No one asked any questions, but, as the Doctor looked in the face of each and then shook his head in the face of all, they knew for certain that which they nearly knew before. Crowder did not come out; but I, as in some degrees his backer in this case, went immediately in and found Dan's old pard sitting by his bedside, upon one of those clumsy wooden stools so common in mining camps. We were silent for some moments, when Dan, poor fellow, as stoutly and cheerily as he could, said,

"Boys, my driving power is a total wreck. I'll never get up steam again."

Nobody responded. Nobody knew any true word suitable for response, and death will not accept a flattery.

"Crowder, old pard, you needn't introduce me to this gentleman. I couldn't offer him my hand, but I know him—I saw him once before—and I'm glad to see him again; but if he'll excuse me a little while, I've something to say to you."

"Certainly, certainly, Mr. Calvert! i'm glad to see you again—that is, I would be glad if I wasn't so sorry," said I in a confused way, as I left the cabin; while Dan replied:

"Thank you, sir. It's a mixed case."

I don't yet know what took place between Dan and his old pard. Perhaps I never will know. But I left them there, and after standing outside among the boys for awhile, talking about how the staging —or scaffolding—gave way and dropped Dan to the bottom of the shaft, I said, through the doorway, to Crowder, that I would be back presently, and went by their invitation up to the mine, to be showed how it all happened, and to be told that no one would have supposed that such a thing could happen—so singularly surprising is often the last summons,—and yet that it did happen.

After it had all been explained to me, I met the Doctor at the mouth of the mine, and asked, as much for the relief there is in saying something, as for any other purpose.

"Doctor, is there the least show for your patient?"

"Not the slightest, sir. He may linger till morning. Let me see" —and taking out his watch, he added, "it is now twenty minutes past four—he may linger till morning. The reaction has set in, but there is nothing to react on. His light will soon burn out. But he may linger till morning—linger, linger till morning, sir."

And the doctor walked away, kicking the broken particles of rock in front of him, as studious men sometimes do when they have run against a disagreeable moral certainty.

I went down the trail repeating to myself, "linger till morning, sir —linger till morning" and sat down on the rough wash-bench which is found always outside a miner's cabin, beside the door. I could hear the low mutter of indistinguishable words from within, as I sat gazing upon the ragged, gnarled, and cheerless mahogany trees that maintained an arid foothold in the jagged seams of the opposite side of the canyon, while the white wandering fleece-clouds came and went across the dry blue opening of the sky, between the mountains overhead; but there still kept throbbing in my mind the dull, sad chorus of death—"linger till morning, sir, linger till morning."

At length Crowder came to me where I sat by the door, and said, in a low voice and subdued manner:

"Go in and stay with him; he won't last long. Beginning to wander in his mind. I must go up to the mine and see the superintendent."

"Certainly," I replied, and stepped inside the cabin. Dan, being so crushed by his fall that he could move neither hand nor foot, made no demonstration further than to show by his expressive face that he recognized me. I sat beside him on the stool and gave him such attention as his sad case would permit. Presently he said:

"That time I was tight in the saloon—you remember—you read a

letter for me. I have not tasted a drop since; I was getting along
first rate. I've had two letters from my little girl since."

There he paused a long pause and, not having the use of his hands,
I had cause to assist him with a handkerchief about his eyes.

"I had hopes of going to see her this coming winter, but—but—"

He paused again; I laid my hand upon his forehead, and found it
hot and throbbing. Talking more to himself than to me he continued:

"Poor girl! poor girl! no, not little now. That's good—that's
good—not little. A woman—my daughter; my daughter—a woman.
Good woman, too; writes like a good woman—no humbug—no frills
—head level. Give me some water, Cally. Throat dry—and hot—
as Death Valley. Yes, yes, Death Valley—but I didn't mean that,
Cally. No, no. If I'm going—of course I'm going—I'll not whine.
I'm ready, ready, don't cry, Cally—no use. Got to be, you know
—got to be."

Then he remained silent again, but soon resumed in a wilder key:

"Hot! Johnson, there'll be an earthquake. Everything is hot
and close and still—be an earthquake, sure. Look out! There she
goes! Didn't I tell you! We'd better get out of this—this shop
will come down. All right, Johnson, old boy; we're a heap better
out of that. Here she goes again! That was a bumper! Look!
look, the Spanish running into that stone cathedral! Why, d—n
'em, that's no place in an earthquake; it'll come down, sure! Now
she goes again—whoop! it makes me sweat like a horse. How do
you stand it, old boy?"

Evidently he was away in South America, going again through
scenes of terror with that queer compound of courage and curious observation so common to our countrymen. After another pause the
scene changed with him.

"Johnson, there's a storm upon us—a terrible storm. Let's put
the blankets over the hut and fasten them down, for it's coming—
coming fast. Hark! don't you hear the thunder over the tree-tops?
It's going to be a hell of a night. If we're alive in the morning we'll
bid New Granada good-bye. Now she comes! Don't you hear that
panther howl? Listen! yell, old fellow, you'll get a drenching.
Whew! how it pours! Tie the blanket down, Johnson—let's keep
dry if we can—it'll be cold here before morning—getting cold now."

Thus he continued from scene to scene of his varied life, until

Crowder came and desired me to go to supper. Leaving Dan still muttering, but weaker and weaker each moment, I went; and when I returned again he was silent—not dead, but collapsed and surely dying.

The boys of the day shift, being off work, came and went; and, among the rest, Dan's spirit went but came not, for before midnight he was cold and dead.

The saw and plane and hammer of the carpenter of the mine gnawed, squeaked and rang busily for hours in the night; then all was still as the man who lay roughly clad in the new-made coffin, save the regularly recurrent spells of coughing of the engine, as with a rapid che-ch-ch-ch she raised the car of rock from the depths below.

A short sleep for all except the watchers by the narrow-box, and morning dawned bright, clear, warm, and dry. Quietly and steadily we arranged for the funeral, without ceremony or officious mannerism. Not a hammer clinked upon the head of any drill—not an explosion of blasting powder to reverberate into a roar amidst the naked, rocky peaks—all silent—or that silence disturbed only by the low, slow throb of the pumping engine of the mine.

When the sun was up full and round, we brought forth the unpainted, unvarnished, undraped, and unplated, heavy box, and by the aid of a hundred willing and able hands, passed it down the narrow trail over the rocks to the wagon-road, that winds with the feeble stream of willow-fringed water out of the canon, into the dry waste of the valley below.

Voluntarily, without command, we moved onward and downward; not toward the grave-yard, but toward the grave, wherever that might be, among the sage-brush of the foot-hill, where never before had a grave been made. Six at a time, strong men relieved each other for a distance of two miles, and the regular tread of iron-shod heels crunched, crunched the gravel underfoot—the only music of the march. Then we rested a moment to drink where the road leaves the stream as it winds directly out upon the hills.

Heretofore this had been a cheerless, sombre funeral; no bit of color brighter than black, brown, and gray; no gaudy female headgear; no glitter of coach-varnish; nothing but the subdued strength of brawny men, clad in the useful colors of respectable labor, marching silently between the everlasting rocky walls of the canon, to the echo of their own firm feet and the tinkling treble of the stream. But now, as we took up the load to move forward for another and last mile, the six Cornish miners who carried the corpse were accompanied by a seventh with a book in his hand; this seventh, placing himself in front of the coffin as we started, opened his book as he walked, and read aloud two lines of the burial hymn of his home people. Reading these lines aloft with a clear, ringing voice, he chanted as he marched, and was joined in the chant by as many of his countrymen as were in the procession. Thus reading and singing, we marched our way slowly out of the canon, leaving the echoes flying and dying behind us.

Arrived at the grave—the grave alone in the desert—(and many, in many deserts, such there are)—we found the native Indians, drawn by emotionless curiosity, gathered in a picturesque and tattered group of men, women, children, ponies and dogs, at a short distance from the two miners who awaited our coming, leaning on their shovels by the fresh-turned earth.

Slowly and steadily we lowered the coffin and settled it firmly in its place; and there being no ministers, no ceremony, no near relations to cast the last tearful look into the open earth, the shovels were grasped by skillful hands and in the briefest space the final work would have been over, had not one of our number, doffing his hat, said "Gentlemen."

Instantly the shovels stopped in the gravel, and all heads were bared to the sun and sky.

"Gentlemen:—In the absence of all customary funeral services, it may not be amiss in this case if I say a few words—words not of balm to wounded hearts—words not of religious comfort; but words to indicate that however far we may be from the cradles of civilization, we still bear in our hearts the elements of that civilization which distinguishes our people from the wild man who now holds us under the observation of his untutored eye.

"There is another land, known to some of us, which, though kindred to this where we now stand and shadowed by the same bright flag, is not, as this is, a waste of wilderness. In that land, where the great forests of many trees and the wide prairies of grass and flowers are nourished by generous and mighty rivers, this our

dead, now in the open grave was born; and there he learned, at his
mother's knee, not only the common prayers, too easily forgotten, but
the humanity and kindliness of man to man, which endures through
life, and is best represented in sickness, death and burial.

"It is well for us, in scenes like this, to remember what we have
been, to consider what we are, and to see what we must be; and, from
these facts, to be advised that life is not all a battle-field where man
goes armed against his fellow, but that it is and ought to be, a season
of peaceful industry crowned with a degree of mental trustfulness.
Here is the place—or one place at least—to call to mind that we are
dependant upon each other; that the life of each man is some support
to the life of all men. Here is the place to learn that if we are not
our 'brother's keeper,' we are at least his pallbearers no less than he
is ours. 'We are responsible each for the final repose of the other.

"Who, my friends, looking now into the grave and thinking of
home—aye, home—to us more dear when distance heaves its moun-
tain-breast to shut the picture out—who, I say, looking into this open
grave, thinking of home, of childhood, of mother, can go away to
belt upon his hip and nurse in his heart those designs upon human
life which are too common—too frequent—in our days and nights?
Let us strive here to take a lesson against anger, illwill, and violence!
Let us cultivate peace! Let us foster contentment! Let us bear
with the hasty spirit of others, to the end that we may ask forbear-
ance!

Gentlemen, here we must leave the dead, as, erelong, the living
will leave us. Let us now do so, with admiration for his courage
and ability as a true soldier in the army of intelligent industry—with
a regret and pardon for his errors—a tear for his fate, and a new re-
solve, born of this tenderness, to stand by each other in all good and
peaceful endeavors.

"Now, to the unknown and undiscoverable designs of the All-
keeper of the universe, who has written around us in mountain-lines
the evidence of his exaltation above the reach of our most majestic
thought, we leave, with the simplicity of childhood, the future of
this mystery we call—the dead!"

At the last word the speaker replaced his hat, and simultaneously
all hats were replaced; and then, by those long used to handle earth,
the grave was quickly filled. Crowder drove down at the head of

the new and narrow mound the plain board with its rude black paint markings—

DANIEL CALVERT.

BORN

In Alexandria, Virginia,

June, 1826.

Age, 47 years.

  With the shovels, picks and ropes distributed among us, we wended our way in orderly disorder, with the noon-day sun high above us, back to the mine, where the scream of the engine soon summoned the appointed laborers to their task; for the link lost out of the chain of industry is ever replaced by a new one from the shop of busy, effort-fostering nature.

  Crowder and I—the Doctor having returned at once—left the camp and rode far into the night to reach home. On the way, as we rode along, Crowder requested me to ask some friend of mine to assist him and myself to look over Dan's papers, fix up his business and communicate the sad facts to the daughter; because, he said, he was not used to writing long letters, and would not spell just proper, always. Bidding Crowder a mid-night farewell, I went home to bed full of reflections upon the matter of man's wanderings, both bodily and mental. I wondered much what the pious people in the older States would think about on the morrow (Sunday) while they congregated in the soft light, among the easy seats of highly-finished churches, to listen to a sweetly toned and well-rounded rhapsody upon the redemption of the world by preaching the Word. I said to myself,'' Alas, these very respectable, pious, Sunday people have no notion of the grandeur of their own vast country; no notion that their piety is a mere beautiful rainbow-hued bubble, floating upon the surface of the heaving, earnest active depths of life that bears it up, and make its beauty possible.

  While they listen in their painted play house, to the artificial graces of vocal and instrumental music, dashed with studied, eloquent, displays, the great harp of the west wind playing over thousands of lonely and manly graves, sings through the aisles of the many mountains the true, unpainted glory and goodness of the unexplained and unpreachable All-keeper.

J. W. Gally.

MEA CULPA.

CHAPTER I.

"Pass the coffin varnish this way, Lieutenant Miles O'Riely, and then spread the contents of the swill-tub you raided to-day."

"Coffin varnish, indade? I'd have you to understand, Major Kintook, that it was meself that paid fifty cints, this very day, for that illigant bottle o' spirits. And ye ought to have seen me a-beggin' the widda, up at the big house beyant, for these four bits! I tould her I had a big family of six to support—and the divil a lie was it aither, for there ain't one of yees can beg worth a cint—and we hadn't a mouthful for three days. She shelled out as illigant a lot of grub as iver a gintleman thramp flopped his lip over, and there it is jist wrapped up in my ould coat anent ye. Och, Major darling, ye never had a better male in ould Kentooky than I'll sphread before ye in a minute. When I seed she was affected loik, and had swallowed me whole batch of lies, I tole her, God bless her, that I wanted jist four bits to buy some medicine for me poor sick baby. She shelled it out so aisy loik that I wished I had made it a dollar! Begorry, I ain't no lieutenant, me name is not Miles, neither is it O'Reily, I haven't raided no swill-tub to day, nor have I the contents of a swill-tub in me ould coat. So, old fel, subject as ye are to mistakes, ye niver made more of them in one short sintence. Coffin varnish, indade! But, I say, Major darlint, it will be precious little varnish that the country that has the honor of burying ye will put on your coffin! So if it is varnish ye loik, ye had better give that beautiful nose of yourn another coat! Begorry, Major, it's as beautiful a nose as I iver——"

"Oh, shut up that fly-trap. Pass the appetizer and spread the banquet. Does that suit your humor any better?"

"Considerin' the hard work I've had, and the imminent success that attended me efforts, couldn't ye as well say plase?"

"Please."

"Loik a gintleman."

Six men were lounging around a camp tire under a growth of wild grape-vines which covered a thicket of young oaks, so dense as to shut out almost entirely the rays of the sun, as well as all sign of the bleak north wind that was sweeping down the Sacramento valley. The public road at this point was about one hundred yards from the river, and the thicket extended from one to the other. The camp was about midway between the two. It had for some time been a resort for gypsies and those "gentlemen" who make a great show of hunting work while hoping never to find it. The fall had been a very dry one, so that even at the approach of winter there was no difficulty in camping out in such a protected spot. These six men were all poorly dressed. Some were positively ragged, while others wore clothes that had evidently been made for some other person. They were "tramps," but a close observer would not have taken either one of them for a thief or a bad man. The one addressed as "Major" in the above conversation, and with whom we shall have more concern than with the others, was six feet and an inch tall, broad shoulders, well made in every particular, and weighed about two hundred pounds. One could easily see even beneath his uncombed hair and heavy beard, that hung in tangled masses nearly half way to his waist that he had been a strikingly handsome man.

The luncheon spread out by the individual addressed as Miles O'Riely—and we may as well call him Miles, for his real name at this time is of no importance to our narrative—while is was composed more or less of the scraps from the table, was substantial, and might have tempted the appetite of those far above the professional tramp.

"Now, be me sowl, this is what I call entirely illegant. There is that home-spun light bread! I bet a pipe o'tobacca the widda made it with her own swate hands. And that slice o' cowld corn beef! And ham! Och, Major, and if this be the schrapes wouldn't ye loik to be a rigular boarder at the table? Did ye ever see the widda, Major?'

"I never did, and I think it is hardly worth while for me to call on her, as you seem to be completely taken up with her, and I should stand no chance against one so eloquent as yourself."

"Chance, is it? Listen, bys, to the loiks o' that? A thramp talking about chance! But I tell ye, bys, I believe the Major did make an impreshun. To-day while I was a stuffin the widda wid me lois, who should walk by the house, big as life, but our Major.

He stopped for a minit until I could show him my purty countenance, so he could know the claim was being worked. The widda she looked at this thramp through the window, and turned a little red in the face, and ses she to me, "Do you know that man? Considin' I had the precedent of St. Peter before my eyes in denying his master, I sed, 'No, mum, but I suppose he is some drunken thramp.'"

"Then," interrupted the Major, "you improve somewhat on St. Peter."

"Of course; isn't this the age of improvement? As the chap wid the puddin' head said at the Dimocratic spaking, Ain't this the nineteenth cintury? But, Major, can ye improve on that other character?"

The conversation was interrupted by the appearance on the scene of another personage.

"Good evening," said the Major; "won't you have a seat?"

"No, thank you; I left my team standing in the road, but I wanted to hire a man, and hearing you folks in here, I concluded to see if I could get one of you to work for me."

There was a silence of half a minute, when one of the men asked: "What do you pay?"

"Well, considering there is not much doing, now, I think about twenty-five dollars a mouth is about all I can afford."

"What do you expect a man to do?" asked another.

"Drive team, milk the cows, plow, harrow—or in short, farm work generally."

A derisive chuckle went round the camp. "All that," exclaimed one, "for twenty-five dollars?"

"And I guess a fellow would have to eat in the kitchen at that!" put in another.

"And sleep in the stable!" said another.

"I guess," said the Major, "you have come to the wrong place to find the man you want."

"It seems so; but I tell you what it is, such men as you are forcing us ranchers to hire Chinamen," and the rancher walked off in no amiable frame of mind.

"There is that everlasting Chinaman again," said one of the men. "Whenever a decent man refuses to take beggarly wages, he has a

Chinaman thrust in his teeth. The cussed ranchers ain't willing to give a white man a chance."

"That's what's the matter with this country. If it wasn't for the hellish Chinamen this State would be prosperous like the Eastern States, and—"

"With wages at twelve dollars a month," interrupted the Major.

"What's the matter with you?" exclaimed several in a voice. "Why didn't you take his beggarly twenty-five dollars, and take care of his horses, and milk his cows, and plow and harrow, and sleep in his barn, and eat in his kitchen with his Chinamen?"

"I didn't do it because I am a tramp; because I am a vagabond on the face of the earth; because I long ago *lost my grip!*"

Here the Major took another long pull at the four-bit bottle of "illegant spirits," and continued: "There was a time when I would have taken that man's offer, and I would have made myself indispensable to him; I would have saved my money and become independent. But we who have grasped for better things, and waiting for somebody to 'give us a chance,' as my friend just said, to make something without the slow process of earning it, cannot bring ourselves to accept decent wages, and do honest work."

"Hoorah! That's better than a Dimocratic speech," exclaimed Miles: "let's run the Major for Governor!"

"Each one of you," continued the Major, "has a history. Yo dreams of the land of gold have failed to be realized. You are n satisfied to take the world as it is, and hence you have become—"

"Tramps and vagabonds," exclaimed Miles.

"I did not intend to say that; but let it go. I will submit the question to the candor of each one of you, and ask if disappointment has not made you what each one of us is to-day—a wreck of human society, a drone in the busy hive, a consumer of garbage, a wearer of cast-off clothes, a guzzler of rot-gut, a—"

"Say, Major, darlint, there is a wee bit left; won't ye be after agiving your stomach another coat of that same 'coffin varnish?' It'll loosen up your tongue loik, so you can spake them hard words be'ther."

The Major held out his hand, grasped the officers bottle, took a long pull at its contents, and continued: "—a disgrace to the mother who bore him, a walking reproach to the God who made man in His own image."

During the conclusion of the sentence the Major held the bottle firmly by the neck, and as he finished speaking, as if to drown the recollections that seeemed to be crowding upon his memory, he drained it to the bottom, and then threw the empty bottle into the bush. "Go!" he exclaimed; "Go! You are as valueless as a man with the spirits all out of him!"

"But, be gory, it's no aisy job to fill it wid spirits agaiu!"

"It takes money to fill the bottle, and money will put spirits into the worn-out bulk of a man," grumbled one of the others.

"But there is a command," suggested Miles, "agin puttin' new wine into old bottles. And I am afraid the spirits of prosperity would burst such an ould leathern canteen as yourself, Jimmy Fiske! Yees couldn't stand the pressure!"

"There is too much truth in that remark," said the Major. "It would be hard to find a man who had lost his grip on life entirely who could stand prosperity. I imagine one would be constantly pinching himself to see if he was not dreaming. He would always be timid, halting and cowardly. That is, unless he was by nature endowed with an extraordinary amount of good sense."

"Good since, Major; good since! Do you think a man of good since would even be such a thramp as all of yees are, barrin and excepting myself of course?"

"That may be a debatable question, but I am inclined to take the affirmative."

"Be me sowl, I'd take the other side; but see the jury we'd have to leave it to?"

"I have seen men whom the world said were talented, so overcome by a single reverse of fortune as to commit suicide. I have seen others recover from shock after shock until their money was all gone, and they were left dismantled hulks on the sea of life, carried hither and thither by the varying winds and changing tides. Men of the finest talent have become inmates of the lunatic asylum. Of course, if a man could always maintain his mental equilibrium he would never lose his grip—his energy would never lag; but that is impossible. That one loses his equilibrium is no sign he never had it."

Here the man whom his companions had named Jim Fiske, because he had at one time exhibited to their astonished gaze a twenty-dollar gold piece, raised excitedly to his feet, gave the fire a vigorous kick and said, vehemently: "Suppose an infamous crime had been committed and circumstances pointed to you as the perpetrator, and wove around you a network of proof you dare not face; and then suppose you should assume the guise of a tramp, in fact become one; who would dare say you had not sense, to begin with?"

"I should say," replied the Major coolly, "that such a one would be a romantic sort of a tramp, and he might make his fortune by relating his adventures in a dime novel. But Jim, did you ever see such a tramp?"

"Yes, I met such a one a few years ago. He is dead now, poor fellow. I helped to bury him." And Jim stretched himself on his blankets, which were half unrolled, filled his pipe with tobacco, took a coal between his thumb and index finger, placed it in the bowl of his pipe, and gave a vigorous pull at the stem.

"Now" said Miles, "for the story. We hain't had a dacent story since we have been in this camp."

"Yes," said the Major; "the story. We have all had an 'illegant male,' as Miles would say; the shadows of evening are creeping on apace, and as we haven't said our evening prayers and are not ready to be tucked in our little beds, we will while away the time listening to the 'Story of an Unfortunate Tramp.' I suppose from the prologue that would be a good name to give it."

"It is not a long story, gentlemen, and, as I have never attempted to write a dime novel, you will excuse me if I fail to interest you for any great length of time. In fact my friend did not know the whole story, and became a tramp, and died because he did not."

JIM FISKE'S STORY.

Some years ago this friend of mine—never mind his name—was a bright, intellectual young man, who had just reached his majority. Buoyant with energy, health and a firm self-reliance, it seemed to him and his friends that life must be a success. But never mind sentiment; a tramp's camp is not exactly the place for that, anyhow. He left Lake City, Nevada county, one autumn afternoon, on foot for Nevada. It was after the first rains, and the roads were a little muddy and the streams somewhat swollen. Near the top of the hill, just before he began to descend to the South Yuba, a deer ran across the road. He took out his revolver and fired at it, but it bounded on. He walked on down the grade, building many a castle in the air, until within less than a quarter of a mile of the river he suddenly came across a man lying in the road, dead. He took hold of him, and found that while there was no pulse, the body was still warm. If you ever traveled on that road you will remember that there is a water trough in a little ravine that crosses the road about a quarter of a mile from the river. It was not over fifty miles from this that the man lay. My friend went back to get a cup of water. He took the man's head in his lap and bathed his temples, but no sign of life appeared. In doing this his pistol fell from his belt and dropped into a pool of blood, and his clothes became more or less bloody. He started on, intending to give the alarm at the bridge. He had not gone far when he heard the voices of men coming up the hill. For the first time he became frightened. His clothes were bloody, and he would be found alone with the murdered man. "Those men have not seen me," he said to himself, "and I will dodge out of the road and avoid observation."

He had not a moment for reflection, but climbed out of the road on the upper side, and from behind a clump of bushes saw four men pass by, and then come to a halt at the dead man. They examined him critically. Then one of them said:

"We can do this man no good: besides this knock on the head, the ball has evidently pierced his heart. Let us capture the murderer. As we came up the hill I got a glimpse of a man leaving the road."

My friend did not hear this then, but he heard it afterwards. They were all armed, and two of them carried Henry rifles. While he was debating with himself the propriety of going down and making an explanation, he saw the men preparing to move towards him. Two of them tied their horses and started up the bank on foot, while the other two rode down the hill where they could get out of the road on horseback.

My friend then thought there was nothing else to do but keep out of the way, and he fled. For nearly half an hour he eluded their vigilance, but at last one of them got sight of him, and then a ball from a Henry rifle came whizzing past him; but he sped on down,

down the hill, toward the canyon below the crossing. Another ball struck the calf of his leg and crippled him. He was then captured, put upon one of the horses and carried back toward the scene of the murder. When they arrived there the body was gone.

"This fellow was not alone in the murder," said one. "He has had some accomplice who has boldly carried the body to prevent identification and an inquest."

They found where a man had gone down the grade towards the river, and one of them remarked that, heavy as the dead man was, he had been carried off by a single man, as but one track could be found.

"It is hardly possible." said one, "that a man could carry such a weight all the way to the river, and we shall find where he has laid the corpse down to rest."

As the road and river are nearly parallel at this point, it was not over a couple of hundred yards from the road to the river. It was now getting late, and twilight was coming on, but the men were rewarded by finding a pool of blood on the ground, and from there down the steep incline to the river they found where the body had been dragged and thrown over a perpendicular bank, some fifty feet high, into the rapid current below.

The lateness of the hour compelled them to give up any further search for what they supposed to be an accomplice of my friend, and they carried him over to Nevada and lodged him in jail. At the examination before a Justice it was shown that some men working near by heard one shot at the spot of the murder; one chamber of my friend's pistol had been recently discharged. The dead man had a mark on his head apparently made with the butt of a pistol; the butt of my friend's pistol was covered with blood. All four men identified the body as that of—well, no matter about the name—who had left the bridge a short time before with several hundred dollars in his pocket.

My friend told his story; but no one—except his mother—believed it, and he was committed without bonds. As the Justice announced his judgment, my friend's mother gave one piercing shriek and fell, dead. It was a broken blood-vessel, or heart disease or something of the kind; but she was dead, and the prisoner was hurried to jail,

and not allowed to attend his mother's funeral. She was a widow;
he her only son.

He languished in jail a couple of months awaiting the assembling
of the grand jury, but found a chance to break jail. He skedaddled,
and wandered around the country in disguise. The family of the
dead man was rich and offered a large reward. I could have gotten
it if I had peached on my friend, even when he was dying.

During the recital of the story, the Major had been much affected,
and during the latter part of it Fiske had noticed it. When he had
ceased speaking, the Major sprang to his feet, strode up to Fiske and
exclaimed:

"Are you sure that Allen Campbell is dead? By the eternal, come
what may, justice shall be done."

"You are one of those sneaking, mercenary sharks in disguise,
hunting for a reward, are you? But you can take that!"

The report of a pistol rang out on the evening air, the Major
staggered and fell, and Jim Fiske left the camp in the direction of
the river.

CHAPTER II.

In an elegantly furnished bed chamber a lady is sitting alone in front of a grate, in which is burning a bright wood fire; the thumb and forefinger of the right hand press either temple; a sclitaire diamond ring, held on the middle finger by a simple band of gold, reflects the light of the fire and adds brilliancy to the scene. Her left hand lies, in her lap clasping a roll of manuscript, which is more or less soiled. The lady is dressed in plain black, and the rings we have mentioned are the only ornaments worn. The rain is falling in torrents, and a stormy south wind is driving it hard against the window near her right side; but she hears it not, neither does she hear or see the servant when she enters and places a lighted lamp on the table on which her right elbow rests. The clock on the mantle strikes five; the pendulum swings back and forth, marking the flight of time with a monotonous tick, and once more the clear tones of the little bell announces that another hour has been added to the dead past. This woman, almost as motionless as a statue, is thinking, thinking, thinking. Several years of her life's history have passed in review, in her mental vision; a question of some moment to her has been debated, and, as the tone of the clock's stroke dies away, her fingers nervously grasp the manuscript, and she says audibly, "I will read." And she reads:

THE MANUSCRIPT.

Dead, yet living ! Dead to all a man may hold sacred on this earth; dead to family, to friends; dead to ambition, dead to hopes. Living for bitter memories, for an aimless purpose; living, in fact, because God wills the intensity of the punishment and holds back the dagger that might end it all in sweet oblivion. One may court death, aye, long for it, yet tremble at the idea of self-murder. While one may have forfeited every claim on God's goodness and mercy, and be void of all hopes for the world to come, yet it seems an awful thing to go before the great Judge with one's own blood on our hands. Oh, that I could be certain that death was a blotting-out of one's life; that that which we call the soul of man could end, like the body, at the grave ! How many, many times have I been tempted to follow th

advice of Job's wife, curse God and die; but I am here, and I suppose
I must listlessly and aimlessly follow the thread to the end.

Why have I commenced to write? What purpose can it serve?
Would the pleasure or the pain predominate in writing down, just for
my own eye, some of the reminiscences of the past? Pleasure! How
dare I talk of pleasure. That's a good joke. Pleasure! Dare I even
hope for pleasure? For ten long years I have throttled every offort
of memory to dwell on the past; but to-day, in the solitude of this
wilderness, I feel an ungovernable desire to call up visions of the past.
Yes, I will try the experiment. I will write me down something of
the past and destroy the paper before the eye of man can see it.
Who knows? There may be a bonanza of pleasnre in it after all.
Let me see. Who am I? From whence came I? I remember
myself first as an orphan boy working for $5 a month during the sum-
mer, and going to the old-field school during the winter. Tho·e were
lonely days. In fact my life has been a desert, with not a single
bright oasis in all its dreary length. As a boy, I was subjected continually to oppression and wrong. One year, when I was about 15,
I worked for Judge Underhill. The Sundays and holidays of the
autumn were spent gathering nuts, which I intended to sell during
the winter to increase my little stock, so I could afford a Sunday suit
of clothes. I was going to where I had them stored in an out-house,
one day, when I found the Judge's wife busy removing them to her
own store-room. I came by on the outside of the house in time to
hear her little daughter say, "Oh, mamma, those belong to John."

"Never mind," said the mother, "he is working for us and his
time is ours."

"But," persisted the little angel, "he gathered them on Sunday;
then his time was his own."

Without noticing the last speech of the little one, the mother and
her elder daughter walked off loaded with my property. The little
one—God bless her! God bless her!—tarried for a minute or so, and
sobbed as though her little heart would break, and then walked off
to another part of the elegant grounds, and began to play with the
Newfoundland dog. I never told that sweet little angel what I had
seen and heard, but it gave me something to live for. I worked hard;
I studied hard, and the day I was twenty-one I grasped my license
to practice law, signed by Judge Buckner, the closest examiner in

the State. For some reason I became popular. The year after I reached my majority Judge Underhill was nominated for the Assembly by the Democratic party. The county was Democratic. The Whig convention was composed principally of young men, and they put me on the ticket against the Judge. I began a canvass without any hopes of an election. I made some happy speeches. The young men of all parties began to flock around me. The old men of my party saw a chance to get even on their ancient enemy, and the canvass became intensely exciting.

All the years since I had worked for the Judge I had been thrown more or less in companionship with his little daughter Inez I would constantly hear those noble words, "Those belong to John," and see the image of the little one weeping over my wrongs. I loved her as a superior being. Aye, I worshiped her as never Indian devotee worshiped his idol. I had never thought of making her my wife. In fact, while she was growing up and budding out into womanhood, I looked upon her still as my little angel.

One evening, when the canvass was beginning to get very warm, I met Inez at a party. We danced together, and then somehow found ourselves out on the veranda alone.

"Do you know, John," she said, as she hung confidently on my arm, "that this political contest is very unfortunate. My father thinks that you are going to beat him, and he is furious. He looks upon it as an indignity to put a mere boy against him and then defeat him. I wish, John,, for my sake, you were out of it."

"I would die for your sake, Inez," I said vehemently.

"I know you would, John Henderson," she replied caressingly. "There has not been a time since I was 12 years old you would not have done that."

"And how did my idol know that I had been worshiping it all these years?"

"Know it! You great, big, awkward booby! You did not think I was blind, did you? Haven't I seen what was spurring you on to such extraordinary exertion? I have seen you look happy so often when I have given you a word of encouragement or a smile of approval."

"And can it be possible, Inez Underhill," I said excitedly, with my heart almost choking me, "that you love me, the orphan boy, without fortune or family connection?"

"Why, of course I do. You did not expect I loved somebody's fortune or family connection, did you? Oh, I have been awful proud of my big, gawky, talented lover when I could see that he had set me up as his queen, high above all the world. Don't you know your first political speech, when you took the town by storm, was made entirely to me? You were not caring a fig what anybody else thought of it. I knew by experience that I could bring you out by looks of encouragement, and I took that particular seat I there occupied to be able to do it. No man ever looked more searchingly back under the shadows of a sun-bonnet for tokens of encouragement, and as each smile of approval brought forth new bursts of eloquence from the boy-speaker that shook the house from center to circumference with applause, I concluded that no one ever got more encouragement from under a bonnet! You have your idol, John Henderson, as I have mine. People who bow to idols must expect to offer sacrifices. Let us see which will be the truest in his worship!"

"Then the first sacrifice shall be mine. I will go out of this canvass."

"I am not certain," said my little idol, "that you can do so honorably. As for the honor of being elected, you and I could forego that; but we cannot afford to do anything not strictly in the line of honorable dealings with man. I understand enough of politics to know that you are leading your ticket, and that there are others who expect you to pull them through."

"When I accepted the nomination I did not expect to stand a ghost of a show of election, and never once dreamed of making your father angry. I thought I would make a little canvass as an advertisement for the little office across the way, that you must understand is not crowded as yet with wealthy clients."

"I know just how that all came about, and I was foolish enough to become elated, too; but since matters have taken the turn they have, I find it rather uncomfortable to have my idol dissected every day by some member of my own family. It must all go straight along now. Vex my father as little as possible, and we will have to trust to luck and a little good management for the balance."

Conscious of the fact that we would be missed, we sauntered back

to the ball room. Inez was instantly claimed for a dance, and I was
left to my own reflections.

I was in ecstacies of delight and dejected by turns. The being in
whom my whole soul was wrapped was mine, but I was so poor as
to be hardly able to take care of myself. What would I do with a
wife reared in the lap of luxury? I could not entertain the idea of
becoming a pensioner of her father. What could I do? I wished I
was well out of this cursed political race. I felt that I must work—
that I could not give time to complete the canvass or to serve if elected.

At my next appointment, after finishing the political part of my
speech, I said: "Gentlemen, when I was nominated I did not expect
to be elected, and, as God is my judge, I have no desire to be now.
I have had no experience, and my judgment would be at fault in a
hundred contingencies sure to arise. I am as yet a boy. On the
other hand, my opponent is a gentleman of mature years, of large
experience, of scholarly attainments and ripe judgment. He is acquainted with all the public men of the State, and his influence in
carrying local measures would be very great."

I then represented myself as an humble advocate of the grand old
Whig party, but as one who did not wish to be placed above his
years in merit. The speech was well received, but I was assured
that it made me many votes. The Judge was furious when he heard
of it, and said that that upstart of a boy had been so certain of his
election that he could afford to patronize him. When I met him he
was coldly formal. I tried to explain how I happened to accept the
nomination. I assured him that I did not wish to be elected.

"Then, sir," said he, "why don't you withdraw?"

"Judge Underhill," I said, "I have on more than one occasion
looked to you for advice as to a father. If you will lay aside any
feeling you may have in the matter, and will, with an unprejudiced
mind, view the situation and advise me as you would a son under the
circumstances, I will follow your advice."

"Fudge! All hypocrisy and deceit. Why should you desire to
save my feelings in the matter? Why would any young man be
willing to forego such a triumph as an election under such circumstances? I will not believe you sincere, sir, unless I can see some
motive."

"I can show you that also. I love Inez Underhill; she loves me, and we expect to be made one some of these days. I know that this situation is disagreeable to her, and I would sacrifice anything, save honor, for her sake."

The Judge turned pale with anger, and it was a full minute before he spoke. Then he said, with a curling lip and bitter sarcasm in his voice: "Pray, then, why did you put yourself and Inez Underhill (without the formalities) in such a predicament?"

"Because, sir, I did not expect to be elected."

"And you count yourself already elected now, do you?"

"I hope I shall not be; but, Judge, you are aware of the fact that the probabilities of it are very strong."

"And when, may I ask, do you expect to make my daughter a beggar?"

"Never, sir! Never!"

"Ah, you are a man of fortune, then; your pretense of poverty has been only for effect!"

"I do not intend to claim her, sir, until I can offer her a home."

"When a child of mine," said the Judge, angrily, "contracts an alliance with a beggar without consulting me, she must renounce it, or no longer seek shelter in my house."

"Beggar, Judge Underhill! Beggar?" I exclaimed, no longer able to conceal or control my anger. "When, sir, did John Henderson ever receive a single dollar he did not earn, and earn honorably, too?"

The Judge turned on his heel and walked away. At the election I had a large majority of votes. I had no further conversation with the Judge, and had not met Inez. In fact, I did not like to meet her, as it would only serve to make her father more angry, and I supposed from the fact of not hearing from her, that he was not in earnest about driving her from his roof, if she did not renounce her lover. After the election I was called down into Tennessee to attend a protracted trial, and did not return home until a few days before the convening of the Legislature. I saw Inez once, and asked her if her father had talked to her about our engagement, and she said he had not. Thinking it best not to trouble her about it, I simply said that we had talked some on the subject.

After I had been in Frankfort about a month I was astonished to see Inez in company with an aunt of hers in the lobby of the Assembly chamber. I went out to see them, and was going to escort them to a seat on the floor, when the aunt whispered, "Poor Inez is in trouble; let us walk down towards the hotel." Of course I knew instantly what was the matter.

"Well," said Inez, when we reached the street, "father and I had a little discussion the other day, which ended in my being at your side. My sacrifice has come first. Aunt Helen, here, is very kind and offers me a home, but I come to consult you about what I am to do with myself; you are my legal adviser, you know."

"Sweet one," I said "the world is before us—we will make a living some way. I am getting the munificent sum of $3 a day from the commonwealth of Kentucky; but that lasts only a few weeks longer." We walked on in silence to the hotel, and when seated in our room, Aunt Helen said: "My children, I love you both very dearly, and I think I can come to your rescue without wounding the feelings of either. In the first place, I could offer Inez a home with me, but her staying with me as Miss Underhill, and not visiting her home, would occasion remarks which might be detrimental and unpleasant to her, and hence we must have a wedding—a very quiet little wedding. I will then make some advance of money to John Henderson, which he can pay at his convenience. It shall be strictly a business transaction."

"Or, better still," I said, "if you will board my wife until I go to California and make a raise, I think I can remit from the very start."

"That shall be as you please."

There was a quiet wedding that evening in the parlors of the hotel. Aunt Helen concluded to remain with us until the end of the season. I began to make ready for my departure for California. In four or five weeks after our marriage came the adjournment. My wife and her aunt went to the house of the latter.

This was 1852—eighteen long years ago! Oh, Inez! Inez! how I loved you! How I love your memory still! But for ten years until this very day—I have not allowed myself to think of her—her name has not escaped my lips. How happy we could have been but for—me! Yes, *mea culpa, mea culpa, mea maxima culpa!* But I cannot think long of her. I would go wild and throw myself into the Sacramento, and drown memory with a worthless carcass. Shall I tear up this paper here and indulge in no more bitter, bitter memories? Well, here we go to California. Accursed be the day I ever heard

the name California spoken. It has brought ruin to me and to mine.
And I am but a walking image of tens of thousands more. Of all the
ills of Pandora's box, the thirst for gold has brought most misery to
men. Men say they want gold to buy pleasures with. Pleasure
may be bought with gold, but it has bought more misery than pleasure. It has : t times been an implement of civilization, but it brings
with it the inevitable seeds of sin, of crime, of destruction. The
more gold there is sown on the field of civilization, the more of the
tares of destruction must fall upon the soil. I fancied that happiness
—"our being, end and aim"—sat upon a golden throne, and that
none need woo her except with an offer of gold. I made the common mistake, and have paid the penalty thereof.

When I got to California—this land of gold—this land of wretch
ed hopes, suicides, and drunkards' graves, I could not think of wait
ing to build up a fortune by the slow process of professional life
Every day away from the side of my angelic wife seemed a year.
must make money quick, and get back to her. I therefore wen
into the mines—the accursed mines!

When I left my wife I told her that I should be satisfied to return
with ten thousand dollars, if I could get no more in three years, but
she need not expect me until I had at least that amount. On the
steamer coming out I had fallen in with one Tom Allen, a regular
'49 miner, who had made some money and was returning from a visit to his friends in "the States." He told me about what a big time
he had, and how he spent or gave away his money, because, he said,
"I know just where to go and dig plenty more."

When I told him who I was and where I was from, he familiarly
called me "Kentuck," and said I would find that all the boys had
nicknames up in the mines.

"I fell in," he said, "with a lot of Missourians, and because I
was from Massachusets they called me 'Yank,' although I am not
one of those blue-bellied chaps you find up in Connecticut."

Before we left the steamer the mining firm of "Yank & Kentuck"
was formed, and the exact spot marked out where we were to take
out our everlasting pile.

Poor Yank, a better heart never beat in the breast of man, but he
came to California too soon!

We purchased our mining outfit at Marysville, and perched on top of a Concord coach we struck out for the mountains. Up the hill-side we went, past mining camps and up among the tall pines. When at the summit Yank announced that our stage-ride was at an end, and we must take it on foot. We had a couple of sacks of flour, four pairs of blankets, a side of bacon, a ham, pick, two shovels, a couple of rifles, pistols, nails, an ax, hammer, saw and some fifty pounds of et ceteras, such as salt, saleratus, etc.

"Now," said Yank, "we will just take them little traps on our backs and strike off toward the Feather. It is only five miles down there. We can make it before night."

Just about dark we reached the river, tired and worn out, for the descent had been fearfully steep.

"This is the spot," said Yank, "where we are to make our pile. Prospected here before I went away. Nobody been here since I've been gone. If the winter don't set in too soon you can go back to that little wife of yourn by Christmas."

Having confidence in my companion's words I slept soundly on this my first night in the mines, and dreamed of a happy "old Kentucky home."

Next morning, as I was a good hand with an ax, I set to work getting out material for a shanty, while Yank went prospecting for the best place to begin mining operations. By night he had collected in all about an ounce of dust, the result of his panning around in different places. "With a Long Tom," said he, "we can take out at least two hundred dollars a day. Only a hundred days to get your ten thousand, my boy."

I was overjoyed, and felt a full confidence in being the luckiest of men. "My good angel and Inez's good angel," I thought, "sent this treasure of a partner across my track."

In five days we had our cabin built and everything ready for mining in good earnest. On Sunday I wrote to Inez a letter, giving an exact account of the situation, and walked up the hill to the stage road to send it out. In a fortnight or so prospectors began to call on us, and soon shanties began to spring up around us. Mining laws were made, and we were restricted as to our claims. In couple of months we had taken out about ten thousand dollars and I sent two thousand dollars to Inez.

"There," I said proudly, as I saw the stage leaving with the check, "my wife need not be a beggar any more. She can live on that until I get home." Would to God that I had followed it! But I did not.

Our claim did not pay so well. We dropped down to about thirty dollars a day, and we both became dissatisfied. But still we had taken out a great deal of money. One day, along in September, Yank came into the cabin, as I was placing dinner on the table, and said: "Look here, Kentuck, I have been prospecting a little and making some figures. If we could turn the river a little with a wing-dam just below our claim, we could take out a bushel of gold. It will cost some money to do it, but we have now about twelve thousand dollars, and we can turn her nicely for that sum. We will say nothing about that small sum sent to the little wife, but what is here belongs to both of us."

After dinner we went to the river and figured out just how we could turn it. We hired all the men we could and put them to work. Yank was almost as large in stature as myself, and had been brought up to work, and we worked, too.

No two men ever did more work in the same time than we did, and we were wet all over from morning till night. In about six weeks all our money was gone, but we had the river turned. The first day we took out over one thousand dollars, and had a regular jollification in the cabin that night. The miners all flocked in to congratulate us, and they were all true and sincere in what they did and said. I do not believe there was one in that camp that envied us. But while the congratulations were going on it began to cloud up, and by morning it was pouring down rain; but we worked in it all day, and several of our friends volunteered to help us, so that we cleaned out about two thousand dollars that day. The next day we went to the site of our works, only to find them all gone!

"Never mind," said my jolly partner, "the gold is there, and we will commence on it earlier next year. It knocks your going home for Christmas, though, pard!"

We found we could not work our claim on account of the water, and finally concluded that we would go out to Marysville to spend the winter. When we got there I found a letter announcing the birth of a daughter.

That daughter is perhaps still living. She is a young lady, yet for ten years I have not dared to seek to know one word of her. If she is living, she thinks her father dead, as he should be. I have not dared to think of her; but oh God ! what a yearning seizes me to see that child. For the last few days I have imagined she was near me. Sometimes I have started and turned, expecting to see her —but I never will ! I never will !

"Look here, Kentuck," said Yank, on Christmas day, "you had better take them slugs ($50 pieces). I am no good banker any more In trying to make expenses off the monte bank last night I sank all the balance."

I was disappointed and somewhat provoked, but of course said nothing. Our claim up in the mountains was worth a great deal of money, and we would work in the spring. But why had I not taken that same money when I first came down, and gone to see the baby? I saw there was a great opening for me in my profession at Marysville, and when I mentioned it to Yank he urged it very strongly. "Send for the wife," he said. "She can come on what you sent her before, and I will go up to the claim in the spring and take out half a million or so, in no time·"

The secret of my not doing this was that I wanted to take out that half million or so, and go back to my old home and show what I had made under Judge Underhill's nose. This was a wrong feeling, and some over-ruling providence may be punishing me for it now.

The early spring found us upon our mining claim making ready for our wing dam. We had not a cent of money, and had to work our placer claims to pay expenses, and do most of our preparations for our winding dam ourselves. We had offers of partnership by men who had money, but we preferred to carry it ourselves. By the middle of August we had the river turned and commenced to take out the gold. We took out easily from one to two thousand dollars a day.

While at work at this we conceived the idea of carrying the entire river in a flume through a canyon below our claim. The more we thought of it and discussed it, the more practical it seemed. The bottom of the canyon we argued was like the bottom of a sluice box; every little corner would gather in the gold. We said nothing about this, however, until we had worked our claim out, which was in the first part of September. We had then sixty thousand dollars. We were certain that with this sum of money and our own work we could flume the river in a month—long before the rains.

I argued with myself that as I had three times the sum that I had made up my mind to be satisfied with, I ought to go home, but Yank was so enthusiastic over our project that I did not mention it to him.

"Now," said Yank, one morning, "let's begin our flume. We will make out a bill of lumber, and get out the square timbers while it is being sawed. The mill just above us has just been completed, you know. But I was thinking, Kentuck, that it will take about all our money to make a proper success of our flume, and he had better make a small remittance to the wife and baby. Suppose we send them a thousand, and this fall, when we clear up our claim, and get half a million or so, we will go back. Durned if I don't want to see 'em about as bad as you do."

For more than a year this man and myself had been as inseparable as the Siamese twins. Every night we slept together; at every meal we ate together; and when not at work, we read to each other or talked together. The greatest joy either had was in the other's society. All expenses, every remittance to my wife, was from a common fund.

Often when I have been tempted to curse the world and swear there was no truth, no disinterested friendship in man, I have thought of Yank—noble, true-hearted Yank—and have repressed its utterance.

The eyes of the miners opened wide when our plans began to develop themselves, and all prophesied success. We therefore went boldly on with it. We could have sold out for many thousands advance before the work was completed, but the spirit of enterprise, or of madness, whichever it might be called, seized each of us. The work was begun, the flume was finished and carried the water beautifully—but, when we went into the dry bed for the gold, it was not there. All our money was gone, and we were in debt. We had the bed of the creek, or river, as it was called, and a flume. When we realized the whole truth of the situation, we went to our cabin.

Tears stood in the eyes of my big-hearted partner, and as he threw his arms around my neck he sobbed out, "It is not for myself, Kentuck, that I am a-caring; it is for the wife and baby. God knows I would lay down my life this minute to put you in possession of as much gold as we had six weeks ago."

"Never mind, old boy," I said, "we will make it up again; I don't care anything about it." But my voice belied my words, for too, was thinking of the little wife and baby.

"You have told me your first lie Kentuck. You not only care, but your heart is breaking, all on account of the time for seeing your wife and baby being postponed. But come, cheer up old pard—it is mighty strange it two great big, stout chaps like you and me can't make a living for one little woman and her baby. And the next ten thousand we get you shall take it back, and if I can't make it by myself I will come and live with you. We must now go further out in the mountains prospecting. There is nothing around here any more; and, Kentuck, to quiet your mind, I will promise that if anything happens to you I will work my fingers off for that little wife of yours. I have no one to care for but one sister back in Massachusetts, and she has been married several years, and I did pretty well by her when I was back there, you know; gave her all I had."

Well, we packed up our blankets, strapped them and a prospecting outfit on our backs, and struck out. We tramped, tramped, over mountains, rivers and canyons, for days and weeks, but found nothing that suited us. We struck several places where we could make ten or twelve dollars a day, but we were after something better. When winter overtook us we were high up in the Sierras. When we found we were about to be snowed in we built us a rude cabin and wintered beneath the snow.

I began here, during this long night, to get discouraged; to imagine that I had had my opportunity and had failed to grasp it. I began to think that "there is a tide in the affairs of men, which, taken at its flood, leads on to fortune," and I argued that if that tide is missed it will never come again.

As soon as the snow melted off sufficiently we struck out again on our prospecting tour. Of course I sought the earliest opportunity to write to the dear little wife to account for my long silence. We struck over on the North Yuba, and there found a claim out of which we took several hundred dollars in a few days, and we were much elated; but it "petered out" before we had as much as one thousand dollars. The depth of my discouragement, as we pulled up to leave this place, can hardly be imagined. "If we can find a claim where we can get ten dollars a day each, let us stick to it," I said.

"That would take it about two years longer to get back to the little wife and baby," said Yank. "It won't do. There are better diggings in California, and we must find them."

And we resumed our tramp again. It would seem that the rich strikes were being made just ahead all the while, and we flattered ourselves that it would be our turn pretty soon. If we had only looked about us we would have seen hundreds of others tramping around following the same Jack-o'-the-lantern.

I felt discouraged beyond measure, but could not make up my mind to give it up. I could not think of taking the time to go to some place and build up a practice at the law. It might require years at that business to make the money I wanted. And, when I felt tempted to go back without it, I could see in my imagination a sarcastic smile on Judge Underhill's face and hear him say in most withering tones, "I told you so."

Another whole year passed by and we were still hunting for that better mining claim in which we were to make our fortune. The regular letters we got from the dear, dear little wife, always full of encouragement, and an occasional one from Yank's sister, kept us from becoming bar-room loungers, as too many of those who set out "to find better claims" about the time we did had already become. Our remittance to the wife had now come down to $50 and $100 at a time and they were far between. I got ashamed to write the same, same old story over again, and my letters home became less frequent. Not that I had ceased to love, to idolize my dear wife, but when I had nothing to tell but failure I could not write. In the summer of 1856 we struck a claim on the south Yuba that began to pay us fair wages and we concluded to stick to it. One unlucky day he went to San Juan. "I am going to take $100," said Yank, "and try the little wife's luck at monte. If we lose that amount it won't hurt us, and if we win it shall go to her."

I expostulated, but it did no good, and into the monte game we went. Yank put the one hundred dollars on the card and won. He then staked the two hundred dollars, then the four hundred dollars, and then the eight hundred. Each bet was won. The excitement around the table became intense. "Once more," exclaimed Yank; "five successive winnings is not impossible. Here goes the sixteen on the queen of hearts."

Yank had looked the dealer constantly in the eye since the first bet. This time he pulled the cards off until he found that the queen of hearts must be the winning card. Then he held the pack in his hand and said, "You cannot bet that way. Take your sixteen hundred and go."

"Thirty-two or nothing," exclaimed Yank. "Pull out that other card. I have seen it, and know what it is."

"I will not," said the gambler.

"Then I will," and Yank seized the dock and exhibited the queen of hearts to the crowd. A cheer went round the house, but with it the sharp report or a pistol. I was on the other side of the table, and saw my faithful friend fall. I was not armed, but I seized a chair and struck the gambler on the head. The crowd tried to interfere, but I used the chair so furiously that no one dared to approach. I broke it to pieces over the gambler, and then with my boot heel mashed in his skull.

Talk about emotional insanity! I was as mad as any lunatic that ever wore a straight-jacket. I felt that I was strong enough to pull the house to pieces. Several shots were fired at me by the friends of the dead gambler, but none took effect. I felt that I was bullet-proof. If repentance is necessary to salvation, I am afraid I shall never be saved, for that is the great and only crime of my life unrepented of, and I am afraid it will always remain so. I took my dead friend in my arms and wept like a child. I saw, in my boyhood, my father and then my loved mother laid in the grave; but I had never had my heart-strings so completely torn asunder as now. It came so sudden, so unexpected, upon me, that I was overwhelmed as by an avalanche.

There was but one other that I loved better than my poor dead friend, and I loved both better than my life. He had been tried in prosperity, tried in poverty. In all our privations for years it had been a pleasure for him to endure more than his share. I had never a thought that was kept secret from him. He knew all my hopes, all my ambitions, all my despondency, all my fears. When I had been ill his touch was as gentle and loving as a wife's; and now, when I felt that I needed such a friend most, when almost on the point of losing my hold on life, he was so rudely snatched away from me! But, Sam Allen, you are happier in that silent grave than your surviving friend. Oh, God! What have I not been through!

The gambler was dead, and an officer came in to arrest me, but a shout went up from the miners, "Let him alone; he was right!"

"I know the law," I said to the officer. "Let me bury my dead friend, and then take me where you please. These hands must dig the grave—these eyes be the last upon earth to look upon him."

That night, as I sat watching by my friend, the expressman brought a letter addressed to him. I opened it, and found that it was from his sister. She wrote that her husband had been sick for a couple of years; things had gone ill with her, and now she was a widow, with no means. Her son was a fine lad, who must now leave school and go to work.

What could I do, without money and without friends to help me? And besides, there were other claims upon what little I could do.

Next morning early I was waited upon by a committee of miners, who said that they had had a talk with the dead gambler's partner, who had admitted that thirty-two hundred dollars of right belonged to my partner, "and," continued the spokesman, "as you may need a little we thought we would bring it to you." Should I take it? was the question I began to debate in my mind, until I remembered the sister's letter. I took it and sent it to her, telling her her brother had died, leaving that much money, without telling her how or when he died.

As luck would have it, no one knew the real name of either of us, and the word "Yank" was all that appeared on the pine board at the head of his grave, and the law had to be satisfied with the alias Richard Roes in my case.

Now to the lock-up! A year consumed before my trial came. The Court asked if it should appoint counsel. I said: "The defendant will be content with his legal right to appear in his own behalf, without the production of license." Several able lawyers volunteered, when I said I might call on them for books and advice, but I preferred to take the management myself.

I was much applauded by the bar and audience in the management of the case, and the jury brought in a verdict of "not guilty" without leaving the box.

Never a word of all this had I dared to write to the little wife, but at the outset had said that, being obliged to take a long journey, she need fear nothing if she did not hear from me for several months. After that I did not write until out of jail.

Then it was the same old, old story of baffled hopes.

How utterly wretched a man feels when he has to begin to acknowledge to himself that he is a failure. That not only is his life to be miserable, but he is destined to have those whom he loves drag along after him. When he begins to feel that his miserable life is all that stands between him and comparative happiness! When he begins to think seriously of whether it would not be better to end one's blighted existence. When one contemplates any undertaking and finds himself saying: "What's the use? There is no success in that for me," he's on the down grade.

It was thus I argued with myself. But I must go to work again, and went back to the old claim. The miners had preserved my rights inviolate. The ground was worked out all around, but that piece was left untouched. It made my heart ache to work without my old partner, but I drowned all recollections as far as possible in hard work. The claim paid just ten dollars a day, and I determined to be content. The first hundred dollars taken out was sent to the little wife; so was the next and the next. But these amounts seemed so very small. She kept writing not to worry, that Aunt Helen was more than a mother to her. Aunt Helen was childless and rich; but this did not satisfy me. What would Judge Underhill say to my failure to provide for my family? In a few months five hundred dollars had accumulated in the box buried in the dirt floor of my lonely cabin, and as much more had been sent to my wife. This was a small amount, but it encouraged me, although the claim was fast being worked out. Some of the boys in the meantime had made some fabulously rich strikes in the old river channel by drifting, and I bought into such a claim, paying my last dollar therefor, and once more hope began to find a resting place in my breast, and the blessed little wife got the first hopeful letter that had been written for many a day. For months and months we worked on taking out next to nothing,

while others that seemed to be similarly situa'ed were getting gold by
the thousand. I felt discouraged, but worked on harder than ever,
as we were liable to strike it rich at any minute. Letters to the
wife grew far between again. No more remittances could be made.
She wrote me that her sister had died, and that her father had pre-
tended he could not live without her, his only child, and wanted me
o come back and live with them.

This set me back more than ever; it was impossible for me to ac
cept the offer; and was I—unsuccessful, worthless I—to stand between Inez and her father? Was I to drag her down further with
my worthlessness? It caused many a pang to write the letter advis-
ing her to accept her father's offer, but it was written.

Mouths passed. The year 1859 was drawing to a close, and often
came the words to my lips: "What's the use? My life has been a
failure, and it is destined to continue so." More and more did I realize the fact that I was "losing my grip." That is the way Californians express it; and there are no three words, coined by people seeking force at the expense of elegance, that express more. Thousands
of men are every day illustrating the *lost grip!* Our mine was
worked out. It seemed that he had staked everything upon it—even
our future hold—our "grip" upon life, and the game was against us.
We quit with nothing.

But there came an unexpected turn in my affairs. A man by the
name of Bates, who had been on the jury in my case, was accused of
murder. About the time utter and complete despair had taken possession of me, he came to engage me to take his case. It was a case
of mistaken identity, but the witnesses were positive. Bates had
recently made a big strike and had plenty of money. He told me if
I would drop everything else and help him for a few months he
would give me a large fee. "Go into it with a vim," he said, "and
if success crowns our efforts I will make you well off."

The case was to come off at Marysville, and I was to go there, or to
Sacramento or San Francisco, or wherever else I could, to find authorities and draw on him for all expenses It was to be my duty also to
help him hunt up testimony. We traveled together for weeks hunting up every circumstance that could have a bearing on the case. I
wrote down all the testimony that could be brought in on either side,
and studied the weakness and strength of every point.

It was getting late in the fall again when our trial finally came on for a hearing. All this while my client had had no attorney, but acting under my advice, had attended to all minor matters himself. We had concluded that it would be better, for effects sake that I should not change my miner's garb, and I stalked into the Court-room wearing a red shirt, duck pants and a pair of miner's brogans.

"If your Honor please," I said, "I desire to be entered on the record as attorney in the case of the People vs. Stephen Bates, set for to-day, and I suppose a license from the Supreme Court of Kentucky will entitle me to do so."

A titter went round the Court-room, and a smile spread over the faces of the attorneys. Three or four of the best lawyers had been retained for the prosecution, and the Marysville bar at that time was counted the best in the State.

The Judge examined the paper passed to him, and said to the clerk: "Enter John Henderson as attorney in this case. Have you assistant counsel, Mr. Henderson?"

"None!"

The name "John Henderson," pronounced by the Judge, sounded strangely to me; almost frightened me. I had not heard it a dozen times in almost seven years, and it was hard to realize that I was the person named. I had no books with me in Court, for I had for months delved into everything I could find that could bear on the case, and I had it in my head. I could repeat whole pages of law on questions of evidence arising in the case, for I had so studied all that could bear upon it, as to be prepared for any and all emergency.

In my opening address to the jury, I called attention to the fact that I was a miner who had paid no attention to law for years, and showed them as hard and horny a pair of hands as handled a pick. We did not expect to bring a law book into Court, but relying on the justice of our case, we were willing to put inexperience against experience; a rusty memory of the law against the library the gentleman had brought into the Court. I tried to make no points that could not be maintained. The attorneys themselves were astonished at my familiarity with the law on every point raised, and before the trial was half over I could hear such expressions as "Wonder where the deuce they dug that chap up?" "He is a nail-driver," etc. I took no notes, for I knew as much about the case before as after the evidence was in. When I was to make my argument every available space in the room was occupied. The speech was a magnificent success. I surprised myself, surprised my client, surprised everybody. It was with difficulty the officers could keep the applause from bursting forth from the crowd. The verdict was in our favor, and before I left the Court-room a lawyer who had the largest practice of anyone in northern California, offered me a copartnership. I could step right into a lucrative practice.

What a fool I had been not to have gone into the practice of law sooner. But I came to California, like many another fool, expecting to get rich in a few months and go back to the "States." The ordinary way of making money was too slow.

But once more I was buoyant with hope as the day I first got my license to practice. I returned to the hotel to write Inez a long letter, and then I began to think it had been three months since one had been received from her. But I wrote her one full of hope for the future, telling her that she must make up her mind to come out here; that my fee in this case was ten thousand dollars, a portion of which I would send her in a few days to come out on. . In fact, as soon as I got my new partnership fixed up I might go back for her. I went to bed and dreamed of a brilliant future.

Next morning three letters were laid on my table. One was from my client, containing a check for $1,000, and saying that he had been called suddenly away, but would remit the balance in a week. The next was from Tom Allen's sister, saying that she had moved to California and was living in Lake City, Nevada county, and from the report of the trial had learned for the first time where her brother's old friend could be found; the words of the third burned into my very soul—dried up, as it were, the marrow in my bones. In the agony of my despair I cursed God, that I might die. These words burn in my memory like the branding iron in the flesh. I can see them standing out in bold relief now in that delicate hand. I have not dared to think of them for years. I wonder if I have courage to write them over again. Let me see.

LEBANON, Ky., September 2, '60.
Sir: I am pained beyond expression to find that all these years I have been cruelly deceived in you. I had no idea of the depth of de-

gradation into which you were capable of falling. Your way through life lies in one direction; mine in another. Henceforth you must not cross my pathway. I hope this is plain enough for you to comprehend.

INEZ HENDERSON.

I scrutinized the writing—there could be no mistaking it; I could swear that it was hers. The address on the envelope was certainly genuine. Then it stated a simple fact—I had gone down, down, until I almost hated myself. Well, of one thing I was certain—she would never hear from me again. I was astonished at my own calmness. After the first few minutes it was the calmness of despair. I could only say "God bless her she is right."

Then came the old saying, "What's the use? Why hope against hope?"

Listlessly and aimlessly I took the stage for Nevada City, and from there to my old claim on the South Fork. From there I started out on foot for Lake City, to see the sister of my old friend, intending also to visit Tom Allen's grave. I had most of the thousand dollars with me that my client had sent, and while at the bridge took out my purse to pay a trifling bill. I had not gone far when I was struck on the head, from behind, by some one I did not see, and fell senseless to the ground. When I came to I found I had been shot immediately over the heart, but that it was a mere scratch; the ball had glanced round. Two horses, which I recognized as those of two of my best best friends, were standing hitched near the road side. I had left these men at the bridge, and they were going my way. From this I concluded that they had found me, thought me dead, and were gone for assistance. My money was all gone, so that robbery was the cause of the attack. As the world was then no more to me, I concluded to go and throw myself into the river; but as I went down towards the river I found a recently slain deer. While death never had any special terror for me, and I would on more than one occasion have welcomed it, still I had a dread of self-murder.

An idea seized me; I would drag this deer down to the cliff and throw it over. My friends would find my traces, find where a bloody carcass had been dragged along and thrown into the river. As my name was well known there, Inez would learn positively that I was dead, and I would leave the country, and she would never, never know any better. If the robbers were captured and hanged for murder it would serve them right.

When the deer fell over the bank I fled from the spot, and kept going. I went down into Mexico and stayed until the war broke out, and then joined the Southern army, and courted death through all that terrible struggle. Never one word have I heard of Inez. God bless her, I hope she is happy. I am afraid to hear from her; afraid to think of her, because, oh, my God, how I love her. Hers was a just sentence passed upon me. If my worthless life would give her one moment of pleasure how gladly would I surrender it, by any means except self-murder.

But now I am a listless wanderer on the face of the earth. Everywhere I strike a lot of tramps—those that labor and those that loaf. They give me the best they have, and I have never suffered for a meal and have never begged one. I always give them that old name "Kentuck," because that was Yank's christening. Out of respect they sometimes call me Captain, sometimes Major, and occasionally I get to be Colonel.

I said I was listlessly wandering over the face of the earth. That was true a short time ago, but not now. I have a purpose now. I learned accidentally, that Allen Campbell had been arrested for my murder: that he had escaped from the jail and had never since been heard of. This is the son of Tom Allen's sister. There is some fearful mistake somewhere, and I will travel this earth all over to find him if he is alive, and clear the stain off the nephew of the truest man God ever made. I begin to feel some energy in me as I think of the work before me. But even if I should find him how could he be completely vindicated and I *remain dead?*

CHAPTER III.

The sun rose bright and clear on the morning of December 25, 1870, and as he sends his rays through an elegant farm mansion near the town of——, in the Sacramento valley, a man in one of the upper rooms thereof walks across the floor of the room absorbed in some mental struggle. After a time he goes to the window and looks upon the outer world. His eyes rest first upon an orchard and a vineyard, a short distance from the house, now entirely divested of both fruit and foliage. A little beyond he sees a field of wheat, which, a few weeks after the heavy rain, has covered the ground with a rich carpeting of green. Then he lets his eyes fall upon the scene immediately beneath his window, and gazes upon grounds covered with blue grass and ornamented with trees, shrubs and flowers. Nearer still he observes a conservatory in which can be seen tropical and semi-tropical flowers and plants in great profusion. He stands there leaning against the window-facing, enjoying the scenery before him; yet his mind is not at ease. As he stands there, lost in contemplation, with his mind sometimes upon things away back in the misty past, a servant enters the room, spreads a cloth upon the table and brings in an elegant breakfast. This being done, the servant touches him on the elbow and calls attention to the fact that his meal is ready. Mechanically he partakes, and when it is cleared away, and he is once more alone, he resumes his walk around the room. Finally he exclaims: "This is too much! Too much!" Then throws himself into a seat at a table before a grate, in which burns a cheerful fire, rests his elbows upon the table, and covers his face with his hands, and his thoughts become audible:

"I am more and more mystified by my surroundings here. Sometimes it seems that I am only dreaming, and that I will yet wake up at the old camp in the brush; and, at other times, I question if what purports to have been a long period of my existence is not, has not in reality, been all a dream, and I may wake up a young man by the side of the truest wife a man ever had. Who am I? Do I really exist? Let me see. How does the mystery stand at present? I wormed out of Miles (that is, if there is a Miles and I am myself), the other day, that I was shot, that he squealed murder, and that just then the "widda," as he calls her, came along in a carriage, took me in and brought me here, where I have been ever since. I was delirious, he tells me, for a week or so, during which time this widow waited on me with her own hands, but I have not gotten a glimpse of her yet. It seems to me that when I first came to myself, that I frightened a young girl almost out of her senses by throwing my arms around her and calling her my own sweet wife. She vanished into thin air, and I have not set my eyes on her since. Miles and one of the best old ladies I ever knew have been my nurses. Mile says the nurse is not the widow, but that she is young and handsome; but Miles has been so mysterious lately that I can get nothing out of him. When I ask him why I am not allowed to leave this room, he says the doctor ordered it; but I am now as strong as I ever was. I have just drifted along on the current of events. O, this mystery, this mystery! No king could fare better, he could not have more attention paid to all his wants than has been paid to this poor miserable hulk of a man. Paintings that I admired most in my youth have been brought in and hung up in my room; fresh bouquets of costly flowers have been daily brought to me. I have only to wish for anything and it is here. The clothes brought me to wear were evidently cut to my measure, and I have been barbered and fixed up until when I look into the glass, extending from ceiling to floor, I can find no trace of the tramp. Well, I have been told that this day is Christmas, and I could to-day go whither I pleased. But where can I go? What is in store for me? Miles, the sly rascal hinted to me last evening that my hostess was much smitten with me, and that I could marry her and become possessor of all her wealth. But, oh God! I hope this is not true! I must be true to my Inez. She may have married again and have forgotten me. I have never dared inquire about that; but I would not for a million dollars put another in her place in my heart. But what if my hostess should be Inez married and widowed? What if she should love me still? But no, no; I must not think of such a thing. I have wronged her too deeply for that. God would not be a just God if he sent such happiness to so great a sinner—to one the burden of whose song must be: '*Mea Culpa, Mea Culpa, Mea Maxima Culpa.*' Oh, Inez! Inez! Could you ever forgive me?"

When he first seated himself at the table, a lady had stolen softly into the room and stood near him unseen, and as he uttered the last exclamation she put her arms gently around his neck, kissed him on the forehead and said; "Yes, dear husband, I can."

The man sprang to his feet and stood for a moment or two and glared at her like a maniac. Then he seized her in his arms, as though she had been a baby, and walked across the floor, covering her face with kisses. "Oh, my God!" he exclaimed. "How can it be possible that I once more hold my darling in my arms! It would be too cruel to have *this* turn out to be one of the mad dreams of a broken-down tramp!" Seating himself in a chair by the window, still holding her in his arms, each hand, each finger, received its separate kiss and caress. When he became more calm he looked lovingly down into her eyes, and saw the love of old reflected back.

"John," she said playfully, and if to reassure him, "John, you are still my great big, awkward booby ! Here I have been for more than an hour curling my hair and dressing my self so as to look my very best, and in two minutes I look like a fright. One would not suppose it had been combed for a month ! Look at it !"

"Oh, Inez, do tell me —do make me know that I am really with you, and that I am not in the midst of one of those dreams of happiness that will follow the poor, broken-down creatures who have lost all hope of the future ! Oh, I have had so many, so many just, such dreams in which the maximum of all earthly happiness would be reached, only to be followed by the realization of bitter degradation and shame !"

"Let us hope, dear John, that it will be a long, long dream this time, extending from this anniversary of our Saviour's birth to the moment when one or both of us shall stand at his feet to receive the sentence of eternity. But, John," she continued, while a mischievous smile played around her lips, "I have forgiven you for letting ill fortune befall you. Now, dear, can you forgive me ? Forgive me for that letter, and for that—that—other marriage, you know John !"

'There is nothing in the wide world, darling to forgive. *My* idol can do no wrong. When I received the letter to which you refer — your last—I could but acknowledge its overwhelming justice, and I had to bow down in humiliation and exclaim, '*Mea Culpa!*' But, Inez, it cannot be that you belong to some one else; that would be too cruel. But what else can expect? All my pleasures have been like the apples of Sodom—touch them, and they are gone. No, No ! it cannot be. Miles said you were a widow, and besides you said we would be always together. Thank God for that !"

"But Miles was mistaken. I am not a widow, but am, a I have been for eighteen years, the true and lawful wife of—well kiss me and I will tell you his name. There! there! that will do, I said one kiss, not forty, John Henderson ! And now, dear husband, not to keep you in suspense any longer, permit me to say that I have read that sketch you wrote just before you were shot, and until I read that I did not know that you had received such a letter as the one which caused you to become dead to the world!"

"Then it was all a forgery! Oh, the fool that I was!"

"I cannot say that it was exactly a forgery, for I have not been without my crosses and trials, John. That letter business came about in this way: After I went back to my father's to live, I became acquainted with a man whom I learned to regard very highly. I was open and frank in my friendship; and presuming that it was love, he wrote me a letter, proposing that I get a divorce and marry him. Smarting under the insult, I wrote him the note you received. As my letters failed to reach you, I suppose he must have had some clerk in the postoffice in his employ, and captured them. It would then have been an easy matter to change the envelopes."

"Who was this man—this villain?"

"To prevent trouble in the future, I prefer to keep that to myself."

"But Inez, tell me how you ever happened to come to California?"

"A strong impulse, with a faint glimmer of hope, moved me in this direction. I did not dare to hope to find you, yet I did not feel that you were dead. Aunt Helen passed away some time ago, leaving me her sole heiress; and when some five years ago my father died I found myself in possession of a large fortune, and entire mistress of my own actions. I immediately set out for this State, and purchased this farm, which I have since improved. The impression or presentiment, or whatever name the feeling may be called, that you were still living and keeping out of the way for some unknown causes grew stronger and stronger, until about two years ago I organized an effort to find you. I had paid emissaries in every walk of life. James Burns, or the man you have nicknamed Lieutenant Miles O'Riely, who had been in my employ ever since I came to the State, undertook the task of searching among those men, of whom there are so many in this State, who have given up life's battles and settle down in the belief that there is nothing more in store for them. Although he firmly believed that the proof of your death was beyond a cavil, he went to work as earnestly as though he shared my impressions. He had been most of the time for two years on the tramp. He had pictures and descriptions of you as minutely as I could give them with your complete history. When he found you at Los Angeles last summer he felt encouraged, and the longer he stayed with you the more he felt that he was right; but he could not draw you out enough to make him certain enough to inform me of the progress he was making until the day you were brought here, shot. Under one pretext and another he kept bringing you nearer and nearer to me. He wanted me to see you. If you remember, you saw him here when you passed by on that day. Up to that time he had not told me of his suspicion; but as you looked toward the house, and hesitated a moment as you saw him, somehow my heart told me who it was, and I took an eager look after you.

"'I am right,' he said; 'that must be John Henderson.' My heart stood still, the room whirled around and I staggered and fell. It was the only time in my life that I had ever fainted; but never mind that. James, or Miles as you would call him, said he would find some pretext for bringing you around the next day. When you were shot, he sent one man to town for a doctor, and hailed a passing wagon and brought you here. With all this ingenuity he said that he had never gotten anything out of you except that you had once practiced law, and that there was a woman somewhere, dead or alive, whose memory you worshiped. It was his talks to you that put you to writing that sketch I read. Oh, the ecstacy of knowing that through all your trials and misfortunes I have reigned queen of your heart!"

Henderson again covered his wife's face with kisses, and she nestled her head against his heart.

"Why have you not told me all this before?" he said.

"Because, John, in the first place, I wanted you to get perfectly strong before subjecting your feelings to the strain of such a discovery; and in the second place, Christmas, the anniversary of our dear Lord, was so near that I thought it fitting to give you a happy Christmas. There are others in the house besides ourselves who will acknowledge this day as the merriest and happiest Christmas of their lives"

"Others, Iuez? What others? Oh, yes, we have a child. O, wife, tell me if that child is still alive."

"I will show you in a minute." And Mrs. Henderson went to the door of another room and said: "Jennie, you can come in now. This," she continued, as the young lady appeared, "is our daughter." She had hardly finished the sentence before he had gathered her in his arms.

"And this is another accusing angel," he exclaimed, "come to bear witness to my want of manhood; one whose young life has been robbed of its happy childhood, and whose young heart has been oppressed with sadness—and all through my fault; my most grievous fault."

"Why not allow me, dear papa, to be a messenger of light, if I am to be clothed with celestial attributes?"

"Ah, here is my little Inez over again. Whatever I once made of myself was owing to the inspiration received from a little girl who looked just like you, and the great mistake of my life was in getting too far away from her influence. "But," he continued, putting one arm around his wife's and another around his daughter's waist, "I am yet comparatively a young man and with God's help I will wipe out all the past and will devote every moment of my life to making up to my wife and child the years of happiness of which I have robbed them."

After a little more conversation between the three, the wife remarked that some company awaited them in the parlor, "and remember," she added," "this is your house and you are the host to-day and must act accordingly."

"My house, Inez! Impossible! It cannot be! I am a beggar, a tramp, a vagabond on the face of the earth! Do not, oh, do not, say that anything is mine until I shall have an opportunity of earning it."

She put her hand across his mouth to stop further utterance, and said: "This is our merry Christmas; we must have no more such talk as that. There are further explanations to be made to-day that will satisfy you on every point."

As Henderson walked into the parlor with his wife and daughter on either arm, a middle-aged gentleman arose to meet them. "I believe, Mr. Henderson," she said, "that you have met Mr. Stephen Bates?"

"My old client, my dear friend; the man who once raised me from the depths of despair to think something of myself. Who would have made something of me, even after I had lost my grip, had not other unfortunate circumstances intervened. From the bottom of my heart, I can wish you a merry Christmas!"

"You do not know yet how good a friend he has been to you,' said his wife. "But here is another gentleman waiting for an introduction. Mr. Henderson, let me introduce you to Mr. Thomas Allen Campbell."

"My God !" exclaimed Henderson; "can this be true? Have I, indeed, the good fortune of meeting under such auspicious circumstances the nephew, the almost son, of the dearest and best friend I ever had?" He threw his arms around his neck and wept like a child.

"Can you forgive me, Mr. Henderson, for that shot I gave you, while in the character of Jim Fiske?"

"Forgive ! "Don't anybody ask me to forgive anything ! All the hardships, all the mistakes, all this unhappiness has been brought about through my fault. It is ever with me the same refrain—*Mea Culpa !* But let us drive dull care away, and make the merriest Christmas California ever saw !"

"But here is yet another," said the wife. "Let me introduce Mr. James Burns, for several years the business agent on this farm."

"Oh, Miles ! You rascal ! How will I ever get even with you for toting me several hundred miles, to get me into such a scrape as this !"

"I am thinking that if you had known as much about the place I was a-bringing you to as you do now, I should not have had such hard work of it. You were the hardest person to get anything out of I ever tried. When I told you the story of John Henderson's murder, and Allen Campbell's hard times, I watched you closely all the time and got but slight reward for it; but that one swallowing down of a lump in your throat gave me encouragement. I was going to follow up the Fiske story with one that would have pressed you for an introduction next day, had it not been for that little episode which followed."

"Did you know that Jim Fiske and Allen Campbell were one and the same person?"

"Not until after the story was told and the shot was fired. Then I knew that the two men I wanted to bring together had met, and that I had not been quick enough to avoid a disastrous consequence."

"I see, Miles, that you have left your brogue out in the camp with the other accouterments of the tramp. But there is one other person to whom I want to be introduced. Where is the old lady who nursed me so kindly?"

"I am afraid you would want to kiss her," said the wife, "and I would be jealous. But if you will wait until I can go and pad up, and get on a wig and some paint, I will try and represent her."

"Well, I'll kiss her any way," said he, suiting the action to the word.

"Well, now," said Jennie, "don't you want to be introduced to the little girl who was sitting by your side when you came to yourself one day, and who you wanted to claim as your little Inez?"

After a while the conversation turned upon Thomas Allen, when Allen Campbell said: "Don't you know, Mr. Hendeson, that the fact of a monument having been erected over my uncle's grave after your reputed death puzzled me no little. I could not imagine you living yet, as with my own eyes I had seen you dead; but I could not imagine who did it."

"Yes, I hewed that granite out with my own hands, but did not put it up for fear of discovery; I had energy enough to hire that done."

"And I," said Mr. Bates, "thought that monument an evidence that Allen Campbell was still around, and caused me to redouble my my efforts toward capturing him. All of which, I now believe, has led to good results."

"It may be more satisfactory, both to my husband and Mr. Campbell," said Mrs. Henderson, "if I should enter into a little explanation just here. Soon after the supposed murder of my husband, Mr. Bates sent me the rest of the fee he had agreed to pay, and hence Mr. Henderson can see that he has quite an interest in the property hereabouts. In addition to this, he proposed we should jointly offer a reward of five thousand dollars for the capture of Allen Campbell, the supposed murderer. This reward was offered by the Sheriff, Mr. Bates not being known in it, which gave him a better chance of working to the same end himself. Some five years ago, one Thomas C. Allen discovered and located a rich quartz claim. A company was formed and the mine was opened. Mr. Bates was interested in mining property, and became a large owner in this mine. Although the heavy beard of the man had taken the place of the smooth face of the stripling, Mr. Bates began to think that Thomas C. Allen and Thomas Allen Campbell were one and the same person. He communicated this to another gentleman interested in the mine, but it happened that this gentleman was a friend of Mr. Allen's, and intimated to him that he was suspected, and that detectives would probably be on his track. Allen left the mine, and Bates concluded that he left because suspected, and set a guard on all the avenues of escape from the State. Allen, in the guise of a tramp, fell in with my husband, and what followed they both knew. After that sad event I sent for Mr. Bates and explained to him the identity of each. We knew that Allen Campbell would not be taken alive, and we wanted to avoid a collision with the officers. He went to see Allen's friend, whom he was satisfied could find him. That friend came to see me, and to satisfy him that there was no trick about, I had to show him my husband, show him the manuscript he had written, and bring Burns in to tell all that he had done, before I could get this cautious friend to agree to anything, and then he only said may be so. In a couple of days Allen called on me, and satisfied himself about the truth of the matter, and has since walked in the light of day, feeling lighter and happier than he has felt for years. It is through the activity of Mr. Bates that we are all here together on this happy, happy Christmas Day!"

"He came near being too active for me," said Allen, "but I honor and respect him for his straightforwardness to the memory of a friend whom he supposed dead."

"And now," said Mr. Bates, "I have the strangest part of this story to tell: A few days ago one Chas. Guthrie died, and on his death-bed confessed that he had instigated the murder of John Harrison, for which I came so near suffering through a mistaken identity. He said that his man had mistaken Harrison for John Henderson, both being known by the said name of 'Kentuckg' The object he said of getting Henderson out of the way was that he might get his wife. He then, he said, proposed a divorce to her, which she stoutly refused, and after stealing letters from his wife to Henderson and *vice versa*, he concluded to have the killing job perfected, and the attack for which Allen Campbell was arrested was the result?"

"*Mea Culpa!*" exclaimed Mrs. Henderson, 'it is through my fault this time. This man came to my father's house, and I treated him as a prince, the same as I have James Burns and Mrs. Bates: but the poor man lost his mind. Let us hope and pray that God will not hold him responsible for his acts."

The recital of this last episode threw a gloom for a few moments
over the assemblage, but they all felt in a happy humor, and soon
laughter, and music, and song reverberated through the house.   This
was kept up until dinner was announced, and when they had arranged themselves around the table, and before they were seated,
John Henderson said: "This is the first time I have ever been called
upon to preside at my own family table, and as we are brought together under circumstances in which the finger of God is plainly visible, let us return thanks."

Then with this tall form erect, and with eyes and hands uplifted,
he said, "Oh, God! Thou who holdeth myriads of worlds in place
by the power of Thy will, and yet who marketh the fall of the spar-
row, look down upon this family and the friends assembled, on this the
natal day of the Savior of the world, around this board spread with
Thy bounteous gifts, and incline each heart to return thanks to Thee;
and may each be so impressed with Thy Divine goodness that he may
go hence strong in his faith in Thee, and an earnest soldier of the
Cross."

John Henderson was master of elocution, and this simple prayer
brought an earnest "amen!" from each one present.

At every Christmas since the above, the anniversary of this jovial
reunion has been commemorated by the Hendersons, and the same
guests have met around the festive board.   The name of one of them
however, has longed since been changed.   High chairs have to be
placed at the table for the grand-children, and Mrs. Allen Campbell
has a seat by her husband.   John Henderson holds that, as one cannot enjoy a good meal who has never felt hunger, so one cannot fully
appreciate genuine happiness who has not seen the reverse; and he
and his are reaping the benefit thus arising, by comparison, of those
bitter days when in anguish of spirit he cried out: "*Mea Culpa*"—
through my fault.

"LIZ."

It was midsummer in the heart of the Sierras. All the air was full of quivering heat, which beat against the mountain side, withering the petals of the wild-flower and forcing the ferns to bend their heads and drink from the clear streams that trickled down the slopes.

The birds, overcome by the heat, were too indolent to sing; and only occasionally could one see the bright wing of a blue-bird or the red breast of a robin, as it darted through the air, half eagerly, to snap at a fly asleep in the purple and white wanothies thicket.

The miners put down their picks and shovels to wipe the perspiration from their brows, then lay down to doze under the pine shade, for it was too hot for work. They looked longingly up at Sugarloaf, whose summit, almost touching the clouds, seemed so inviting and cool.

It stood, like a rock, boldly out in relief from the undulating sea of foothills covered with dry grass, and the sight was as tantalizing as the mirage of the desert to a worn traveler.

The dust in the roads was yellow and thick, and when the stage made its daily entrance and exit into and from Nevada City, their leaders were obscured in a fine, penetrating mist of dust. It covered their flanks until they looked as if they were emulating the poetical bee, who "powders his wings with gold." It settled over the passengers, until the most renowned physiognomist could not well have discovered a line of distinctive character in their dirt-grimed faces.

Nevada City lies in a gorge in the mountains, a town born of the mines, and of mushroom. Men in the old days of California chivalry had little time to waste in architectural design, and the cabins and houses scattered here and there were without regard to any regular plan. The town was built by men who had come to work, to wrest from the earth by muscle power, their fortunes—men of indomitable will and courage, who had little time to spend on the mere comforts of living.

All the heat was concentrated in that spot, and poured down in full vigor upon the rude cabins, scorching the leaves of a few previously guarded rosebushes in the gardens, even exhausting the energy of the hardy pioneers, who were content to sit indoors idly; while the chickens drooped about the yards, and the ducks reveled in the waters of the ravine, which were very low and muddy, for the sun had drained it almost dry, and only a shallow stream flowed over the yellow clay.

While the men dozed, a young girl worked steadily, panning out dirt in the upper part of the stream, with her head bare, in the scorching sunlight. She was tall and brown. Her eyes were dark and expressive, and her rich auburn hair fell down her shoulders in unkempt profusion. Her shoulders were broad, but her face was young—the face of a child, who had lived more in the years of her existence than was well for her. She looked as Joan D'Arc might have looked when she knitted in the cottage of Lorraine, while France lay bleeding, and the nameless ambition was stirring in her breast.

Her feet were encased in an old pair of men's shoes. There was something pitiful about the expression of those shoes, supporting her slender, bare, brown ankles, which looked too slight to bear such a weight. They were aristocratic-appearing shoes, but their original color was lost, for they were torn, patched, run down at the heel, the soles ragged; still, they had an air of gentility, as if they had seen better days.

They turned up at the toes, as if they shrunk in disdain from their surroundings.

They rolled over at the ankle, as if they shuddered at contact with bare flesh, and had been accustomed to silken hose. The tracery of arabesque patterns on their instep stood out clearly, and reminded one of Mrs. Skewton's frippery and artificial roses, after the decay of youth.

Liz did not mind the shoes as she worked, although they were so large they impeded her progress, and gave her a sort of shuffling gait. She loosened the handkerchief around her throat, twisted her mass of hair carelessly on top of her head, tucked her ragged, calico dress further up from the water, and shook her rusty pan to and fro, her eyes bent eagerly in their search for particles of gold. She glanced occasionally from her work at a figure sleeping under a tree near by, which filled the air with a chorus of snores that reverberated through the mountains like distant growlings of thunder.

"Well, Liz, what luck to-day? I see the old dad is quietly snoozing. It's a burning shame you are working out in this sun. It is hotter than Hades."

She blushed, as the speaker came in view from behind a clump of manzinita bushes, but answered:

"I'm sort of used to it. I can't get much blacker—and poor dad's head ain't just right, you know, Dick."

Dick whistled significantly, but his countenance did not express much sympathy for the aforesaid head, for he thought rightly, whisky and laziness were the things that were not "just right."

Dick Beech was one of the numerous crowd of young men who had drifted along with the tide in the the early days, landed in California, and patiently sat down, waiting for fortune to come to him instead of troubling himself to search for her. He counted on stumbling on a big thing some day, so despised the humble panning for gold dust, but somehow or other he always managed to obtain a share of the world's goods.

A man down in Grass Valley had found a nugget as big as his fist, one day, without any effort on his part, and Dick Beech reasoned 'that if the man from Grass Valley found a nugget as big as his fist, there was no reason why Dick Beech shouldn't pick up one as big as his head.' He therefore quieted his conscience by this questionable logic, and spent most of his time in waiting for the above mentioned result.

He possessed a smattering of a college education, and was consequently looked up to as an oracle of learning by the simple-hearted miners. He had befriended "Drunken Harry," as Liz's father was dubbed by his associates, and so had earned her eternal gratitude.

She was not accustomed to being noticed, and did not court it, for the few women in town drew back their skirts in pharisaical dismay when she passed near them.

The daughter of a drunkard, a girl who could shoot a deer, ride a bronco like a man, and work in the diggins, was a thing never dreamed of in their philosophy.

Liz was a waif, motherless and alone, she had flourished like a

weed in rich soil, and had grown into a tall, handsome maiden, de-
fiant of the laws of society and the creeds of man, "free as the mountain winds," a true child of the Sierra.

The mountains and her dissolute father were her sole companions.

His faults were only forces of circumstance to her and she idolized
him.

She had been taught by an old man named Hugo who lived a her-
mit's life in an old cabin, so she was not entirely ignorant.

Dick Beech was a revelation to her. He belonged to a class she
only saw in her dreams and while she often treated him scornfully as
she did the rest, she reserved a higher place in her heart for him because he had helped her father.

"I'm used to the heat," she said: "I like work only there's nothing to pay for it to-day."

"Come Liz! Your dad's asleep. Come sit in the shade. I want
to talk to you."

She shook her head determinedly.

"I shall stay here all night, until I get something when I make up
my mind to do a thing I intend to do it if it kills me."

"Dear me! Heroism in calico. A new Judith—a coming Portia
of the Sierra!"

"I'm just Liz Byrnes. No fooling, Dick Beech," she said stopping her work, her dark eyes sparkling, as if he had intended an insult.

"Well," he laughed, "don't show fight. It's honorable company
I placed you in."

Then he stretched himself out full length on the dry grass idly
stirring the water with a stick; and regarding Liz curiously.

The sunshine brought out every tint clearly on the hillside—the
blue green of the pine tassels the purple brown brinks, the rich red of
the manzinita wood, the gloss of the madrona leaves mingled with the
emerald of the live oak foliage and the surrounding mountains revealed dark against a sky of intense cloudless blue.

The granite bowlders sparkled like monster diamonds in the strong
sunlight which beat down upon Liz's head causing each hair to shine
like a thread of gold.

She would have well served for a model of the vestal Tuccia as she raised the pan over her head to relieve her arms from their cramped constant motion.

Dick Beech lay there listlessly watching, anathematizing her drowsy father but never imagining that he might relieve her for awhile.

"You will have a sunstroke," he said. "I insist upon you covering your head, or I shall borrow that inverted basket from that China-man down there."

"Liz, do you know that you are very pretty?"

She opened her eyes wonderingly.

"You are as bad as the boys who call me names. I never looked at myself."

"I wish I could paint you just as you are. Unfortunately I have never learned how."

"These duds would be pretty things in a picture," she replied touching them. Why don't you go 'long and talk to Nancy Brown? I'm busy."

"Because you interest me, and she don't like you Liz, just as I prefer a wild flower to a cultivated one. I'ts a matter of taste. I think we were intended for each other and I love you Liz "

He moved a little farther into the shade as he looked at her stead-ily.

She laughed though her heart beat fast with happiness.

"I could work and you be a gentleman. I would like a man like old Hugo used to read of—a knight who would fight for me, go through everything for me, die if need be—and kill bears," she said merrily.

"Dick, I heard about your hunt the other day. If I had had your chance I would have shot him instead of climbing a tree. I will love you on one condition: that you bring me a young grizzly for a pet."

"I don't care about sharing affections, and I'm afraid the bear would be the strongest party Liz," he said suddenly. "One of Ham Jones' girls is going to be married to-night. Going to the wed-ding?"

It was intended as a Roland for her Oliver, she looked at him, her eyes snapping with anger.

"How dare you ask me? I'm not good enough for them. Any-way weddings are curious things. I see them dancing and kissing; in a year they fight like wildcats, then two to one they leave one another. It's like dad's game. Head or tails. I don't believe in weddings."

"But Liz, suppose two people love one another?"

"Well Dick, what is love?"

"That's a stunner. Oh! I don't know exactly. A sort of a—a kind of a feeling when two people care for each other, and one can't live without the other. There was Abelard and Heloise, Romeo and Juliet."

Liz tossed her head scornfully.

"I can tell you. It's always sorrow and trouble for one of them. There was the baker's Lize. She was in love and stepped round as if she was walking on eggs; but Tim married another woman and instead of eggs. I reckon she thought it was pretty heavy and now she is a half-witted creature. That is what love does. Don't talk to me of that nonsense. Weddings and funerals are mighty like. Sometimes the first is a living death, the other a restful one."

A slight breeze blew down from the summit of Sugar-loaf, stirring the pines into motion, fanning the air and creating a purer atmosphere.

The shadows of the pines were lengthening and the color of the mountain crests changing to a golden purple in the setting sun.

Liz pulled down her sleeves, called to the figure underneath the tree, which grunted in reply, and, grasping a black bottle, started to its feet. The rags, unfolded, developed themselves into a resemblance to clothes, and a man rose, blinking in the light with blood-shot eyes, and waited until Liz shouldered the pick, shovel and pan; then lazily joined her.

She whispered to Dick: "Go! Dad can't bide you. He gets in such temper sometimes, he might hurt you."

Dick obediently slipped back through the thicket from which he had come.

"Got anything to-day Lazybones?" he growlingly asked.

"Not much, dad," Liz answered, gently; for her voice was always soft to him.

They walked together up the lonely path to their board shanty, which stood across the ravine opposite the town, in a grove of madrona trees. No miner ever possessed such a rickety, desolate old cabin as "Drunken Harry," and like its owner, it looked as if it was intoxicated and on its last legs. The planks were nailed on the frame unevenly, at a tipsy looking angle; the nails were half out, as if bound for a spree, and the shingle roof was patched in uneven heaps with cloth, brush, odd bits of lumber and old petroleum cans, until it appeared as if it were suffering from a mild form of delirium tremens. Handsome Liz looked as much out of her place in the hovel as a queen in a stable-yard, or a yellow primrose growing out of the barren rock cliffs by the sea.

"Dad," said she, leading him in, "don't take any more of your medicine to-night, it makes you so cross."

"Shut up! tend to your pertatoes. This is jest the stuff that puts life into a fellow. When I feel sick or down sperited, I jest take a sip from this bottle," patting it affectionately, "then I feel straight, and says to myself, 'Harry, you're a gentleman.'"

Liz left him while he continued talking to himself in a maudlin way. She suspected the quality of the medicine but said nothing, because he was her father, the only person in the world, near to her, the only one who had spoken kindly to her during the lonesome nineteen years she had lived in the world.

The women in the town were cruel to her and avoided her as they would a crotalus on the mountain rocks, so she lived a strange life alone, with nature and a drunken father. She had learned the lesson of silence, and however hard she worked, however heavy her burdens, she never complained.

"Dad, supper is ready," she called.

"Ugh," he growled, "a few asby potatoes."

"There's a bit of meat for you."

"That's well; your pore dad's sick, Liz; you wouldn't take it from him, would you?"

She pushed the morsel towards him.

"I'm going down town; mind you keep close to the shanty. Got any dust 'bout you?"

She took the little she had found from her pocket, and looked at him beseechingly, laying her hand on his arm.

"Do you think, dad," she said, looking up into his face, "that you need more *medicine*," slightly emphasizing the word. "This is all I have for bread, and we have no more in the house."

He pushed her roughly from him and whined : " You'd let your pore old dad die and you'd never keer."

She handed him the dust silently and went out of the room, while he slunk down the trail quickly toward the town, for his throat was dry and parched, burning for liquor to moisten and relieve it.

Tears gathered in her eyes as she watched his shambling figure disappear down the slope, but she brushed them away impatiently and returned to the house, to straighten up a bit, which did not take her long, for Liz had not been taught that great principle " which is akin to godliness," and is never inherent.

She went out and sat on a stump of a pine tree which stood near her door. The air was sweet and balmy, redolent with pine fragrance and odor of plumy buck-eye blossoms. The feverish heat was gone. Nature's pulse beat faster, and a pleasing cool reigned over valley and mountain. Venus peeped over the tops of the pines, and peered down upon the girl sitting all alone in the forest. The new moon, bent like Diana's bow, shone in the skies, while all around clustered myriads of bright stars, like golden-winged bees round a wondrous tropical bloom. The lights twinkled down in the town like glow-worms' lanterns, and the breeze wafted up to the heights faint echoes of laughter and merry life. Liz gazed at the stars, and wondered " if beings who lived up there were ever poor and lonely as she was." Hugo had told her " they were other worlds," and she conjured up many fantastic fancies in her mind in regard to their inhabitants. " They were so bright, people must be happy there," she sighed. " There is so much misery here, I know the world cannot shine like that."

She looked down at the town, and rebellious thoughts stirred in her breast as she thought of Dick Beech and his pretty speeches. Putting a shawl on her head, she concluded that she would go down and see the wedding, where she could see him also. She walked down the hill, crossed the narrow flume that spanned the ravine, and went to the house where the merry-making was. It was a typical miner's wedding. The fiddler was sitting on a chair placed on an old dry goods box, busily spinning off reels, Tom Tucker's various medleys, and calling out " alaman right, alaman left."

Some of the miners who had slept in the daytime were dancing in their best style, cutting innumerable pigeon wings as they swung their partners. The windows were open and Liz crowded close to the wall, watching Dick Beech eagerly as he danced with the rural belles.

Her eyes burned with jealousy as she watched him look at Nancy Brown with the same tenderness he had bestowed on her in the afternoon, and she felt as if she could gladly plunge a knife into Nancy's heart. "Indian blood flowed in Liz's veins," they said, and surely she possessed a haughty, deep, passionate nature, that might well have descended to her from an Indian princess.

She watched them as they played games and drank whisky. The noise grew louder, the men more hilarious, and when the fiddler called out, "salute your partners," they availed themselves of a liberal interpretation, and imprinted a rousing kiss on each buxom maid's lips. She did not know how long, but the company showed signs of dispersing, and she stole away home.

When she reached the bottom of the hill she noticed a light burning in the cabin, and her heart almost stood still, for she knew her father's moods were not pleasant after he had been indulging too freely in "medicine." As she came near she saw him walking back and forth, looking very savage, but Liz did not know what terror was, so she went boldly in.

' Where hev you ben this time o' night?" he growled, showing his teeth like a wild animal. "A pretty time fur an honest gal to be prowlin' round the country."

He came near to her, raising his arm as if to strike her, but she looked him steadily and defiantly in the eyes. "It's no matter; I'm used to looking out for myself."

"A fine care you take. They are talkin' 'bout you, an' that curly-headed, smooth-tongued chap down town; and I tell you, Liz Byrnes, if I ketch him 'round here, I'll crack his head quicker than you can say 'Jack Robinson.'"

She did not answer, biting her lips to keep down the angry words. "You defy me, do you? I'll show you!"

Then in a sudden fit of rage he picked up a gnarled manzanita log and struck her. Its aim was sure, it hit her on the shoulder and the blood oozed through her thin calico dress.

He looked at her as if afraid. She started to speak. Her face turned deadly pale, while the red blood slowly dropping, stained her dress.

A look of hatred flashed in her eyes; then she turned away silently, wiped off the blood, while he slunk into the next room as if afraid to meet her gaze. It was the first time he had struck her. He had cursed her, but the sound was familiar to her. That one cut burned into her very soul, and she felt she could never forgive him.

The next morning she went to her work as usual, and he sneaked off down town before she was up.

The July sun had gathered a renewed force, but she worked sullenly on, only stopping once in a while to pour some water on her throbbing head. The heat was so intense a steam arose from her damp hair. She worked savagely, trying to stifle the bitter feelings in her heart, which hurt far more than the burning pain in her shoulder.

"Harry's Liz has struck a good streak to-day," the miners said as she found an unusual quantity of dust, but she never heeded nor answered them.

Dick Beech sauntered down about the usual time in the afternoon.

"How goes it, Liz?"

She vouchsafed him no answer.

"Liz what's the matter? Sulks to-day?"

Still no answer. She kept on working.

"Don't be so hard on a fellow. It's confounded hot, I wanted a sight of you to refresh me."

She lifted her eyes for the first time, and looked at him with a peculiar, searching expression and answered: "I think you could find refreshment nearer home. Nancy Brown is good enough for some folks to look at."

" 'O, Jealousy, thy name is woman!' " he laughed. "Why Liz, your little finger is worth her whole body. But you know," he continued, "a fellow has got to have some fun. He can't sit in a corner. Some day when I get rich it will be different. What makes you look so fierce? I believe you would be equal to the Moor of Venice, if I loved any one else, and smother me as he did poor Desdemona."

"I could smother you or kill you, Dick Beech, if you were false to me. I suppose I am not good enough for the likes of you, but none of them will love you any better, Dick." And her expression grew tenderer as she said the words.

"I wish that you didn't have such an awful temper."

Mr. Richard Beech's private opinion was that he was too good for Liz Byrnes; and they were both attracted to each other by the law of opposition. She was handsome and strong. He was polished and weak, and an ardent admirer of the beautiful. He was kind to her, and she placed him in a niche of her heart, with her father, as the priests place the images of the saints in the cathedral, giving to each a shrine above the world below.

"What is that stain on your dress? It looks like blood. Has anybody hurt you?"

"No," she answered, looking away from him. "I only fell down on a stone and cut myself."

She despised a falsehood, but was too loyal to expose her father, even to the man she loved.

"Liz, if it were not for your father we would be married."

"Yes?" she said dreamily,

"But I never could stand him."

"The knights, Hugo read of stood everything for the ladies they loved. They killed giants and overcame dragons. They were strong to stand everything, and Dick, they would have waited patiently, with brave hearts. Poor old dad would not trouble you. You don't know him as I do, and—I can never leave him alone."

"In this nineteenth century, Liz, knights are not as plenty as black-berries. The Round table is a romance after all. Their wonderful Sir Lancelot, was not so fine, he was human."

"But," she said earnestly, the color creeping into her cheeks, like the rosy glow over the summit of the Sierras in the eventide, "people don't need to fight battles with their hands, old Hugo says. The beasts are in the heart we must conquer. Sometimes I feel as if a lion was caged in mine, and it is hard work to keep him quiet."

Then, as if half confused at her own confusion, she worked on.

"Life is short enough, without so much trouble. I will see you again. I must go, for I have an engagement."

She nodded good-bye cheerfully, and her heart felt lighter as she went home in the evening.

The cabin was deserted, no signs of her father anywhere.

She lighted a fire, and tried to cook an inviting meal. She waited for an hour; still he did not come, and, being tired from her work, she laid down on her cot, and fell asleep.

When she awoke it was dark, and the moon was shining in her face. She looked out of the door, down the long aisles of pines, but he was not there. The night was misty, so she thought she would walk down to the flume, where he usually crossed, and wait for him there. She sat there for hours, it seemed her heart filled with tender hopes and fears. "Dick loves me. He loves me," she said over and over to herself. The words sounded sweet to her. Her heart softened towards her father, as she sat there breathing in the pure mountain air. The air was heavy with the intense odor of wild azalea blossoms. The moon had gone down and it was very dark. She did not mind the blackness, for Dick loved her. She knew it, she felt it. The wound on her shoulder smarted, but she smiled, as she drew her shawl closer around her, and half laughed to herself, when she thought that yesterday, she had minded so small a thing—so small a thing.

At last through the stillness, she heard a step coming towards the flume. The trail was covered with dried pine needles and every step was very distinct. She saw as he came nearer, that he staggered more than usual. She rose and called to him through her hands.

"Don't cross. Go up to the bridge."

He answered her with an oath, and stepped on to the narrow enclosed flume, which was just the width of a plank. Liz started to go to him, but he waived his hands wildly, commanding her to "go back."

Through fear for his safety, she obeyed· Her heart beat fast as she watched, with strained eyes, through the darkness, and saw his form swaying from one side to the other.

She saw him stumble, and regain his balance. He reached the middle. She breathed more freely. He stopped, and continued gesticulating. Throwing his arms up he missed his balance and fell. Liz heard a sickening sound as he struck the rocks below. He groaned once—and all was perfect silence—a terrible quiet. She stood on the bank alone, as one petrified. She tried to move, her limbs seemed bound with icy chains. At last she screamed, and scrambled down the steep declivity as rapidly as possible. Her cries reached the ears of a passing miner, and he hurried to the spot, and peered down into the darkness with his lantern. Liz was sitting there, helplessly holding her father's head on her lap, and beseeching him to speak. The man went to her, and felt old Harry's pulse.

"It's all up with him. Wait till I get some help. How did you find him?"

"Lying with his face in the water. But he is not dead. It was so shallow, and he has only one cut on his head. He is not dead," she cried, wildly.

The miner shook his head, and said roughly, but kindly:

"I've seen 'em drown in an inch, when the jim-jams was on 'em, and it's as good to die by water as whisky."

Liz wrung her hands. She could not cry, and her eyes burned like fire. The miner obtained assistance, and they bore the lifeless body to the cabin, and proffered their rude help, but she preferred to be left alone.

There was no woman's hand to soothe or comfort; not one came near to whisper words of consolation to relieve her aching heart. She hoped Dick would come to her, but she was left entirely alone with her dead, and when the men came to bury him, they said:

"She was so white it was hard to tell which was the corpse."

She grieved for him passionately, mourned because she could not tell him she forgave. Her pan lay idle in the corner; money was so little to her that she had no incentive to work; still, unless she roused herself she must starve. She started out one afternoon more with the secret hope of seeing Dick than with any other object. She looked white and worn, a mere shadow of herself, walking in the sunlight like some poor soul, out of place in the world. She sat down on the bank and a familiar whistle startled her, which brought the color into her cheeks.

"Hello, Liz," he exclaimed, "so you have crawled out of your shell at last." His face had an uneasy expression. "I thought that I wouldn't disturb you," he said apologetically. "I could not do any good, and I hate funerals, and such reminders. Now, Liz, what are you going to do?"

She looked at him earnestly, but he turned away, on pretense of
plucking a cluster of manzanita berries that hung above his head.

"I—well, the fact is, I'm poor, Liz. We must wait for a while
still."

A disappointed expression stole across her face for a moment; then
she replied simply:

"I can wait, Dick."

O woman! thy faith is infinite, thy heart long enduring, long suffering; when love enters it it is blind, and feels not fault or defect in
the loved one, content to be happy, even in waiting.

Liz took up her work and said to herself: "I shall work for Dick;
now I have another object in living."

August, with its heat, passed by, and the few orchards were laden
with ripe, red-cheeked peaches and golden pears, a fortune to their
possessors in the early days of California, when peaches and pears
sold for a dollar apiece. Gold was more plentiful than fruit.

September's breezes were cooler, the young quail filled the canons
with the whir of their wings, the dog-wood fruit clustered ripe and
red as berries of coral, and the dry grass waved long and yellow in
the sunlight.

One morning Liz went down town to obtain some supplies, for
Dick had sent her some money as a present by a boy that day.

She was quietly making preparations little by little, when she
could spare a hard earned dollar, for the happy event she looked forward to as being near.

She saw knots of men gathered in the street, discussing something
very excitedly. She went into a store and asked:

"What is the matter?"

"They jist took Dick Beech up to the calaboose for stealin' Long
Tom's pile last night, who lives above you, and they are going to
try him right off. Better go down to the court-house. He is a tri-
flin' sort of chap, anyhow."

Liz put down her purchase, took up the money, and walked out.
She saw a man she knew on the street.

"Is this true I have heard?" she asked.

"Bet yer, it is. There's bin lots of theivin' done here lately. I
hope they'll string him up."

She turned away, and followed the stream of men, women and children who were running toward the large, wooden courthouse. A crowd was already gathered there, the judge seated a platform, the prisoner on one side, the two attorneys on the other—miners who possessed a smattering of law, law suited to their prejudices, who were acting for the prosecution and defense. The court preserved a semblance of order.

The jury was impaneled, the men constituting it, of course, were miners, and their threatening looks towards the prisoner at the bar did not tend to reassure him. Liz stood in the back of the room listening breathlessly.

Dick sat with his head bowed, trembling like a man with the ague. The prosecuting witness was called.

Long Tom shuffled up, attired in his Sunday best, a suit of butternut which his hair and eyes matched exactly, proclaiming his descent, unmistakably, "from Pike county, Missouri." He appeared as uneasy as a young barrister wrestling with his maiden speech.

"Waal," he began, "I jest handed over the dishes and truck, for Topsy, my dawg, to lick, when I thought uv somethin' I wanted down town, so I left my pile in an 'ole sack under my bunk, some dust and pieces of silver, 'bout a handful, I reckon. I was gone jest 'bout an hour. When I come in the bag was settin' in the middle of the floor. I tuk it up and shook it. It was as empty as Job's turkey, and I'd seen Dick Beech skulkin' 'round thar awhile before, and no one else was near. I'd know that silver this side uv Halifax, 'cause I cut an X, my mark, on each of them four bit pieces."

Liz started, and looked at the money in her hand. There was the mark, ill cut and jagged, but plain as day.

She closed her fingers tightly over the pieces, and a faintness came over her. She staggered, caught hold of a bench near, for now she knew Dick Beech was a guilty man, a criminal, and—she loved him.

Long Tom descended from the stand with a well satisfied air. The attorney for the defense spoke a few moments, evidently as a matter of form, for his argument was lame and weak, showing his spirit was not in the work. The jury returned, and rendered their verdict of guilty. The judge said:

"Prisoner at the bar, the court has found when a man is found guilty of the crime of theft, he should be hanged by the neck until he is dead."

Being prompted by a man standing near, he hurriedly added, "May God have mercy on your soul." This was a first case and the honorable judge was not quite posted.

"Do you know any reason why the law should not take its course?"

A hush fell upon the crowded room, and they looked intently at the prisoner who never lifted his head. The flies buzzing in the sunshine on the window panes were the only sounds that broke the intense silence. The expression of the faces of the people was as eager as that of the spectators in old gladiatorial conflicts, for the animal was rising in their natures, and they thirsted for blood. To them a human life was very little, but a man's property by the laws of the mining camp was sacred.

Dick lifted his head, looking haggard and appealingly towards the crowd as if seeking sympathy, but there was none for the guilty in all those upturned faces. Before he could reply Liz pushed her way through the crowd, and stood before the judge, who regarded her sternly. Two bright spots burned on her cheeks. She looked straight at Dick when she spoke, and the people listened breathlessly.

"If it please your honor, I am guilty," she said proudly, looking steadfastly at Dick. A gleam of joy and relief passed over his countenance. The color died from her face. A weary look came into her eyes.

"Does the man recognize this?" she asked, holding out a few dollars in her hand.

Tom came forward. "Yes," he said joyfully, "that's my mark. I could swear to it."

Dick covered his face with his hands and would not look at her, but her eyes never left him, looking at him as if she could read right through his cowardly soul.

"I am willing to die, judge, only let it be soon. You shall have the rest. Only let me speak once to this gentleman."

Groans of derision burst from the crowd. A boy threw a stone

which struck her, but she stood there as if turned to stone and did
not utter a word.

"Bad blood, bad stock coming out," she heard them say, and
there was not one voice in all the town lifted in pity or sympathy for
her.

"What you've got to say, say quickly," commanded the judge.

She went to Dick and whispered to him. He tried to kiss her
hand, but she snatched it quickly away, rubbing it as if his touch
contaminated it.

"You will find everything in my cabin to-night," she said quietly
to the judge. "I have nothing more to say. I am guilty.

Dick Beech walked out of the room a free man. He was pitied
and praised while she was reviled by every tongue, and he did not
say even one word in defense of her. As the officer was escorting
her to jail, they passed by a door of a saloon where he was in the act
of drinking. The glass was raised to his lips. She merely glanced
at him, but there was a world of love, misery, disappointment and
reproach in that single look. He let the glass fall. It shivered in a
thousand atoms on the floor, and he went home to his room.

Far sweeter and calmer was her rest on the straw in a prison cell
that night than his.

They mitigated the sentence because she was a woman, but many
long years Liz Byrnes expiated Dick Beech's crime in the Nevada
jail. He left the town. They said he prospered well in 'Frisco,
while she worked hard and endured patiently for his sake. Surely no
human love could be greater than this, for she bore disgrace, was
willing to suffer death, while he lived honored in the world. She was
so young, it was pitiful.

After her term was served she went back to her old cabin on the
hill, an outcast, an object of scorn to all people; a martyr, a saint
in the eyes of angels above.

She waited for him, hoping that he would come back to her some
day, and she would forgive.

It was winter time, and the rain descended from the heavens in
solid sheets. The wind swept around the mountain peaks like
mighty monsters, seeking to wrest them from their foundation. The
pines mingled their voices, sighing and moaning, while a torrent

roared down the ravine, in mad frenzy, dashing over rocks and leaping over bowlders.

Liz sat with hands folded, watching the storm; but she was not afraid, though the wind threatened to blow down the old shanty at every gust. Through the storm some one was beating his way to her door, and, as a fierce blast blew it open, it blew a man with dripping clothing into the light.

"Tom," she asked, gently, "what do you want here?"

"Liz," he said, hesitatingly, "won't you shake hands with me? I know all; Dick Beech is dyin' down at the tavern. He's told us," he said, wiping a suspicious moisture from his eyes. "You're an angel, Liz, which wimmin folks ain't often; but if ever thar was one on airth, you're that one, Liz Byrenes. He wants to see you 'fore he pegs out, the scoundrel."

"Is Dick Beech there?" she asked excitedly.

"Yes; he came back a day or two ago. I never seed sich a change; and he deserves it."

"You shall not say anything about him," Liz retorted, angrily.

"They sed how he was doin' well," Tom said, "but it seems now he wasn't. It was well in whisky, I 'spect. He got shot in a row at Black's saloon to-night, and he keeps callin' for you."

She hastily threw an old shawl around her shoulders, and followed Tom. The rain and wind beat in their faces, but they kept steadily on, Tom holding a lantern before them, which illuminated the wet and slippery trail. At last they reached the saloon. It seemed hours to Liz, who threw off her dripping wrappings and went into the room where he lay slowly dying. Men were laughing, drinking, betting in the next room, one life was very little to them.

"Liz," he said, feebly rising up as she entered, "I knew you would come to me. Don't look at me so. It was that look that maddened me, it has haunted me day and night," he moaned falling back on his pillow.

"Only say you will forgive me. I have told them all. I would scarcely know you, you are so changed. May I kiss you once, Liz? For I love you," he said, looking at her wistfully.

She clasped his hand in hers, while a light, bright as a halo round the head of a saint, shone in her face.

"Yes, Dick, I forgive, freely, freely, if you will only live. I don't care for these years, they are gone, and my life was not meant to be like other women.

The wind swept around the house like the wail of a lost spirit, and Dick held her hand in his and smiled peacefully, for he was too feeble to talk any more.

As morning neared, the storm died slowly away, the embers faded into ashes in the fireplace, and Dick's life ebbed quietly away. His soul was summoned before the Higher Tribunal. Liz sat there motionless by his side, through the long day, praying in her heart for death to be merciful unto her.

The Judge shook hands with her; the people crowded around bringing offerings. They tried to make amends for their wrongs to her, but she only said wearily:

"It is too late now. It is all the same to me. When you could have been merciful you turned away. Now it is all over. Justice can never make amends for my sufferings."

And then she said softly to herself:

"It was all for his sake."

Mary Willis Glascock.

MIRANDA HIGGINS.

He was a drummer; a moon-faced, big-eyed, round-cheeked, inno-cent drummer. He had been in California but a short time, and had been forwarded by his firm to secure the trade of the then booming town of Josie.

He drove a span of greys attached to a light spring wagon, loaded down with samples of dress goods, dry goods and small wares. He was innocent, I say, because this was his first experiment in that line of business, and his saucer eyes had not yet become contracted and steeled by unflinchingly gazing in the clear depths of honest pur-chasers; his peach-blow cheeks were not yet browned by the sun and conscientious resistance to insinuating bargain-drivers.

He sat back on his seat, permitting the lines to lie loosely on his knees, while he read a volume of Bret Harte's stories of California life.

"Well, here I am at last," he said to himself, "among the very scenes he pictures; breathing the very mountain air once inhaled by Tennessee's partner; rattling over the very road that may have been trodden by Jim and Kentuck. How strange it all seems! To think that I, Samuel Kingston, am here among the genuine Californians, where I can see M'liss, and the rest of his heroines and heroes. No-body ever opened up the pure, untainted streams of human life as did Bret Harte. Simplicity, honesty, honor and classic ignorance com-bined with rugged beauty and unadorned sweetness must be, as he represents them, found in their purest forms among the denizens of the grand forests, and—ah—ah—gr-rand canons. I am wearied of the stilted formalities of city life; I am tired of the assuming beauty of civilized females. Sam, my boy—you have struck it! If you can find one of the simple, pure children of nature, with a generous heart, a self-sacrificing nature, and, of course, of the female sex, *marry* her, and be happy. I'll do it! I will search for one of the untamed savages, and she shall share my lot as certainly as my name is Sam-

uel Kingston. How we will astonish the natives at Sacramento !
Bret Harte was right. Here is the place to find the feminine soul
untainted and pure as the leaping waters of the mountains. Get up,
you lazy brutes !"

Sam jogged along, leaving first the fig and nectarine, then the oak
trees behind him as he climbed higher and higher toward the divide
which overlooked Bobtail Canon. His horses squirmed up the
dusty, stony grade, puffing and blowing, as they worked from side to
side of the ever ascending gimlet. Sam, deeply engaged in following
the equally winding careers of Bret Harte's characters, looked up
only now and then and bent searching glances to the roadside. His
whole being was on the alert for the appearance of some of these
peculiar individuals.

Bret Harte's work was his guide-book; it was his Murray. He
was fond of Dickens, and had he visited London, he would have
taken Pickwick as his model of an English gentleman,

Sam's notions of Californians, simon-pure Californians, were not
derived from California or Montgomery street, or from the business
men of Sacramento. They were but hangers-on, but excrescences.
Genuine Californians, according to his views, as derived from his
constant perusal of Bret Harte, were to be found only among the
everlasting mountains, in the gulches, canons, and among the
sluice boxes of the mines.

Sam reached the top of the divide, and, as his greys spread themselves loosely in the harness, swished their tails and tossed their
heads, delightedly at the prospect of the downward trot, his eyes
caught a glimpse of the gulch below.

There they are, just as his imagination had pictured them ! Ramb-
ling, straggling streets tumbled up, jumbled up, rickety houses.
Windows of glass and wood and potato sacks. Chimneys of stone,
mud-plastered wood, kerosene cans and fire-proof, but rusty and con-
tradictory, stove pipe.

"Bobtail Canon"—said Sam to himself, "Harte never wrote
about it that I remember, but how unique it looks, how breezy, how
picturesquely suggestive, the name ! What legends must cling
around such a distinctively characteristic California name as that."

The team of greys drove downward and around until, after rattling over a decidedly nervous bridge which crossed the creek, they trotted gaily in among the houses of Bobtail Canon.

A sign attracted Sam's attention. "Miners' Roost," it said in big black letters on a sign-board which wearily rested one end upon the ground and hung convulsively with the other to a rusty hook on the equally wearied porch which leaned against the bosom of a disgusted looking tavern that stared at Sam with wide open doors and windows. Not a soul was to be seen. The place was as silent as a grave-yard at full moon.

Sam, somewhat dazed, got out of his wagon and pounded vigorously upon the front door, which stood invitingly open, with the butt of his whip.

"Hello! Hello the house!" he bawled.

A cloud of dust floated through the corral rapidly, and a figure vaulted with a handspring over the fence.

"Hello y'self an whart's the matter?" said the figure as it came right end uppermost in front of Sam in the shape of a girl about eighteen years old.

She was tow-headed, freckled-faced, pug-nosed and blue-eyed. Her feet were bare as well as a lengthy portion of limb visible above them, bare that is of artificial covering, though plentifully frescoed with dust. She wore a grimy calico dress and was otherwise unadorned.

"M'liss?" said Sam slowly but insinuatingly, looking at the lady in amazement.

"Say it agin an' say it louder, stranger," said the girl placing her hands on her hips.

"How artistically simple!" muttered Sam. "Isn't your name M'liss?"

"No—'tain't! my name's Randy, whart's your'n?"

"Mine?" answered Sam. "O mine is Sam Kingston. But tell me, isn't this a hotel?"

"Twar onct, but tain't now."

"Can't I put up here to-night?" asked Sam; "I have come a long way to-day."

"Reckon so. Whare yer doin' up hyer anyhow? Say you Long Jim an you Snakey Jake c'm yer an' see te ther horses. Reckon ye'll hevter put up't our cabin if yer stay hyer all night. C'm long."

She led the way around the remains of the old tavern to a cabin, rather more substantial in the rear, and introduced Sam to the interior without further ado.

The furnishings were rough but neat and clean enough and Sam was soon in the wakeful dreams of "Hartey" romance.

Here was everything as described. He rambled around through the little straggling streets and made mental note. Here was a bar room, the bar indented with a multitude of arcs of circles where whisky Bill and Snorting Jerry had slammed their glasses down in emphatic argument, and there in the ceiling were bullet holes where some Black Daisy or one-eyed Tom had applauded the emphasis.

Kingston was in ecstacy. It seemed to him that he had but to touch a hidden spring somewhere, and the slouch hats, long boots, revolver belts, clinking glasses and historic dog fights and human conflicts, would all put in an appearance and begin their operations. It was a group in marble, it needed but life to make it a romantic feast.

"Anyhow," said Sam, "I have found the girl. She is a thoroughbred. Such eyes, such freedom from conventionality, I never saw. What a heroine she would make for Harte. I'll capture her if I can."

He labored hard for the three days he stayed, during which his firm suffered from his negligence, and the siege he laid to her heart was something tremendous.

He opened treasured samples of Smith, Brown & Co., and gave her a choice of knickknacks. It was a heavenly joy to him to hear her little screams of delight as she tried on the buttoned boots and displayed one trim booted ankle in contrast to its begrimmed comrade.

"Keep them ,Miranda," he said with the air of a prince.

"Shore yer ain't jokin', stranger?" she whispered sliding up to his side.

"Now could I joke with such a creature of nature as you are?" said Sam. "But you must call me Sammie."

"Call yer Sammie? Course I'll call yer anything for them boots,

Yer a snakin' good feller," she whispered again as she threw her brown arms around Sam's neck and implanted a resounding kiss upon his cheek, much like in sound to the pull of a horse's hoff from an adobe road.

A quiver of delighted conquest went all over Sam. He drew her frowsy head to his manly bosom and said, "Oh Randy, did you ever love?"

"No," whispered she.

"Don't you love me just a little?" plaintively whined Sam.

"Yer bet," she replied anchoring her head on his shoulder.

"Will you be mine?" asked Sam trembling with apprehension.

"Your'n? Yer mean will I tie to you?"

"Yes," said Sam, "marry me,"

"Ya-a-as," answered Mirande dropping her plump form into Sam's arms.

"Your father will not object, will he?" inquired Sam.

"My ole man? Wal now yer whispering. Te! he! He'll be something doggoned new ef he does. Count me in as your'n, Sammie."

Samuel Kingston, Esq, drummer, drove off the next morning to hasten through the business of his firm at Josie, which he accomplished in three or four days and returned to Bobtail Canon.

Agreeably to the arrangements privately and previously made, he took Miranda Higgins and drove to the nearest Justice of the Peace at the county seat, and was duly made a happy man in the possession of the untamed savage. He persisted in insanely calling her M'lies, much to the disgust of Miranda Kingston.

Sam was on the constant outlook for the outburst, which he expected, of some remarkable self-sacrificing deed on Miranda's part, and even meditated deliberately upon getting himself into some serious physical danger just for the sake of arousing the mountain spunk of his heroine, so that he might relate the wonderful prowess of this piece of unpolished nature to his friends at Sacramento.

The opportunity came, but not exactly as laid down in Sam's programme.

They had started on the grade to the valley. Miranda was profusely decorated in brilliant calico and gay streaming ribbons, and perched her buttoned shoes upon the dash of the wagon, where they were ever present for her constant admiration. Sam complacently smiled and delighted in the happiness of having given this unsophisticated lady an opportunity to breathe the first breath of worldly fashion.

They were winding around up the grade when suddenly the sound of clattering hoofs and rattling wheels was borne on the breeze down the mountain to them. Sam looked up quickly, and up the grade two turns of the road from him he caught a momentary glimpse of a span of wild eyed horses and a buggy tearing down in a cloud of dust. In a minute they would be at the next turn and be upon him. The grade was wide enough for one wagon only. On one side a deep and precipitous wall fell away for two hundred feet; on the other a sheer precipice rose fifty more. There was but one crevice in the upper wall where a foothold could be had.

Miranda clinched her teeth, turned pale, and screaming, "a run-away!" climbed down from the wagon.

"Ah!" thought Sam, in the flash of a moment, "she is a heroine; she goes to throw herself upon the brutes and stay their course."

Miranda did nothing of the sort. She made 2:15 time for that crevice in the upper wall, and perching herself safely there, shouted as the cloud of dust drew nearer:

"Shoot! Yer blamed fool, why don't yer shoot?"

"Sure enough," thought Sam, and as the wild team came round the bend he blazed away with his revolver. One horse fell, and in the twinkling of an eye a $400 span and a buggy were crashing down the precipice below.

Miranda climbed down.

"Nothing like such presence of mind, M'liss, Miranda, I mean," he remarked, as she seated herself in the wagon once more.

"Ain't nothin' like cold lead an' heaven' a man with yer at sich times," replied Miranda, with a grin.

They reached Sacramento, and Sam, to give his wife an eye-opener on the wide, bad world, away from the pure atmosphere of the mountains, gave a reception to his friends at the Golden Eagle. They came in claw hammers and white kids. Drummers every one of them.

"Miranda is stunning," thought Sam.

She wore a blue silk, and twined orange blossoms ornamented her head. The wild, sweet picturesqueness of bare and frescoed feet and ankles was gone; the untamed expression of the wide-open eyes was lost under the banged, flaming hair; the freckles, fashionable as they were, glared angrily in contrast to the blue dress.

Sam swept her regally into the center of the room and introduced her:

"This is my mountain heroine, boys. She is a specimen of pure and undefiled nature. She's a mountain gem."

"Kingston," whispered a brazen-faced drummer to him on the sly, "you've done it now, you know."

"I know it," answered Sam, "I always intended to get one of her stamp. I am sick of cultured loveliness, and I found her, a wild rose, blossoming amid the rubbish of one of the most romantic mining camps you ever saw."

. That night, when the guests had all retired, and while Miranda was unbuttoning her boots, she glanced up at Sam and said:

"Say, ain't it about time to let up on this hyer mountain gem business?"

"Why, what do you mean, Randy?" asked Sam, aghast. I am proud of your mountain origin; you are like a fresh breeze on the sandy desert."

"I'm glad yer think so," muttered Randy, with a mouthful of pins, "only 'taint quite the kerrect thing."

"Oh, that's all right," replied Kingston. "The people here appreciate that sort of a thing. You'll be quite a heroine."

"'S'nice fer yer to say so, Sammie,'cause yer see I'm among strangers like. Dad'n' I only kem out from Missouri, from the old Massysip, three weeks ago.

Tableau.

WILLIAM ATTWELL CHENEY.

THE MARQUIS OF AGUAYO.

[The point of law involved in this story needs explanation. In our country a question of fact, such as whether a man committed such and such a crime, is left to the jury. In Mexico, there is no jury, and the judges decide both the law and the fact. However, they require two witnesses to the overt act. In this respect they follow the Mosaic law, which is retained in that part of the Constitution of the United States referring to treason, where a man can not be convicted of treason without the testimony of two witnesses, or "confession in open court." Our readers will appreciate the force and materiality of these distinctions in the story we give below.]

Broad were the lands of the Marquis of Aguayo; far as the eye could see his acres stretched; up to the high ridge of the Sierras, where straight against the sky a fringe of fearless pines were growing, unconscious that, if the Marquis willed, they too might be bought and sold. From Mazapil to Patos, from Parras to Monteclova, and even further, for all we know, did the Marquis of Aguayo's lands extend.

If the traveler had inquired, "To whom does this or that field belong?" as of the Marquis of Carabas of old, for miles and miles, the answer would still be, "To the Marquis of Aguayo!"

The Marquis, to be sure, had tenants; but if they held the land, the land held them; and none would be so bold as to affirm that the Marquis was not their master as well as their landlord. In spite of his enormous wealth, however, and almost kingly prerogatives, the Marquis had little of the luxuries the modern rich man could command. He had more land than money, and more of money than of the things which it could buy. Yet if he had less of the comforts of life, he had at least the proud satisfaction of knowing that whatever he did own he owned absolutely, without let or hindrance from any of his neighbors. He was the best swordsman in Mexico, and when he bestrode a horse, his strength in riding, it was said, was so great that he could make a horse squeal by the mere pressure of his knees. He lived in a rude, middle-age sort of a way, moving to and fro among his numerous *haciendas*, his body-servant sleeping like a hound before his door.

On the 16th of April, in the year 1737, the Marquis of Aguayo was holding court (the expression is not too inaccurate) at his *hacien-da* near Mazapil. The occasion was one of high festivity. The glasses clinked merrily around the board, sparkling with the wine of Parras. Twelve young Mexican girls, in white *chemise*, gay petti-coat, and blue and white *ribosa*, were moving noiselessly about the table, waiting on the numerous wants of the guests. The *menu* was the usual one on such occasions—*Tortillas, Olla Podrida, Guisada*, a dish of olives, eggs and oil, a particularly fine roast kid, and at the finish the inevitable *Frijoles*. In the center of the table was a huge glass of water from which all drank.

The marquis had summoned all his friends, or rather all his satel-lites, for he had no friends. He made it a rule, he said, to avoid these entanglements, and he had easily succeeded in carrying the rule out. For the Marquis was rather feared than loved, and it was whispered in certain circles that, though he could control almost all else, his wife's affections were somewhat errant. Base rumor had it that a certain major-domo, now at Patos, had estranged the beauti-ful Donna Ignacia from her rightful lord and master. But whether this was true or not, the Marquis gave no sign of ether outward ro inward suspicion. He sipped his coffee and smoked his cigarette imperturbably, with a calmness which at least betokened self-control if not self-possession.

It was noticed that on that evening he was particularly affable to his guests. He had even joked and smiled grimly at his own hu-mor. Indeed the lion of Patos, as he was familiarly called, had so relaxed his usual severity that one of the company, Don Jose Ybarra, the young superintendent of the mines at Mazapil, was bold enough to hazard a remark.

"Where is the Donna Ignacia this evening, if one might ask?"

Now Don Jose Ybarra had no cause to love the Marquis. It was he who had sought the fair Ignacia's hand in marriage before her richer suitor came along. It was said—what will they not say?—that the beautiful Ignacia was not averse to the young engineer, and that family influence, powerful in all Spanish countries, had been exerted in his rival's behalf. Be this as it may, every one in Mazapil knew that the young engineer had taken his disappointment much to heart. He had become dissipated and impudent, and the noble and open countenance which God had given him, had been disfigured with the marks of sin's defilement. Many thought, too, that he was lacking in proper spirit in breaking bread with his arch enemy, the Marquis. But others, for the most part women, in whose heart the superintendent had still a soft place, argued that they were friends now, and that altered matters.

There was this much to confirm the latter view; the Marquis would stand from his young acquaintance what he would never have allowed from any other; who else would have dared at such a time to have asked:

"Where is the Donna Ignacia?"

The Marquis gave a puff to his cigarette.

"I believe she is at Patos," he said carelessly.

So reckless had Don Jose become with troubles (for besides his tendency to drink, he had begun to gamble, and was heavily in debt both to his conscience and the world) it was quite in the cards that he should have gone on and inquired the whereabouts of the Major domo, who was also conspicuously absent.

But the Marquis gave him a quiet but terrible look, which seemed to say, "Go on if you dare."

In spite of himself, the young man's courage oozed out; and though he despised himself for the weakness, he felt quite relieved when the Marquis indulgently changed the subject.

After the supper was cleared away the cards were brought out, and the gambling began to run high. It was quite the usual thing at Patos to welcome in the morning light at play. And the present occasion promised to be no exception. But the Marquis held himself aloof from this amusement. He seemed above all petty passions; and, trusting to his guests' absorption, was in the habit of withdrawing well before the midnight hour. This evening he retired even earlier than usual. But what was that to the gamblers? They cared only for what he had to give; feared him for what he might take away; hated them for what he had already deprived them of. The Marquis, too, had the heaviest purse and the coolest nerves. It had long been a standing rule at both Mazapil and Patos that none but guests should play. On one occasion, distinct in the memory of some at least, the Marquis had "taken a hand," but no one wished the experiment to be repeated.

The din grew louder and louder and the evening longer, until finally each player lost either his hopes or his money; and, overcome with the fumes of wine, and oppressed with that sickening sense of self-contempt, which is the ash of passion, betook himself to bed.

The whole house was wrapt in quiet.

In the morning the sun rose as usual and proceeded on his westward journey. Not long after the menials of the *hicienda* also arose and began their daily avocations. Most of the guests at Mazapil were in the habit of taking their coffee in bed and then rising for the *almuerzo* or late breakfast. On this occasion they were later in getting up than usual; but then, on the other hand, they had largely discounted the evening before. One by one they began to collect on the pavement, in the shade of the building at the entrance to the *patio* whence they commanded an extended view of the treeless country and of the road to Patos, by way of the Punta Santa Helena.

They were in no too good humor. But one man had won (and even he, as is the custom in such a case, was out of pocket), Don Manuel Sanchez, the rich banker of Mexico. Stingy, close and unscrupulous, he turned everything to profit, even gambling.

"So you lost like the rest of us," said the irritable Delgado, who could not bear to lose or to keep silent.

"Jesus Maria, did I not have 200 pesos, and what have I now?" said Manuel, with injured innocence.

"Carramba," said Delgado, "your pockets are well filled; I'll dare swear."

Nothing makes gentlemen so impolite as gambling. Self-control, under loss, is not, as is generally supposed, the characteristic of a gentleman at play. This sort of stoicism is rather the characteristic of a professional sharper who makes gambling a business. Consequently, this fine morning when all nature was rejoicing, our gentlemen of Mazapil were out of humor, even rude, if Spaniards are ever so, and were secretly cursing each other in their hearts.

Perhaps, also, their irritation was increased by an untoward event. Strangely enough, the Marquis was late, and had not yet made his appearance; in consequence breakfast was waiting.

"Mine host has been under the weather of late," said Don Manuel wishing to appease the company, by introducing a congenial topic of conversation.

"Family cares," said the superintendent with almost a sneer.

"And the Donna Ignacia not present to console him—too bad," said Delgado.

"Too bad! Too bad!" echoed this arrant pack of cowards, who dared not, even in the absence of the subject of their hates, speak out too plainly the envy in their hearts.

In this instance their caution was not amiss; for, faultlessly dressed in full white shirt, his long pantaloons cut open at the side, and a broad sombréro on his head, cigarette in hand, cool and imperturbable as he had left them the evening before, the Marquis had just shown himself at the door.

"Good morning, gentlemen. I hope you passed the night agreeably," said the Marquis, courteously, holding out his cigarette in the two fingers of his left hand, and calmly blowing out into the air a perfect ring.

As he did so, however, the careful observer might have noticed that he looked toward the west, where a cloud of dust was rising on the highway.

The cloud drew nearer, until finally, a horseman could be perceived urging his steed with his huge spurs, as if some life were at stake. It was Miguel, of the first *estancia*, on the road to Patos.

"Senor! Senor!" cried that worthy man, fairly throwing himself at his master's feet:

"Lopez, the *vaquero*, has been found dead before my door, stabbed in the back!"

The Marquis of Aguayo kept on smoking.

The company, transfixed with terror, looked alternately from the messenger of death to the owner of three provinces, whose slight figure, as if of bronze, stood out so grimly against the sky.

"What did you do with the body?" said the Marquis, quietly.

"I laid it out in my room, Senor."

"You did well," said the Marquis; and then he added: "You may go."

The company shivered with unknown dread, but the Marquis still looked toward the western sky.

Soon again another cloud of dust could be seen, and in time, another messenger appeared, also in haste, and bearing a message similar to the one which had preceded him. This time it was another poor *vaquero* who had been murdered. He had been stabbed, in the same mysterious manner, at a station further on towards Patos.

A third messenger came, and then a fourth, each bearing tidings of a fresh murder still further on towards Patos.

At last came the end.

The unhappy wight who brought the news was too frightened to talk. The substance he stammered out was this:

A *vaquero*, the Marquis' major-domo, the Marquis' wife and his four children had all been murdered at Patos.

When the dreadful intelligence was announced to him, the Marquis only said.

"I am indeed unlucky to-day."

And he went on smoking, stopping even to brush off the ashes that had fallen on his spotless shirt.

     *   *   *   *   *   *

For some time after these occurrences all Mazapil was thrilled with horror. It was an open secret that the Marquis had something to do with the murders; but how were they accomplished? Whose was the hand that, in a single night had, over a distance of one hundred miles, sent no less than ten souls into eternity? Was it not attested by all those present at the dinner given by the Marquis on the fatal night, even by Don Jose Ybarra, that his Excellency had retired early, and that the next morning he appeared only a little later than usual. The knowing ones remarked even this delay was the least suspicious circumstance of all. A man who had been on a death hunt the night before, would be particularly careful not to excite any suspicion by departing from his usual habits in the morning.

But these doubts were all laid to rest by no less a personage than the Marquis himself. The horrid rumor began to spread about Mazapil, and from thence to Mexico, that the Marquis not only was the author of the crimes in question, but that he was openly boasting of it. In his cups he would, with fiendish pleasure, to *one* companion unfold the manner of the killing. This confession was made invariably to one witness, and always in the privacy of his room.

The substance of that confession was this:

When the Marquis retired on the evening in question his plans were all arranged. He had ordered four relays to to be ready on the road from Mazapil to Patos. By changing horses he counted upon making the whole distance of fifty miles in four hours. His calculations were not far astray. Arriving at Patos in the dead of night, he found his worst suspicions confirmed.

Before two in the morning his wife, his major-domo and his four children were all cold in death.

He had left his *vaquero* some distance out of the town.

"I wished to surprise the Senora," he had said grimly to the unfortunate man.

On the way back to Mazapil he rode just behind the *vaquero*, and before arriving at the next station stabbed him in the back. There was thus one witness less to his crime.

Arriving at the next *estancia*, he found another horse and *vaquero* waiting for him. Behind this *vaquero* he also rode, and just before the next *estancia* he also stabbed him.

At the third *estancia* another victim was ready, as well as at the fourth. There were no longer any witnesses to his crime. By seven in the morning the Marquis was in his bed. His ride of death was over.

His plans had been calculated with most fiendish premeditation, and had met with the most complete success. And he took particular delight in detailing them to the one witness who cared to listen.

When asked why he had murdered his children, the Marquis had only answered:

"I exterminate the whole brood. When an Aguayo doubts at all, he doubts everything."

In a month's time, no less than ten men in Mazapil had been told the story; and yet on no occasion could the Marquis be induced to tell it but to one witness at a time.

Don Jose Ybarra was not yet among the number.

Down into the lowest steps of degradation had he sunk. He had lost his position in the mines. His hand, once steady, now trembled

with the excess of dissipation; his bloodshot eyes glared out their
disappointed hate on the very children he passed along the street.
When he heard the fearful story that was freezing to the marrow of
all the people of Mazapil, his heart leapt within him at the thought
of revenge—revenge, the last passion of a wasted life: revenge, the
sweet solace of a disappointed life.

"I will bring this vulture to justice," thought he. "Yes, if there
is law in Mexico."

Then he looked back on his lost existence; he remembered the fair
face of the young girl that he had so hoped to make his bride; he
thought of all the misery the Marquis had brought on them both,
and with clenched fist he leapt into the air.

"Curse him! Curse him!"

That day Don Jose Ybarra was one of those who knew. Merrily,
cheerily, as if it were some sailor's yarn, the Marquis had reeled off
to him the confession of his crime. Ybarra fled from the mocking
laugh; fled from the polluted board which had witnessed his enemy's
triumph and his own shame.

But his despondency was but for the moment. A thought came
to him which cheered his soul.

"The snake will not confess but to one at the time. I will catch
him in his own trap; he shall see but one—there will be two."

Don Jose Ybarra rubbed his hands in glee. And then he stopped.
Who would be the other? An accomplice in such an undertaking
would not be easy to secure. In order to have the plan succeed, he
must manage to entice the Lion of Patos from his lair. Who should
be stool pigeon? The drunken priest of Mazapil came to his mind.

"The very one," said Ybarra to himself. "I will go to him at
once."

When Father Gomez was, by delicate approaches, informed of
Ybarra's intention, he did not take kindly to the plan. The luxurious priest saw no pleasant prospect before him.

"Besides, was not the Marquis a friend?" he said.

"Is he not a murderer?" said Ybarra, with quiet intensity.

"I'll not do it," the priest answered, finally.

"You will do it," hissed Ybarra, "or I will write to Mexico and inform the Archbishop how you cure souls at Mazapil."

Such is the force of persuasion, that Don Jose, partly by threats and partly by holding out the hope of future advancement, succeeded in making the priest an accomplice to his crime—if, indeed, bringing a man to justice can be truly said to be a crime.

In accordance with instructions, the priest called on the Marquis and invited him to dine at his apartments in the town.

The Marquis accepted without demur.

The priest reported the success of his interview to his principal, and the two men took their precautions. A table, with an unusually long cloth was prepared, and a little before the appointed time Don Jose Ybarra secreted himself in its folds.

The Marquis came as he promised. There was a cold glitter in his eye. "Does he suspect anything?" thought the priest. "No it is impossible. How can he since the secret was buried between us two?" So stifling his fear when the guest was in his cups, he led the conversation, with great tact, around to the desired point. The Marquis looked at him with surprise.

"Who do I think murdered my wife and children, and my major-domo, and my four *vaqueros*?"

The priest's fingers grew cold with fear.

"I will tell you who murdered them. I did!" hissed the Lord of Patos, as he leaned over the table with a drunken leer.

"Oh, my son, my son, how could you murder your poor wife?"

"Because she deceived me."

"And your children?"

"Because they were not mine."

"Are you not afraid to confess this to me?" said the priest growing bolder.

"No, why should I be?"

"Are you not afraid that I might hand you up to justice?"

The Marquis laughed.

"What, are you alone? The word of one witness is not sufficient."

With a quick movement the priest disclosed Ybarra concealed under the table.

"Now, Sir Marquis, there are two witnesses."

A flash and a report; 'twas soon over.   Don Jose Ybarra lay dead at the priest's feet with a hole in his head.

"And now," said the Marquis of Aguayo, "there is only one."

Henry B McDuwell

A Sensation in the Orange Groves.

There had long been a sensation in the orange groves of Los Angeles county, on account of the presence there of the notorious Tiburcio Vasquez. On the 16th day of May, 1874, at 4:30 p. m. as the Clerk of the City Council of Los Angeles was about to read the last communication to that body, an unusual stir outside attracted quick attention, and in a moment more City Fathers, City Clerk, City Surveyor, City Reporters, and everybody else in the room, were making for the front door. Instinctively I supposed Vasquez had something to do with the hegira, and I was right. Vasquez was lying pale and bloody in a light wagon, in front of the entrance to the city jail. A surging crowd was gathering around. Two men who were taken in his company, at the time of the capture, were hurried into jail and locked up. In a moment after, Vasquez, himself, was lifted from the wagon and was borne into the city prison. Dr. Wise soon after presented himself; and, assisted by several other medical gentlemen of the city, rendered the wounded robber such surgical services as he required. The result of the examination showed a buckshot in his left arm, one in the left leg, one in the left side of his head, one in front of the pectoral region, passing out under the left arm, and one in the right arm. The balls were extracted, the wounds pronounced not dangerous, and opinion expressed that he would be well in a few days.

During the time referred to, Mr. Charles Miles, who had been robbed by Vasquez near San Gabriel, a few weeks before, entered the room. He was at once recognized by the wounded man—in fact, the recognition was mutual. Mr. Hartley, the Chief of Police of the City of Los Angeles, had taken Mr. Miles' watch into his keeping. It was returned to the proper owner. Mr. M.'s chain was missing, however; Vasquez said nothing about it at the time; but, after Dr. Wise and his associates had dressed his wounds, he requested Dr. Wise to take his portemonnaie from his pocket. It was done, and

Vasquez opened it, and handed the missing chain to Dr. W., and requested him to return it to its rightful owner. He remarked, "It belongs to him, *now*," emphasizing the last word, as much as to say, "he might have whistled for it if they had not caught me." While his wounds were being dressed, Mr. B. F. Hartley, Chief of Police, one of his captors, asked him why he (Vasquez) had asked him (Hartley) what his name was. Quoth Vasquez, "Usted es un hombre valiente lo mismo que yo." (You are a brave man like myself.) He bore the probing and opening of his wounds without a murmur. In personal appearance, this robber chief was anything but remarkable. Take away the expression of his eyes, furtive, snaky, and cunning, and he would have passed unnoticed in a crowd. Not more than five feet seven inches in height, and of very spare build, he looked little like a man who could create a reign of terror. His forehead was low and slightly retreating to where it was joined by a thick mass of raven black and very coarse hair; his mustache was by no means luxuriant, his chin whiskers passably full; and his sunken cheeks were only lightly sprinkled with beard; his lips thin and bloodless; his teeth white, even and firm; his left eye slightly sunken. He had small and elegantly shaped feet. Perhaps 130 pounds was as much as he weighed. His light build made it an easy task for the horse that bore him to perform forced marches. The reign of terror which he had been answerable for was at an end. No attempt was made to interfere with the law by the crowd which surrounded the jail. A feeling more of relief than of revenge or exultation seemed to be uppermost in the minds of all. The history of the capture of Vasquez forms one of the most interesting chapters that has ever been written. The captured robber had defied pursuit, mocked at strategy, and eluded for months the skill of the bravest and most celebrated detectives on the coast. Once afoot or on horseback, with three hours the start of his pursuers, Cuban bloodhounds would not have compassed his capture. A sudden, well-arranged surprise was the only chance to secure him. It had been effected, and in the manner hereinafter related.

After the futile pursuit of the robber up the Tejunga Pass, a short time before, Mr. Wm. Rowland, Sheriff of Los Angeles county, came to the conclusion that any further prosecution of the quest in that manner and direction was a waste of time, energy and money. His subordinates were ordered to desist, and many and loud were the complaints lodged against him for inaction and inefficiency.

Mr. Rowland, however, kept on in the even tenor of his way; and, availing himself of every possible source of information, at length became satisfied that the long-sought-for prize was within his grasp, and he quietly arranged for a capture. On Wednesday night, May 15th, the evening before the capture, he received positive information of the whereabouts of Tiburcio Vasquez.

The pursuers left Los Angeles at 1:30, Thursday morning. About 4 A. M., they arrived at the bee ranch of Major Mitchell, one of the party.' There they took breakfast, and held a council of war. The ranch is up a small canon, off the usual lines of travel, visited occasionally by neighboring ranchmen for wood. After consultation, Messrs. Albert Johnston, Mitchell, and Bryant left the party and followed a mountain road about one mile and a half, until they came to a point opposite Greek George's ranch. Turning square north they climed to a point where, with a field glass, they could obtain an unobstructed view of the covert. A heavy fog rendered satisfactory observations impracticable for hours. When it lifted they saw enough to convince them that their game was at the very point designated. A horse answering the description of that ridden by the outlaw was picketed out as above stated. Twice they saw a man, answering the description of Vasquez, leading him to the monte, and returning, picket him out as before. Another man on horseback went in pursuit of a white horse which tallied with the description given of a horse belonging to his gang. Various plans for the capture of Vasquez were discussed by the trio, but finally it was decided that Mr. Johnson should return to the bee ranch and marshal his forces, while Mitchell and Smith went in pursuit of the horseman referred to, they believing him to be Chaves, the Lieutenant of Vasquez.

Arrived there, unexpectedly, and it almost seems providentially sent, allies presented themselves. A wagon driven by a Californian, and in which there was another man (also a native), was driven up, from the direction of Greek George's. It was a box wagon. It was not long before the plan of capture was decided upon. Six of the party remained. The extra man with the wagon made seven. Mr.

Hartley, who spoke Spanish fluently, was instructed to inform the driver that he was to turn his horses' heads, allow all six of the party and his extra man to *lie down in the wagon bed*, and then drive back to Greek George's, and as close to the house as possible; that if he gave a sign or made an alarm, his life would pay the forfeit. In due time the house was reached. In a moment the men were out of the wagon and on their feet with shot-guns and rifles cocked and ready for what might offer. Mr. Hartley and Mr. Beers went to the west side of the house, the other four to the southern, passing round the eastern end. The foremost of the latter had hardly reached the door opening into the dining-room, when a woman opened it partly. Seeing the armed "quartette" approaching, she gave an exclamation of fright, and attempted to close it. The party burst in, Mr. Harris leading the way, and seeing the retreating form of the prize they sought leaving the table and plunging through the door leading into the kitchen.

Harris was close upon his heels, and Vasquez, with the agility of a mountain cat, had jumped through the narrow window, or rather opening which admitted the light, when Harris fired at the vanishing form with his Henry rifle, exclaming, "There he goes through the window!" The party left the house as precipitately as they entered it. Vasquez stood for a second of time irresolute. Whether to seek cover in the monte or rush for his horse, seemed the all important question. He seemed to decide for the horse—doubtless he would have given ten kingdoms if he had had them, to be astride of him—and started, when Mr. Harris fired; turning, he sought another direction, when one after another, shot after shot, showed him the utter hopelessness of escape. He had already been wounded, just how severely I have already told. He had fallen, but recovered himself; blood was spouting from his shoulder and streaming from other wounds. He threw up his hands, approached the party, and said, with a cold, passionate smile wreathing his thin lips, "Boys, you have done well; I have been a fool; but it is all my own fault." He was taken to the court-yard on the southern side of the house, and laid upon an extemporized pallet. Not a murmur, scarce a contortion of the visage, bespoke either pain, remorse, or any other emotion of the mind or soul. Mr. Beers said to me on the evening of the capture: "While looking for his wounds, I placed my hand over his heart, and found its pulsations gave no signs of excitement. His eye was bright, and there was a pleasant smile on his face, and no tremor in his voice. He was polite and thankful for every attention. Although he thought and said that he was about to die—'Gone up,' as he expressed it—his expression of countenance was one of admiration of our determined attack and our good luck."

The house was entered, and a young man was captured in the north room before described. This was the arsenal of the robber gang. Three Henry rifles and one Spencer, all of the latest patterns and finest workmanship, besides other arms were found there and taken possession of. Major Mitchell and Mr. Smith overhauled the party they went in pursuit of, and brought him back. I have stated that it was well that Mr. Rowland did not start out with the party. Greek George, whose real name is George Allen, was designated as the party who was harboring Vasquez. Vasquez was found there, that is certain. Allen was in town Wednesday night, and while he supposed he was watching Rowland's movements, he was being watched with a degree of wide-awakefulness he could hardly conceive of. He was solicitously attended in his peregrinations throughout the city all that day. Had he attempted to revisit his surburban home before the consummation of Sheriff Rowland's plans, he would have learned the meaning of a writ of *ne exeat* which would unquestionably have been extemporized for the occasion.

As it was, when his distinguished sometime guest had been, by the physicians in attendance, prepared to receive visitors, Mr. Allen was taken into his presence by Sheriff Rowland. He was so much affected by the sight that he forgot to express his sympathy. Had Mr. Rowland not been seen by Mr. Allen Wednesday, the latter would probably have remembered something whi h required his presence at the ranch. Too much praise can never be awarded to Sheriff Rowland for the quiet but effective manner in which he carried out his well-conceived plans. It would simply be invidious to attempt to particularize any member of the capturing party. All that I was able to learn upon the subject, from any and every source, went to show that each and every man acted with consummate courage, coolness and discretion. To all intents and purposes, the approach to the house where the capture was effected was a deliberate approach to a masked battery. That Vasquez was there, was a matter which admitted of no doubt. How many of his fellow desperadoes were with him, no man of the party could know. How well he was prepared to "welcome them with bloody hands to hospitable graves," nobody could doubt; but, determined to capture him, if possible, they "went for him," and they got him.

His coolness in the hour of capture, the fortitude and the uncomplaining stoicism with which he bore his wounds, all went to show that, whatever opinion as to his bravery may have become current with the public, he was a man who would have sold his life dearly if he had had a ghost of a show. I verily believe if he had had a knife or a pistol on his person he would have sought and found death rather than capture. No *posse* of armed men could have approached the well chosen fastness which he had selected. Strategy and a fortunate concurrence of circumstances placed him in the power of the law

While being carried into town he exchanged notes with Major Mitchell relative to the Tejunga Pass pursuit. He told the Major that twice during the pursuit he was near enough to kill him and his party, if he had desired so to do and convinced Major Mitchell of the truth of his assertion. Vasquez protested that he had never killed a man; that the murders at Tres Pinos were committed before his arrival; but he admitted that he led the party who committed the outrages away from that point. After his capture, he inquired who was the leader of the party, and, upon being told that Mr. Albert Johnston was, he delivered to him his memorandum book, and commenced to make a statement to him, not knowing at the time but that his wounds were mortal.

His first declaration related to his two children; when, the preparations for the march into the city being completed, the record was abruptly brought to a close. He showed Mr. Johnston the photographs of the children, and enclosed in the same envelope with them was a wavy tress of black and silky hair, bound in a blue ribbon. This he requested Mr. Johnston to preserve carefully, and return to him when he should require or demand it. What secret heart history was bound up with that mute memorial of days when perhaps the outlaw had his dream of home, and all that makes life beautiful, no one can tell.

At a late hour I visited him in prison. Lying upon his pallet, to all human appearances a doomed man, a price set upon his head, an outlaw and an outcast, he received me and a number of other visitors with an ease and grace and elegance which would have done no discredit to any gentleman in the land, reclining upon his *fauteil* in his dressing-room. After answering quietly and politely a number of questions, he requested those present to retire, as he had something to communicate to the sheriff, relative to certain stolen property. His memorandum book, among many other things, contained a great many extracts, clipped from the *Star*, *La Cronica*, and other papers, containing accounts of his various exploits. They went to show conclusively that he had been furnished regularly by confederates with everything that could interest him or keep him informed of the measures set on foot to effect his capture.

On a small scrap of paper, dated April 3d, was a memorandum in the Spanish language, in which the name of Repetto occurred. Whether it was a reminder of his intended visit to that gentleman, or a credit for the amount of the enforced loan he exacted from him, I do not know. As soon as Vasquez was safely lodged in jail, all parties agreed that Sheriff Rowland and the actual captors of the bandit, the cool-headed and intrepid Albert Johnston, Under-Sheriff; and his brave, energetic, and fearless associates, officers Hartley, Harris, and Bryant, Major Mitchell, and Messrs. Rogers, Smith, and Beers, were entitled to great credit. They had been unceasing in their efforts to effect the capture of Vasquez from the time of the Repetto outrage, and the result is told as above.

William Rowland, Sheriff of Los Angeles county, is a native of the county; was about thirty-three years of age, and was serving his second term. Albert Johnston, Under Sheriff, is a New Yorker by birth, a brother of Geo. A Johnston, of San Diego, and had been a resident of Los Angeles for about five years, having held the office of Under Sheriff since Mr. Rowland's election. He came to this State when a mere youth, and went back to the East and remained several years, but, like all good Californians, returned. He was of about the same age as his principal. Officer Harris was thirty-two years old; was well-known in the city, where he had lived for six years, and had been on the police force four years. He had detective qualities second to no man in the State; was brave, cool and energetic, and just the man to have associated in such a hazardous undertaking. Officer Hartley was a brave fellow, about thirty-seven years old, and a model member of the police force, upon which he had served efficiently and faithfully for two years. He had resided in Los Angeles for five years. Constable Bryant was also one of the best officers Los Angeles ever had. He, too, was a brave and efficient officer, about thirty-five years of age. Major Mitchell, soldier, lawyer, miner, apiarist and journalist, was a young man of talent and education. With what valor and intrepidity he followed the flag of the Southern Confederacy may be seen in his persistent and unrivalled pursuit of the robber chief, from the Repetto event until the achievement related. Mr. W. E. Rogers was a young man of thirty-two years of age, twenty-four of which he had spent in San Francisco. He had been associated with the Sheriff's party from the start, and was as brave as he was genteel and unostentatious. Mr. Smith was, I believe, a farmer, and resided outside of the city. When Mr, Smith went to Greek George's house a few days before, to *inquire if he wanted any barley cut,* the latter not in the least suspected that the would-be hay-maker was taking a survey of the premises for Mr. Rowland, so that, when the time arrived for the attack, it could be made without confusion and without loss of life, if possible, to the besieging party. Mr. Beers, the correspondent of the *Chronicle,* was as gallant as his fellows, and marched up to the scene of attack with rifle in hand, prepared for any emergency.

The next day I interviewed Vasquez. He seemed but little the worse for his wounds. Sheriff Rowland had provided him with a comfortable spring mattress, and the dinner which was brought to him during my stay in his cell, or rather room, was good enough for anybody. He laughed and talked as gaily and unconstrainedly as if he were in his parlor instead of in the clutches of the violated law. In reply to my questions, he gave the following account of himself, substantially:

"I was born in Monterey county, California, at the town of Monterey, August 11th, 1835. My parents are both dead. I have three brothers and two sisters. Two of my brothers reside in Monterey county: one unmarried and one married; the other resides in Los Angeles county; he is married. My sisters are both married; one of them lives at San Juan Baptista, Monterey county, the other at the New Idria quicksilver mines. I was never married, but I have one child in this county a year old. I can read and write, having attended school in Monterey. My parents were people in ordinarily good circumstances, owning a small tract of land, and always had enough for their wants. My career grew out of the circumstances by which I was surrounded. As I grew up to manhood, I was in the habit of attending balls and parties given by the native Californians, into which the Americans, then beginning to become numerous, would force themselves and shove the native-born men aside, monopolizing the dance and the women. This was about 1852. A spirit of hatred and revenge took possession of me. I had numerous fights in defense of what I believed to be my rights and those of my countrymen. The officers were continually in pursuit of me. I believed we were unjustly and wrongfully deprived of the social rights that belonged to us. So perpetually was I involved in these difficulties, that I at length determined to leave the thickly settled portions of the country, and did so. I gathered together a small band of cattle, and went into Mendocino county, back of Ukiah, and beyond Falls Valley. Even here I was not permitted to remain in peace. The officers of the law sought me out in that remote region, and strove to drag me before the courts. I always resisted arrest. I went to my mother and told her I intended to commence a different life. I asked for and obtained her blessing, and at once commenced the career of a robber. My first exploit consisted in robbing some peddlers of money and clothes in Monterey county. My next was the capture and robbery of a stage coach in the same county. I had confederates with me from the first, and was always recognized as leader. Robbery after robbery followed each other as rapidly as circumstances allowed until, in 1857 or '58, I was arrested in Los Angeles for horse stealing, convicted of grand larceny, sentenced to the penitentiary, and was taken to San Quentin, and remained there until my term of imprisonment expired in 1863. Up to the time of my conviction and imprisonment, I had robbed stage coaches, wagons, houses, etc., indiscriminately, carrying on my operations for the most part in daylight, sometimes, however, visiting houses after dark.

"After my discharge from San Quentin, I returned to the house of my parents, and endeavored to lead a peaceable and honest life. I was, however, soon accused of being a confederate of Procopio and one Soto, both noted bandits, the latter of whom was afterwards killed by Sheriff Harry Morse, of Alameda county. I was again forced to become a fugitive from the law officers; and, driven to desperation, left home and family, and commenced robbing whenever opportunity offered. I made but little money by my exploits. I always managed to avoid arrest. I believe I owe my frequent escapes solely to my courage (*mi valor*). I was always ready to fight whenever opportunity offered, but always endeavored to avoid bloodshed.

"I know of nothing worthy of note until the Tres Pinos affair occurred. The true story of that transaction is as follows: I, together with four other men, including Chaves, my lieutenant, and one Leiva, (who is now in jail at San Jose, awaiting an opportunity to testify, he having turned State's evidence), camped within a short distance of Tres Pinos. I sent three of the party, Leiva included, to that point, making Leiva captain. I instructed them to take a drink, examine the locality, acquaint themselves with the number of men around, and wait until I came. I told them not to use any violence, as when I arrived I would be the judge, and if anybody had to be shot I would do the shooting. When I arrived there with Chaves, however, I found three men dead, and was told that two of them were killed by Leiva and one by another of the party named Romano; the rest of the men in the place were all tied. I told Leiva and his companions that they had acted contrary to my orders, that I did not wish to remain there long. Leiva and his men had not secured money enough for my purpose and I told a woman, the wife of one of the men who was tied, that I would kill him if she did not procure funds. She did so and we gathered up what goods and clothing and provisions we needed, and started for Elizabeth Lake, Los Angeles county. On the way there Leiva became jealous of me, and at once rebelled and swore revenge. He left his wife at Heffner's place on Elizabeth Lake and started to Los Angeles to give himself up, as well as to deliver me to the authorities, if he could do so. Sheriff Rowland, however,

was on my track, and in company with Sheriff Adams, of Santa
Clara county, and a *posse* of men, endeavored to capture Chaves and
myself at Rock Creek. We fired at the party and could have killed
them if we had wished so to do. We effected our escape, and arriving at Heffner's, I took Leiva's wife behind me on my horse, and
started back in the direction I knew Rowlands and Adams and their
party would be coming, knowing that I could hear them approaching
on their horses. I did so, and as they drew near I turned aside
from the road. The Sheriffs and *posse* passed on, and I took Leiva's
wife to a certain point, which I do not care to name, and left her in
the hills at a sheep ranch, while I went out and made a raid on Firebaugh's Ferry, on the San Joaquin river, for money to send her
back to her parents' house. I did so, and have not seen her since. I
provided for all her wants while she was with me. I tied ten men
and a Chinaman up at Firebaugh's Ferry in the raid above referred
to."

[Here I digress a moment, to tell what befell Sheriffs Rowland and
Adams and *posse*. They went straight to Heffner's, found their
game had broken cover. They found Vasquez' camp, captured thirty-
six horses and the greater part of the goods, clothing and provisions,
taken from the Tres Pinos, and then divided, Sheriff Rowland returning to Los Angeles with the horses, all of which had been returned
to their owners except two. While at the camp Leiva came up and
was arrested by Sheriff Rowland, on suspicion; was by him turned
over to Mr. Wasson, the Sheriff of Monterey county. Sheriff Adams
and his party kept up an unsuccessful search for the bandit for several days, and finally abandoned it. I now resume Vasquez' narrative where it was left off.]

"After sending Leiva's wife home, I went to King's River, in
Tulare county, where, with a party of eight men besides myself, I
captured and tied up thirty-five men. There were two stores and a
hotel in this place. I had time to plunder only one of the stores, as
the citizens aroused themselves and began to show fight. The num-
bers were unequal and I retired. I got about eight hundred dollars
and considerable jewelry by this raid. I went from there to a small
settlement, known as Panama, on Kern river, where myself and
party had a carouse of three days, dancing, love-making, etc. El

Capitan Vasquez was quite a favorite with the senoritas. It was well known to the people of Bakersfield, which is only two or three miles from Panama, that I was there, and arrangements were made for my capture; but the attempt was not made until I had been gone twenty-four hours. Then they came and searched the house in which I was supposed to be concealed. When I left Panama, I started for the Sweet-water mountains, and skirted their base, never traveling along the road, but keeping along in the direction of Lone Pine. I returned by the way of Coyote Holes, where the robbery of the stage took place. Here Chaves and myself captured the *diligencia* and sixteen men. Chaves held his gun over them while I took their money and jewelry. We got about $200 and some pistols, and jewelry, watches, etc.; also a pocket-book, belonging to Mr. James Craig, containing about $10,000 worth of mining stock, which I threw away. One man was disposed to show fight, and to preserve order I shot him in the leg, and made him sit down. I got six horses from the stage company, two from the station. I drove four of them off in one direction and went myself in another, in order to elude pursuit. I wandered around in the mountains after that until the time of the Repetto robbery.

"The day before that occurrence, I camped at the Pietra Gordo, at the head or Arroyo Seco. I had selected Repetto as a good subject. In pursuance of the plan I had adopted, I went to a sheep herder employed on the place, and asked him if he had seen a brown horse which I had lost; inquired if Repetto was at home, took a took at the surroundings, and told the man I had to go to the Old Mission on some important business, that if he would catch my horse I would give him $10 or $15. I then returned by a roundabout way to my companions on the Arroyo Seco. As soon as it was dark I returned with my men to the neighborhood of Repetto's and camped within a few rods of the house. The next morning about breakfast time we wrapped our guns in our blankets, retaining only our pistols, and I went toward the house, where I met the sheep herder and commenced talking about business. Asked him if Repetto wanted herders or shearers, how many sheep could he shear in a day, etc.; speaking in a loud tone, in order to throw him off his guard. I had left my men behind a small fence, and being told that he was at home, I entered the house to see if I could bring the *patron* to terms without killing him. I found him at home, and told him I was an expert sheep shearer, and asked him if he wished to employ any shearers; tolp him that my friends, the gentlemen who were waiting out by the fence, were also good sheerers, and wanted work. All were invited in, and as they entered surrounded Repetto. I then told him I wanted money. At this he commenced hollering, when I had him securely tied, and told him to give me what money he had in the house. He handed me eighty dollars. I told him that that would do; that I knew all about his affairs; that he had sold nearly $10,000 worth of sheep lately, and that he must have plenty of money buried about the place somewhere. Repetto then protested that he had paid out nearly all the money he had received in the purchase of land that he had receipts to show for it, etc. I told him that I could read and write and understood accounts; that if his books and receipts, and they balanced according to his statements, I would excuse him. He produced the books, and after examining them carefully, I became convinced that he had told me very nearly the truth. I then expressed my regrets for the trouble I had put him to, and offered to compromise. I told him that I was in need of money, and that if he would, accomodote me with a small sum I would repay him in thirty days with interest at $1\frac{1}{2}$ per cent. per month. He kindly consented to do so, and sent a messenger to a bank in Los Angeles for the money, being first warned that in the event of treachery or bretayal his life would pay the forfeit. The messenger returned, not without exciting the suspicions of the authorities, who, as is well kuown, endeavored at that time to effect my capture, but failed. But you know all about the Arroyo Seco affair."

I do, and present it as follows: Mr. Repetto, fearing that his life would be taken, despatched a boy to Los Angeles with a check for the above amount. The boy went to town as quick as ever man flew over the old Mission road, and proceeded at once to the Sheriff's office and gave a detailed description of the robbers and the affair. Mr. Rowland and Under Sheriff Albert Johnson at once made arrangements for a pursuit, entertaining no doubt but that it was Vasquez and his gang of freebooters. In less than a quarter of an hour a number of fleet horses had been procured and saddled, and a party, composed of officers Sands, Harris, Hartley, Redona, and Benites and Mr. Rodgers and Chantes, led by Mr. Rowland, proceeded out toward the neighborhood of the outrage. In less than half an hour the pursuing party arrived within sight of Mr. Reppetto's house, and quick as a flash five men mounted their horses, and galloped in the direction of the upper Arroyo Seco, the Rowland party giving hot pursuit.

While all this exciting work was going on, Charles Miles and John Osborne, who had been hauling some piping material out to the lands of the Orange Grove Association, were quietly jogging on toward home. Now, if you had told these two gentlemen that Vasquez was within gunshot of them they would have laughed in your face. But all of a sudden, up dashed two men, eached armed with a Henry rifle and a six shooter, and, in English, demanded a halt. Osborne thought it was a joke, and carelessly dropped the rein on his sorrel, so as to increase its pace. In doing so he drove right into three more of the bandits, who gave him to understand that he proceeded further at great peril. Vasquez, quick as thought, made his appearance on the near side, and covered Osborne with a Henry rifle, which little maneuver caused the smiling face of Miles to elongate a trifle. Then he smiled again; and then, as a Henry rifle, seemingly as big as a Dahlgren gun, fooled around his left ear, he drew on that Platonic countenance again, and began to view the scene from a "business" standpoint. Two of the highwaymen dismounted, while Vasquez and the two men who did not dismount covered the victims in the wagon with their rifles and six-shooters· "Hand out your money!" said Vasquez, "and hurry up, for there are a dozen men coming this way." Mr. Miles declared that he hadn't got a cent with him, which elicited from the accommodating knight of the road, "Then I'll take that watch!"

At this juncture the urbane City Water Collector looked first at his own English hunting lever, and then at Osborne's, because, you see, he didn't know exactly which chronometer suited the fancy of the California Duval. But the latter, in order to create no hard feelings or misunderstandings in the matter, took both of them. About three dollars and a half in United States silver coin, also, was donated, and then the outfit was permitted to depart, the robbers, in the meantime, perceiving the Harris and Sands party at the top of the hill about a thousand yards off, dashing off in a different direction.

Los Angeles was wild during that afternoon, and all sorts of rumors gained credence, among which was shat "Jeemes Pipes, of Pipesville," had been killed.

About three o'clock Rowland, after locating his forces as best he could, returned to town for reinforcements. believing that, with a proper number of men at his command, he would succeed in effecting a capture. In a few moments General Baldwin and two other men, and Constable Bryant and three others, were equipped, and in the line of pnrsuit.

To continue Vasquez's account: "After my escape, I wandered for a while in the mountains; was near enough to the parties who were searching for me to kill them if I had desired so to do. For the past three weeks I have had my camp near the place where I was captured, only coming to the house at intervals to get a meal. I was not expecting company at the time the arrest was made, or the result might have been different."

The foregoing is a very fair paraphrase of the recital made to me by Vasquez, in the presence of Sheriff Rowland. Almost all of it, except his version of the Tres Pinos affair, is known to be true. Only the leading events of his long career of brigandage and outlawry are described. But my readers can draw their own conclusion as to what manner of man Tiburcio Vasquez was. He protested frequently throughout the interview, that he had never killed a man in his life.

To complete this sketch, I would state that during the September following his capture, Vasquez was arraigned in the Twelfth District Court, San Jose, for the murder of Leander Davidson at Tres Pinos. A continuance was granted until Jan. 5, 1875. On that day the case was called, Judge Belden presiding. Charles Ben Darwin and Mr. Tully were retained for the defense. Darwin withdrew, and in his place Judge Belden appointed Judge W. H. Collins and Judge J. A. Moultrie. Attorney-General Love, District Attorney Briggs, of San Benito county, Hon. W. E. Lovett and District Attorney Bodely, of Santa Clara county. appeared for the people. After a four days' trial Vasquez was found guilty of murder in the first degree.

On the 23d day of January, 1875, he was sentenced to death, and by the execution of that sentence, California got rid of one of the bloodiest scoundrels of the century.

Ben C. Truman

NATHAN, THE JEW.

A girl in years, but a woman in shame, wearied by the night's dissipation, let herself fall upon the cold steps of St. Mary's Cathedral. Her tired eyelids touched each other in repose. The red lips drooped apart. The mist moistened the burning throat. Her hand involuntarily stretched toward heaven. Then she lay motionless—asleep. A nimbus of shame and a halo of glory surrounded her. The ragged dress buttoned before, fell apart, and disclosed the white bosom; but none saw, save the morning star, and no one was sacrilegious enough to caress, except the falling dew.

Robert Oswald, who was passing, stopped, attracted by the arm extended in mute appeal. He saw her bosom rise and fall. As she moved something startled him, he gave a cry of pain, for upon the white breast he saw the Hebraic word,

זונה *

The cry awoke the sleeping girl. She saw the open dress, and with more fear than shame exclaimed:

"Did you see?" and she pulled the dress with a convulsive shrug together.

"No," replied the man, "I saw nothing."

"If you did, Fag will kill you."

"Do not get excited child, no harm shall come to you through me," he replied kindly. The wild light left her eyes and the melting lustre returned and she touched his arm and said: "Go away, you should not come to a girl's sleeping place," and she laughed.

"Come with me to No. 5 Bartlett Place," he replied.

She shook her head so fiercely that her unkempt hair fell about her face, and said angrily: "I am not * * * * Oh, you did see, didn't you, now?"

"My intentions are to give you in my home an honorable place to

*Unchaste.

sleep, a breakfast and whatever your position deserves, and then to
let you go your way. I am a gentleman," he added.

She laughed. "You may be, but gentlemen sleep at this time
o'night."

"Will you go with me?" he asked somewhat impatiently.

"I think you good," she said as she turned her sorrowful face towards him. She then approached him and together they turned the
corner of St. Mary's and started out Dupont street, through the heart
of the city towards Robert Oswald's home.

She found rest and sleep. In the morning her eyes had grown
larger and her cheeks a little paler. Her limbs were thin but stil
graceful. Her eyes had a beautiful pathetic light in them. Her
hands were coarse, but her lips were red, and, drooping with sadness,
were in sympathy with the beauty of her eyes. This was Ivern at
the age of eighteen. Robert Oswald waited for her in the morning.
He greeted her cordially. She returned it with shyness. "I must go
now," she said.

"Where must you go?"

"To my home," she answered.

"Where do you live?" he asked.

"Most of my time on the street. Rest of the time, anywhere," she
replied.

"Have you no parents or friends to care for you?"

"Can't you see," she replied, "I'm a Jewess but I'm cursed. I
don't know why. I always live among bad people, and that's all I
know, exceptin' some how or other I think, and other people like me
don't. I can't say any more, but I've trouble, for see, my hair is
brown and gray. The gray comes from thinkin'. Sometimes I work
and makes money, but I always lose my place because I'm cursed.
You've been very kind to me." As she spoke her wistful face
became radiant. Although she called herself a Jewess, her face
was of the highest German type, small, delicate features, rich lips,
clear complexion and deep violet eyes. Indeed, she was not at all
of the Jewish type, except in her slender, upright, graceful figure.
The expression of her face was bright and intelligent. There is a
Sixteenth Century picture over the door-way in the museum at Bos-
ton of a maiden princess, painted by a German. The original was

a German girl with the sparkle and fire of the Italian. The picture might have been a portrait of Ivern, the resemblance was so strong.

She waited but a moment, then was gone. Robert Oswald called after her but she only turned and gave him a bewitching look.

"I am happy but the scars are still there," exclaimed Ivern when she was out of sight. "Oh, those terrible words—I wish I could cut them out—I will some day!"

Before she had gone far a little squint-eyed fellow, bow-legged and crooked of feature, addressed her.

"Hello! Ivern, don't you know me? I'm same old Fag, even if I be in business,"

"Of course I know you. Still at your old tricks?" she replied.

"No, I've joined the Silver Star Sunday-School, and if I don't get pulled again, I'll be boss of the concern."

"You're too ambitious Fag."

"No, I am not, for the teacher said that often times bootblacks, newsboys and theives become great men like himself."

"I hope you will do well Fag. Did you see Paul since yesterday?"

"No, exceptin' through the winder at the bank. He wasn't a-lookin' fer you at all."

"I must see him, Fag; will you tell him to meet me at the old place near Zeiles?"

"Of course, I will; Fag will do anything for his friends. You see they ain't many, but what there is, I stands by 'em."

Fag was a boy of the world. He was a wicked, and an amusing little fellow, full of dislikes, impulses and kindly feelings. He represented a phase of life to be studied for the good there is in it. Of a fine evening, the narrow streets in the heart of the poor portion of the city swarm with children. Their earlier experiences are of a most degrading character. The mature years fulfill the evil promises of childhood, and the little sins become the crimes of old age. Fag was a resident of Pacific street, and a notable figure, on account of his crooked back with his papers and blacking outfit.

All day long he watched for Paul, so that he might do Ivern a favor. The night approached, twilight glittered around him, the lamps were lit, the people were hurrying home. He was without money, and he dared not hold out his hand in pity. Fag was hungry; he put his hand under his vest and tried to press together the great empty space that called for food.   Did you ever realize what it is to be hungry ?   Not the hunger where a meal is within easy reach, but to want something to eat and be without money, and without friends.   The cry within becomes the howl of the tiger.   You turn and curse the world and cry, "Alone !"   Fag was hungry; he looked around the street corners trying to make an honest bit.   Despair seized him.

"I'll sell my outfit," he thought.   Then he hurried around to 631 Clay street, and entered the store of Nathan, the Jew.

"Ha ! you leetle thief, vat you wants to steal ?" was the greeting.

"Won't you buy my blacken brush ?" timidly asked Fag.

"No, get out; I hab no use.   You stole 'em somewhere."

"I didn't; I bought 'em, with my word of honor."

"Vell, I guess I gifs you dat much," replied Nathan.

"No, I want to get my supper.   I haven't eaten anything all day."

"Vell, I tells you vat I do.   If you go to No. 5 Bartlett Place, an' call out the man who lifs there, an' tell him that you see a Jewess and her child in a saloon singing songs, and calling for Robert Oswald, then I gifs you von dollar for dose tings.   But you mustn't tell vot I told you, or I'll treat yur like this:" "Oh ! Oh !" screamed Fag, as he was whirled around by the ear.

"Yes, I'll do it.   Let go," he entreated.

"Tell him no more than vot I tells you; then run away quick, and I gifs you von dollar when you comes back."

Fag wasted no time in getting away.   He hated the Jew, but started to do his service.

Nathan returned to his work.   He opened his book.   There across the ledger was written the name of Robert Oswald, and after it a red cross, the silent token of the descendants of the tribe of Benjamin of vengeance.   His bent form, still bent lower, and his small, bright eyes sparkled and flashed.   His face which had the appearance of shrewdness in repose, wore the expression of a laughing fiend, as he thought how well he kept his oath of vengeance, and that Fag would add new life to the pain that was killing Robert Oswald.

Nathan is an historical character, a black Jew, born in Barnow, educated in the Bowery, New York, and engaged in a semi-legitimate business at 631 Clay street, San Francisco.

He had gathered about him in his career, trinkets and valuables of every kind. His store was filled with the cast-off truck of the impecunious, and the pledged jewels and goods of those who suffer by the wheels of fortune turning backward. There were diamonds, rings, watches, breastpins, ear-rings, trunks, jackets, coats, skirts, silken hose, fine gloves, gold-headed canes, penknives, silverware, razors, cradles, rare and valuable books, sea shells, bundles of old love letters, which he had accepted on deposit, old clothes, household furniture, from an armless stool to a satin-covered ottoman, worthless fiddles, music boxes, gold pens, old pipes, mosses, innumerable pistols and shooting irons, bowie-knives, brass kettles, silver drinking goblets. What a wonderful story the stock of pawned wares tell ! Who can count the heartaches of each treasured trinket, as the owner reluctantly parted with it for bread? Who can measure the grief of the lonely maiden as she wends her way to old Nathan, the Jew, to pawn her lover's gift? Boundless is the silent grief of the forsaken one. We cannot turn a deaf ear to a tale of woe, but the deepest sorrow is silent and dumb.

CHAPTER II

I can hardly proceed with the details of the story. It seems so incredible. Only the few people who are familiar with the fanaticism and vindictiveness that prevails among the very ignorant Jews would comprehend how such things could really be. All others will doubt. I can only say, the story is true. I did not invent any portion of it. Besides, the story is a sad one, and the hiss of the serpent is heard among the flowers.

Fag found his way to No. 5, Bartlett Place, and bravely rang the bell. The door was opened by Robert Oswald himself.

"I seed a Jewess and her child a-singin' songs in a saloon, and a-callin' for Robert Oswald," said Fag, quickly.

"Take me there at once. It is she; it is ! it is !" exclaimed Oswald.

"Gimme a dollar, and I'll tell you more," replied the ready-witted Fag.

"Here, tell me all, quick ! replied the now excited man.

"Nathan told me to tell you, and I bet it's all a lie," said Fag.

"Curse the Jew ! Will he never let me be in peace ? I will meet him again."

In a minute he was on the street, followed at a respectful distance by Fag. As he entered Nathan's place, the Jew came forward, stroking his long, pointed burnsides, and licking his moustache.

"Meester Oswald, you do me too much honor by your presence. You want to know about your wife, eh, and von leetle girl. Dey be bad, very bad."

Oswald laid a hand on the Jew's shoulder.   "Silence, wretch ! Silence ! I will not listen."

"Meester Oswald not like Meester Nathan's curse.   It bees too much like God's curse on the Jews, eh ?"

A number of people collected about the two men.

"I care not for your curse.   It is my wife and daughter—your daughter and my child—I want."

"My daughter, your wife, and her child, be nothings to me. They are marked with a——"

"Stop, fiend, or I'll choke you."

Then dropping his arm he turned and fled. He rushed home like a hunted creature. He sank half fainting on the stone steps.

"Then, kind Heaven, the mark I saw on the girl's bosom, was put there by Nathan, and she is my daughter.   Degraded or pure I will claim her for she is more of a Christian than a Jew.

He arose and with the painful and suppressed emotion, that the girl he had taken off the streets the night before, was his child.

He did not proceed far until he again met Fag. The little fellow was not averse to seeing him.   Mr. Oswald asked him at once in reference to Ivern.

"Do you know the girl that Nathan told you was singing in a saloon?"

"No sur. Do you?" replied Fag.

"I saw her this morning.   She was at my place last night."

"Golly, I met her, that was Ivern, I know her! Of course I do. Never was a time I did'nt know her. She and me are old 'quaintances," replied Fag.

"Where can I find her? She is my daughter."

"Sure now, you're foolin'. She aint got no father, I heard her say many and many a time. She haint no mother, but I guess you're all right, and I'll tell you where to find her. She allus meets Paul, opposite Zeile's, when the whistles blow."

"Come with me", commanded Oswald, and the two started off together.

A little while before they arrived at the place, there could have been seen walking up and down the street, a young man, of well rounded figure, erect carriage, with a strong German face. He appeared to the observer to be about twenty years of age, but he was past twenty four. Around the corner came a young girl, with quick step, and a lithe graceful movement. It was Ivern.

The young man, Paul Wedekind, met her. "Was ever lover so punctual as I?" he asked.

"I never had any but you to know," she replied.

"I wish I could believe you," he answered.

"And I wish I could believe you," she replied.

"Then why doubt me if you wish to believe?"

"Because if I trust you, I'll love you, then my will is gone and I'm afraid I'd be like . . . the marks . . . Oh, God! there is an awful pain in my breast. There is something here that burns."

"Why, what great mystery do you hide from me? It is terrible, ah, more, it is extraordinary, that you should become so tragic, and always refer to some hidden mark. Does your modesty forbid you to tell me?"

"Do you not understand, Paul, that I am a street waif. Ask Nathan, the Jew, what mystery I hide from you? But it is not that, for I know you would not like me, if I was bad like the rest of them is. I am not good, but I am not bad, exceptin' I never learned anything only from the sea as it talked to me, and the fishes I used to sell, and from the flowers—you know you bought a bunch of violets from me long ago; that's when I first knew you. I am not so awful dumb as not to know that I am not the kind of a girl you ought to make real love to."

"But Ivern have I not loved you ever since you were little; and I have believed, and believe yet that your purity of thought amid such surroundings is due to your birth."

"You have been awful good to me, that's why I let you kiss me. It's not because I think you ought to. You must go now, Paul; I'll never be fit for you, but I always want you for my friend."

"You are fit for me, our love makes us equal; I will not give you up."

"Now, Paul, you forget that I use to talk slang, and how you scolded me when you found me in a saloon jesting with the men. You forget those things. It was you that teached me to talk right and I'll never, never allow you to love just because you think you ought to. Go away now."

"Ivern you do not understand that it is you I love, and once I love it is with my life. It makes a furnace so hot within my heart that steal would melt and run like water. Love is the most intoxicating poison my darling."

"I do not like the word," said Ivern with a shudder.

"Do you not like the word *darling*?" he asked.

"I do not mean that word, I mean poison. It kills. Love seems more like sherry to me. It makes me tipsy with wild joy. Only love is far, far away. I've seen it in pictures, I've read it in other eyes. I've dreamed of it; but it is always over the sea."

"It is near you now and you are too strong willed to have it. Come let me give you my protection and your sweet eyes will lose their sadness, and your face will brighten and never know trouble any more."

"You make my trouble now the dearest thing I have had in life. But I know you Paul. You love me just because I am strong-willed. I saw Fag chase a butterfly, and when he caught it he did not care for it, the beauty was all rubbed off. That is the way with you. You want me, but if you had me you would not want me. I know that life-love is between equals. I once saw a flower tied to a weed, it made the weed prettier but the flower died, that's like me and you."

Paul stood before the girl he pitied in admiration.   He knew that the character born in Ivern was stronger than the one attained by him.   The student of human nature would say, that she combined the best traits of the Irish and the German or that of the inherited, the strength and the craftiness of Jewish character, softened and ennobled by pure American blood.   Paul could not but contemplate the face and then the thought of his own weakness made him silent.   For he would soon leave Ivern, to enter the presence of Anethe, his promised bride.   His dual nature had found its complement in the graceful and intelligent woman of his own sphere, and in the overpowering personality of a street waif.   He had thought that love was but an incident in life, but rubbish in a man's way as he winds tediously upwards, and now it turned him from his course as effectually as the stroke of death.

"There she is!" exclaimed Fag, as she and Mr. Oswald turned the corner.

"At last!   At last!   I have found you," cried Oswald, as he rushed towards her.   Ivern drew back, and Paul put his arm about her as if she needed protection.

"Do not shrink from me.   I am your father.   Is there not a mark upon your breast placed there by Nathan as a curse upon the child of his daughter for marrying me, a Christian.   Speak!   . . . Speak quickly!"

"Yes," replied Ivern trembling with a timid feeling, between hope and fear but Nathan said I had no father and that my mother was a _____ oh, no!   I know it is not true, but only yesterday he said she was of the Jews of Barnow and the mark I wear is the brand of her shame, and it has burned through my breast to my heart.   Do not lie to me.   Perhaps Nathan has sent you to torture me.   Tell me, was my mother pure?"

"As pure as heaven.   Oh Lea! that your child for a moment should think that you were not true and good!"

"You say that my mother was pure, then I believe that you are my father and I will love you."

She kissed her father and Fag and Paul.   "You brought him to me," she said to Fag, "and you saved me from sin," she said to Paul.

On their way to No. 5 Bartlett Place Mr. Oswald told the following story: "Twenty years ago I was passing Nathan's home and I saw him beating a beautiful girl. I rescued her from the torture. She proved to be his daughter. I fell deeply in love with her and without delay we were married. It so enraged Nathan that his daughter should marry a Christian that he cursed her and her children. He inherited the superstition, fanaticisms and bigotry of the Barnow people. He hated all the more bitterly because he lived among other sects. A child was born and for a time we lived happily together, and Nathan's terrible oath was forgot'en. I was compelled to go East. When I returned my wife was missing, my child was also gone. I approached Nathan and demanded that he give me information. He replied: "A Jew never forgets an oath." At last he confessed, to save himself from death, for I would have strangled him, that he sent my wife to Poland. I made immediate preparations for departure. I tracked her to New York and found out upon which steamer she had sailed. I went to Poland. I spent months in search of her, but to no avail. I returned, and Nathan told me that Lea was leading a life of dissipation in the city. Then he tells me she is dead. Thus he lies to me. I have lived a constant life of suspense. A year ago he told me that my child was in the Magdalen Asylum. Yesterday I learned from him that you had burned upon your heart the Hebraic words. Then I knew that my years of search were rewarded.

CHAPTER III.

Paul hurried to the residence of Anethe. An hour after he had poured forth love to Ivern in the shadow of a street corner, he stood in the presence of his promised bride concealed by the rich draperies of a luxurious parlor. He came determined to ask that the sacred bond be broken and to tell the unhappy story of his love for Ivern. The dim-lit parlor cast a charming shadow over her beauty and Paul stood undecided. There was such a rich color to Anethe's lips, such a gentle pursuasive coaxing look in her eyes. The shadows creeping in and out through her sun-tinted hair and across her face made him forget the girl he had left.

Anethe was comely. She was divinely fair. Was man ever so

arrogant as to cast aside the love and treasures of such a woman's heart for the helpless, branded, girl like Ivern? Under the facinating gaze of Anethe Paul forgot his errand. He was weak in the presence of the woman who loved him. Instead of telling her of his faithlessness, he pictured to her the golden dawn of their future. Is it any wonder that men. who think, grow cynical and lose respect for humanity. But Ivern was still uppermost in his mind, and in a moment of thoughtlessness he mentioned her name. Anethe, with the jealous watchfulness of love, quickly asked:

"Who is Ivern?"

"Just a girl I have aided to get employment," he answered.

"I trust you Paul, but I know little of your life. You are too honorable to do anything that is wrong, but I pray that you will not deceive me in the least. It seems odd for you to be interested in a girl in that way, unless she is some particular friend. Have you known her long?"

"I have known her five or six years."

"And never told me about her?"

"Would you like to know about the beggars, street girls and waifs that all men meet in their lives, and are forced to aid in one way or the other?"

"I would like to know about Ivern. Is she beautiful?"

"Not pretty like you."

"I did not ask you for a compliment. Tell me about Ivern, her very name fascinates me?"

"Would you like to know about the people who visit dance halls, low theaters, people who beg, steal and cheat for a living, the low, debased and vicious? Ivern belongs to the class, though there is a spice of nobleness with the taint of shame in her life. Do not look displeased Anethe. I met her through a friend of hers, called Fag, who wished me to give her some money to save her from a greater crime than begging. She was so interesting that in all the years I have not lost track of her. Are you satisfied now?"

"Perhaps there is something more to tell?" replied Anethe.

"Jealous heart, keep silence. If I am a man, I have a conscience, and I would be true to you were you not half so fair."

Anethe was not quite satisfied. She silently determined to find

out more about Ivern.   The reluctance of Paul to talk, his protesta-
tions of love and over-defence of himself against her insinuations told
a story that she, though unwilling, still read.

The next evening found Paul at No. 5 Bartlett Place.   Soon after
he rang the bell.   Fag opened the door.

"Ivern told me to keep you out if you come."

"I must see her.   Let me in."

"Cant, thems my orders, but Paul,you helped me and if you want
in, why just push me away;I can't help it you're bigger than me.'

Paul gave him a push and he fell full length upon the floor.   Before Fag had time to arise Paul had grasped Ivern by the hand.

"Paul, you shouldn't have come,yet I am glad to see you," she replied.

"How greatly improved you are since yesterday," he replied, heed-
less of the rebuke.

"Well you see Paul papa says that I am his real daughter: nd am
not to be nobody any more.   So, he bought me all this trumpery
which makes me look better than I feel.   But Paul——.

"What is it, Ivern?"

"You forgot something."

"What did I forget?"

"Can't you guess?"

"No."

"Then I'll never tell you."

"Please do."

She looked up at him and artfully said: "Do you remember what
you took with you when you went away?"

"I really do not."

"Did you not bring me one?',

"I do not know what you mean."

"Oh, Paul, you're stupid," she said with pouting lips.

"I know what it was," exclaimed Fag.

"You kissed her.   You thought I wasn't looking but I was a
wantin' one myself."

Paul stretched out his arms, but Ivern covered her face and slipped
away from his presence.   She did not want her trembling lips
touched after Fag's jest, even by one she so dearly loved.

"Come Ivern; I want you to go with me to Nathan's, to find some trace of your mother. He will not refuse us."

"I will go," she replied.

It was early when they started. Fag, with a jealous eye, shadowed them. They were about to enter the trade-shop of Nathan when he appeared. A gleam of triumph was in his eye as he stroked his beard with both hands.

"You bring dat girl here! Avay mit you! I be contaminated by a voman like dat. She is——"

"Stop, wretch, or I'll——"

"She is——"

"Stop!" cried Paul.

"She is a——" Before he could speak the word, Paul struck him a blow; but the Jew, like a serpent, coiled about him, bore him forcibly to the pavement. As he lay helpless upon the street, Nathan raised his steel-tapped heel, and despite the strenuous efforts of Ivern, it descended upon his forehead, scraping the flesh away to the bone.

Fag seized upon Nathan's leg with his teeth, but he shook him off like the wind does the icicle upon the swaying branch. Again the heel was raised, this time to descend with murderous force. The dim light of the city lit up his fiendish face. Ivern saw, and cried out, "Murder!" The frightened Jew, at the approach of others, fled.

Paul was badly hurt. He was carried to a surgeon's office near. When he was told that he was seriously hurt and would not be able to be moved for several days, he called Fag, and requested that he should deliver a message to Anethe Howard, so that she would not be frightened by an exaggerated account of the affair.

Anethe admitted Fag, and instead of delivering Paul's message—that the injury was slight—he said:

"Poor Paul, my best friend, is hurt. I'll kill Nathan! He mashed Paul's head with his heel. I'll kill Nathan!"

"Tell me what you mean. Has anything happened to Paul?" asked Anethe, bewildered by Fag's talk.

"I have just been tellin' you what Paul told me to tell you, that

Nathan killed him, but I'll kill the Jew, I will! Fag never forgets what he says. Paul is all bloody."

"For God's sake, stop! Tell me, are you crazy?" cried Anethe.

"P'raps I am. I hope I be, if I don't kill the Jew cause Paul's blood is spilt on the pavement. See here; it has kind o' painted this patch on my pants red."

"My God! do not say any more. Paul is dead!"

Anethe began to scream for help, and with the assistance of her mother, obtained from Fag a more lucid account of the tragedy. They were soon on their way to see Paul.

Ivern did not leave his side. She watched him with painful eyes, not quite tearless. The surgeon came to her, and said:

"He has been severely hurt, but will soon recover. He has, however, lost the flesh from his forehead, and will be badly disfigured unless I get some one who is quite brave to help me."

"I'll do anything for Paul. He is my friend," replied Ivern.

The doctor pointed to Paul, who was now unconscious, and with his finger traced the space cut by the sharp heel of the Jew, as he spoke:

"I need a piece of flesh large enough to sew in there."

"Where will you get it?" quietly asked Ivern, with a slight tremor.

"From your arm," he replied.

"Doctor, you may cut it from my check," and she touched the rosiest spot on her face, and pinched the delicate flesh until it stood out, for the surgeon's knife. The blood of a peculiar people ran in her veins, a people who would demand a pound of flesh for money, and would give one for love.

"No, I do not wish to disfigure you. I do not even wish to pain you."

"It will not hurt," replied Ivern.

"Then the sooner it is done the better."

He had her uncover her arm to the shoulder. The doctor gazed rather tenderly on her.

There was a gleam of coquetry in Ivern's eye, and witchery in her glance as she met the doctor's look of admiration.

"I cannot cut that arm," he replied.

"Then I'll do it," she said.

"Turn your head, please. Your eyes are apt to make a man nervous."

"You are a sentimental surgeon," she replied.

She did not turn her head, but watched amused and pleased with his gentle touch, and blushing, tremulous face.

He would press her delicate skin, then pause. He loitered over the operation like a hawk over unprotected prey. Then with a careful estimate of the flesh desired, he took it between his thumb and finger and severed it with a stroke, and held it up, the blood dripping off on the uncarpeted floor.

"Quick, doctor, you are not a careful surgeon," exclaimed Ivern.

"But see, you bleed. Wait, I will bandage your arm."

"Never mind me, that's nothin' but mean Jew blood anyhow. I wish it would all run out of me."

Just as the operation was complete, Anethe and Fag were announced. As the former came in, Ivern withdrew to a shadowed corner of the room. Anethe went direct to the couch, and bending over Paul, kissed him.

Ivern hid deeper in the shadow, and her nails pierced the flesh in her hands as she listened to Anethe explaining to the doctor, that as she was soon to wed the wounded man, that she was there to watch over him, and would remain at his side. It was a bitter, a cruel revelation for her. She had found her father to lose her lover, and perhaps the paternal instinct in her was not as strong as love. At last all had gone, except Anethe and Ivern. The countless kisses which she imprinted on Paul's pale face drove the iron deep into Ivern's soul. Wearied at last she fell asleep in her hiding place. When she awoke Anethe was asleep. She arose, and going to the bed-side caressed the wounded man's hair, then stooped and touched with her lips Anethe's brow. It was not a warm kiss of affection, it was more like the sunshine kissing the frozen hill, or the humble soldier kissing the wounded commander, or the gentle dove billing an injured robin.

Anethe awoke with a start. "Where am I?" she exclaimed. "And who are you?" she asked as she noticed Ivern.

"I am just myself, that's all," and she passed out on the streets once more. She would not return to her father. The pain at her

heart was too hot. The love of a father is efficient, but not sufficient
to satisfy the feminine nature. In her heart she pitied Anethe, for
if Paul was true to her, he was false to Anethe; and if he was true
to Anethe, he was false to her and to himself. "Well Paul is a queer
muddle anyhow. I'll keep out of his way, and let him be true or
false as he wants to me," she thought. All night she wandered about,
as she had often done days before. The Hebraic words glared at her from
every lamp post. She could even see the serpent, like letters in the
heavens above. Then she would draw her lips closely together to
curse Nathan the Jew; but a little whispered prayer for mercy would
be wafted to the unknown God. After three days of sadness and
wandering she again returned to her anxious father at No 5 Bartlett
Place.

Her first words were about Paul. "He has recovered, so as to be
able to be out," was Mr. Oswold's reply. Then he kindly censured
her. He was afraid Ivern's previous life and habits would always
cling to her. A flower that is left to grow in the shade, never attains
its full beauty and sweetness. He was very kind to Ivern. Not
once did he try to reform her ways. He would win her love first.
And great was his joy, as each day he saw more convincing proof of
her chasteness, and that Paul's love was pure. He had not only
found the flower of his life, but the perfume remained with it still.

One day she was sitting in her new home. Her eyes were sadder
than ever, and her luxuriant hair fell in ringlets about her shoulders.
She gazed wistfully towards the sea, and the cry of the waves seemed
but the echo to her lost spirit. Thus she was sitting when Fag,
dressed in a new suit, clean shirt, polished boots, and washed and
combed until one would hardly recognize the boot-black of former
days.

"I've been looking for you" exclaimed Ivern.

"And I've been looking for you, too," replied Fag. I've something
to tell you."

"Come in where papa is, unless you want to tell me alone."

"Its just for you, and no one else."

"Well then, tell me here. No one will hear you."

"I'd rather tell it in the dark, in some lonesome place."

"I would like to know what it is," replied Ivern.

"Am I big enough to get married ?" asked Fag.

"Yes, I should think so," she replied.

"Are you ?"

"I hardly know."

"I'm your best friend, ain't I ?"

"Yes."

"I have fought, begged, and stole for you. Hain't I ?"

"You have done nobly. I have no true friend but you in the world."

"You forget Paul."

"No I don't."

"That makes me feel good here !" exclaimed Fag, as he placed his hand on his breast.

"You are a darling friend," said Ivern as she gave him a coquettish glance.

"Let's get married," exclaimed Fag, and throwing his arms about her, he kissed her hands, face, dress, hair, and touched her with his hands as gently as a child.

Ivern did not try to restrain him, neither did she smile. She stooped and kissed his forehead.

"I wish it was night, I am ashamed of myself," and he hid his face.

"I did not know that you ever thought of love," she said.

"Let's get married?" he implored.

Ivern was puzzled. Had she really aroused a love passion in Fag. A crippled, ugly, little fellow who had always declared he would die for her. She owed her life to him, yet Paul called her to a higher life while Fag, with a kind of imbecile love, wooed her to the old. With pitying tones she said: "Fag I love Paul, you must go away. Come back after awhile and I will give you an answer," and she pushed him aside.

He coiled at her feet and wept like a girl. Then with a masterful sweep of his hand he brushed away the tears and said half to himself: "Fag's a man, love makes me little, it will make me big, I'll die for you."

He was gone, Ivern would have called him back to weep with him, but she wept alone.

Paul came to her in the evening with his head still bandaged. She kissed passionately the white cloth. Paul smiled at her warmth. He did not know that the bandage covered her own flesh.

"The days of trial are over," said Paul.

"Not as long as Nathan lives. I will never, never be happy until he is dead."

"When you are my wife I will protect you. He will not dare insult you then."

"When I am your wife? I know not what that means. It's in me and no one ever teached it to me that the one you are engaged to is your wife."

"What do you mean?" he asked

"I mean that you have another lover. I heard her say so. I saw her crying at your side. It is well. She is for you. I am not fit, even papa says that good people will despise me if I do not do like them."

"But it is you I want my friendless girl," replied Paul.

"You are engaged to a very rich and, I know, a very beautiful Christian lady, while I am only a Jewish girl and a bad one too."

"You must marry me though."

No," she said blushing, but with great decision, "that would not do. Fag is better suited to me than you with your wealth and friends. And Fag loves me more than you do," she said as she passed nearer to him.

"I have a rival then?" he asked.

Yes, Fag asked me to marry him this morning."

"And you consented?"

"No, until Nathan is dead and the curse removed I will be only Ivern."

"Then you will marry Fag?"

"No, I love you."

As she spoke they glanced at the window and saw the face of Fag. She was frightened for it had a wild fierce look. She and Paul watched for the face again which never appeared, but a small wiry form moved down towards the water front. On and on, with a set face and determined step, the figure moved until the roaring of the waters sounded lone and dismal.

"She'll marry him," said Fag as he contemplated the sea wooing him nearer and nearer its damp embrace.

He listened to the moaning sea and wailed in harmony with its tone. Life had been a series of failures to the poor, forsaken and unloved boy.

Now he stood weeping and irresolute, by the border of the suburbs of eternity. Death would give him unconsciousness—a long, quiet sleep, beginning with time and ending in the fortress of futurity. There was something fascinating about death to him. A quiet rest with no horrible dreams, a delicious sleep to hours of anxiety and pain.

Fag's mind did not penetrate the beyond, though his dreams of a fairer land were consciously sweet, and fascinating. He stood upon the shore waiting to cast himself into the sea, but unconsciousness came to him above the deep, and tired and exhausted with the excitement of the day; he curled himself in a knot and rested. He slept all night.

The morning sun never shone on a more peaceful face, it lighted up his irregular features, and played and sported around the angular frame, chasing its own shadow away from his back, and from under his well-worn hat.

The sunshine warmed the blood in his veins and gave to his thoughts a more gentle tone. He dreamed of the angels at the bottom of the sea, and that they were kind to him, Yes, out of the deep came consolation. He did not contemplate foul monsters feeding upon his flesh; but that the fishes had turned into angels, and all the inhabitants of the sea played with his hair and caressed him with pale white hands. While thus dreaming a hand was placed gently on his face, flushed with the warm light of the sun.

Fag raised his arm and with a slow motion of his hand muttered.

"Go away, angel, don't bother me."

Again the same hand was laid upon his face, and Fag's tone was loud and clear when he said:

"Angel, don't touch me."

Then the figure bending over him drew back, and watched the

tired boy. Her face was wreathed in smiles, and her eyes sparkled as they always did under intense joy.

She again went to Fag, lifted up his head and shook him, not roughly, but to awake him.

"Go away, devil," he said angrily.

Then he put out his hand and felt her face, and said:

"No, 'taint no devil; you're an angel," and then opened wide his drooping eyelids, and saw Ivern stooping over him.

"Why, Fag, what's the matter?" she asked.

"I thought an angel touched me. It was only you, and I dunno whether it was an angel or devil. You are both."

"Why, no, Fag, I am your friend."

"Yes, but you're Paul's girl."

"Anethe is Paul's girl," Ivern replied.

"Then, if I were you, I wouldu't kiss him," and Fag arose from his cramped posture, and looked rather disdainful upon Ivern.

"Why did you come here?" he asked.

"To see you."

"But I do not want to see you any more. Don't you know I love you and can't be your friend now. I hate you. If you marry Paul, and he dies, like old Graham did, then I'll be your friend again, but I ain't a-goin' to live long, so you see what's the use of talking. But since you mentioned old Nathan, the mean Jew, I'll be revenged on him right away, now. You go to Paul, you don't care for me nohow." Fag stopped out of breath, he had spoken excitedly. Love was not a lofty passion with the friendless boy, but it was sincere, it made him weep, it was true, it was unselfish, and unselfish love is perfected passion. Fag did not stop, like the young man, any young man, and estimate the intelligence, the usefulness and beauty of Ivern. He just loved her without asking the reason why. He did not dream even of the consummation of his love.

Ivern was pleased by the passion of this forlorn boy, and she was shy with him as she was with Paul.

"I haven't married Paul yet," she responded in reply to all he said.

"Well, I don't care, you go up that way, and I will go up this way," and he started away in an opposite direction from that which he had pointed out for her to go.

As he started up Pacific street a thought came to him forcibly, suddenly, terribly. "I'll kill the Jew then drown myself. She said she would never be happy until Nathan was dead."

He paused a moment, not irresolute, but to meditate. You know how natural it is to study a project, or with your eye to measure a distance before leaping. Human nature is very subtle and very odd. Once we met two men who were exactly alike in expression, movement, style and manners—they were both dead. Human nature is eccentric. Once we knew a man who died for love—his death was happy. Human nature is true to noble impulse, if the sympathetic chord is touched. We have never lived among a people nor traveled with a company where we did not find the bird in the soul.

Even Fag with murder in his mind and love in his heart was not bad. He was noble. There was something grand in his desire to kill Nathan, the Jew. He had no personal spite against him, he did not crave vengeance for himself, but for others. With the intent of killing Nathan for Ivern, and then committing suicide, he approached the place of Nathan, hedged in between two saloons.

He did not tremble, though his face became somewhat repulsive and his eyes flashed as he asked Nathan for a fine, ivory-handled dirk, that lay with its glittering blade under the glass case.

Nathan gave Fag the knife. In a moment all was over. Fag's hands were covered with blood. He would never again be guiltless, never! A life was ruined. Fag was a criminal. The young life was blotted.

"Now quit your meanness," he said. "Have you forgotten Ivern? Have you forgotten Paul? Have you forgotten one-half the crimes you have committed? I am glad you will forget them now. I killed you for her sake, I knew I could do it. You see now that it don't pay to be low and mean. Hurry up and die before some one comes. I am going to leave you now, for I am going to die too, but it won't hurt me." Then as if in remorse, he stooped down, and raised the Jew's head and according to an old custom, he took from his pocket two coins and placed them upon the glassy eyes. Nathan's arm twitched and he seemed to make an attempt to raise his arm. Fag muttered, "Well, he's trying to steal the bits off his eyes," and he

quickly replaced them in his pocket and hurridly left the store.   He
went to No. 5 Bartlett Place and again met Ivern at the door.

"I'll never see you again, never, Ivern.   I am going away.   I
wonder if the bottom of the sea is cold, and if angels will see me
there.   I often dream of angels, and I am going to die."

"Hush, Fag, you frighten me.   You must not talk wild like that,
it hurts me."

"It is not the dying that hurts me.   It is the leavin' you," replied Fag.

"No, I am gone, for dead is dead, and gone is gone.   If Paul
marries Anethe, then come to me, won't you?"

"I promise you I will," replied Ivern.

"Tell Mr. Oswald, when I am gone, that Nathan the Jew, wants
to see him.   And Ivern, I have fixed it all right so that he won't
trouble you any more."

"How can I ever repay you, Fag, for all the kind things you
have done for me?"

"By kissing me good-bye," he replied.

"I will kiss you if you stop, and don't talk in such a dreamy,
sad tone, just like something would happen to you."   Then she
stooped and kissed him,

"Kiss me good-bye again, Ivern, it is like,—like nothing I ever
had before."

We will not blame her for taking the almost doomed boy in her
arms and kissing him again and again.

Like a frightened deer he withdrew from her embrace and started
away.   When he reached the foot of the stairs, ready to enter the
street, he turned and saw Ivern with tears in her eyes still watching
him; he went back and stood on the step below her.   "Give me the
last kiss?" he asked.

"I will she said," and kissed him again.

It was the last kiss he ever received.   No mother gave his cold
lips a warmer caress.   Born of a low woman, of a father who added
to the list of his crimes by becoming the father of Fag.   Do you
not pity the boy whose morbid sentiment drove him out of an un-
friendly world.

He hurried away.   The thought that an officer was after him,

made him double his speed. He reached the water's edge, and
stood upon the pier. The sea breeze tossed his hair about his pale,
agitated face. He held his arms up towards the sea-gulls as if beseeching them to bear his soul away upon their wings. Then he
looked upon the sea; it wooed him to its depths; it seemed a living,
breathing thing; the waves were laughter, and the lapping waters
were caresses! The whole world loomed up behind him as a colos-
sal stiffening corpse, with a face of night. A glance backward.
A leap forward. All was over. His body sank beneath, and his
spirit rose above the waves.

There is still more to tell. The winter-breath of death has not
placed upon all its victims the ashy hue.

The papers told the sensational tale of murder and suicide. The tearless relatives remained at home, and Ivern watched the sea, with her
face against the pane, hoping that the dead would come back. The
spirit from the air answered, "Never! Never!"

CHAPTER IV.

Paul, trembling and excited, stood once more in the presence of
Anethe. She had been told the whole story of his love for Ivern.
There was no anger, but there was a trace of pain upon her face as
she said: "Here I gave you my wounded heart. Here I pronounce
our separation. Go! but not in anger. Go! from the one who loves
you to the one you love. Not go, you say? You must. A woman
knows a man's heart. Perhaps, you will tire of the new love as you
did of me. If you do, come back. Know that love alone forces
from me such an invitation. Not a word. Go!"

Such a look! The very richness of love arose to her face, and hal-
lowed it as she spoke the last word. He went reluctant, but satisfied, and Anethe's serene, like Patience, smiling at grief, lived on.

For Ivern and Paul there followed days and days of pleasure.
Sometimes a jealous pang would drive its cruel point through her
heart, and then she would complain; "Poor, dear Fag, he loved me.
He died for me. Some day, Paul, I will drown my love for you
like Fag who drowned his for me. Only for papa's sake I'll keep
the rest of me dry."

Paul would strongly advocate his love. He would protest until falling tears hung on his eyelids. At last there was peace between them, and mutual love brought its own happiness. Perhaps, somewhere in the book of life, it is recorded that they were united.

When the winter and summer had passed, and the grasses were springing up, Ivern grew sad again. The night frosts of life were with her. She and Paul were sitting quietly in the dark, mutually occupied in divining each other's thoughts, and lost, half in their hearts, and half in the sublime night. Ivern placed her hand tremulously upon his. Then, blushing and hiding her face, with a voice low and musical, thrillingly painful, she talked, not once turning her face towards him:

"There is happiness coming to us, Paul, under the shadow of a cloud. You wanted to marry me, but I wanted you to wait until I had given up all my old habits. Then I thought our love married us just as well. Now, Paul"—he tried to see her face—"No, do not look at me," and she placed her hands over his eyes. "Last night I dreamed that a little bird, entangled in the folds of a cloud, broke away and flew to me, bringing me token after token. When it flew away for the last time, it sang that it would bring me a token of your love. Then I became deathly sick, and the bird returned with the token, a little child, and it lead me from you to the spirit world. Oh, Paul, you know, it was not all a dream!" Her face was confused with a heavenly mildness, for Paul understood. My words cannot add to the picture of the one who was bird-like in her love, nor express the mental anguish of the other.

Again Paul pleaded that she would allow him to have the marriage solemnized, but the strong-willed girl would not listen to him or her father. A strange presentiment had taken possession of her. She believed that she would soon follow Fag. Mr. Oswald did not offer her a word of reproach. His hopes for her happiness remained. She was all that he had in the world. The records of Nathan, the Jew, proved conclusively that Lea, his wife, had died many years ago. Ivern's disgrace was not shame. The sorrow stricken father loved his wayward child. All that he asked of Paul was: "You are not married to her, are you? He answered:

"There is no record of our marriage ou earth but there is in heaven."

Ivern seldom left her room. All day long, many weeks she would watch the sea. At last she would not see Paul except when the room was darkened. Then one night she asked him to say good-bye until she would send for him. She lived now in a world of love within the rind of the real world. "Paul," she said, "I took you from Anethe. Sometime when I am gone return to her. Do not mourn for me. Do like me, when Fag died I gave you all of my love, and I think for the last brief year we have tasted all there is of love. It is wrong for me to dread the future, but let us part to-night as though we should never meet again. A little child will lead me from you to the spirit world."

Then in the silent night with no candle to lift the veil of their happiness, with their souls altogether lost in each other they parted.

It was a night of mortal agony for Ivern. In the morning the sharp, physical pain was over. The mother and babe lay side by side—dead.

*   *   *   *   *   *   *

Paul loitered about the grave of Ivern for a year, fatigued, not freshened by tears. Alas! that death should so sully the blossoms of life. "Ivern! Ivern!" he cried, "lead me to you." Then he tottered away from the grave, where knelt the father of the buried one, to return to the living. From death he turned to life. The words which Fag often used seemed written above him across the sky: "Dead is dead; gone is gone." Then, as he approached the home of Anethe, it seemed as though he heard her singing: "Dead is dead." "Life is life. Come! Come!" He paused as he neared the house.

"Not yet, not yet," he muttered and passed on. Another six months passed. Again he approached the home of Anethe, but the shadow of the dead crossed his path, and he tottered away. Winter had come, and he was standing once more in the luxurious parlor waiting for Anethe.

"Do you welcome me back?" he asked, as she came very near to him. Her love and sorrow prevented her from answering.

"Anethe, bid me stay with you !"

"I have lost and found you again !" she replied.

"O rapture ! O God ! Am I still loved by **one so** peerless as you Is there no shadow between us ?"

"There is sunlight from the grave," she answered.

"Yes, and the light is eternal. Our happiness is complete. The end is the beginning of our eternity of love."

HARR WAGNER.